Fury

by

Christopher J. Ferguson

Angels of War (vol 1)

Fury

Cover Art by *Jennifer Greeff*

The Wild Rose Press, Inc.
PO Box 708
Adams Basin, NY 14410-0708
Visit us at www.thewildrosepress.com

Publishing History
First Edition, 2023
Trade Paperback ISBN 978-1-5092-4992-3
Digital ISBN 978-1-5092-4993-0

Angels of War (vol 1)
Published in the United States of America

"She killed a man twice her size in fair combat not three hours ago," Spiro assured.

"Did she?" The piercing blue eye turned to her. Tisiphone made herself hold the woman's gaze but said nothing. The interaction between slave-soldier and free-soldier had not been lost on her. Abeiron had not lied about the potential. A woman and slave treating a veteran soldier like an underling. It amazed her. "I'll see for myself!" Like a claw, Chloe's hand reached out and plucked Tisiphone from the cart, hurling her roughly into the dirt.

Tisiphone's heart lurched with shock. She fell hard, but rolled with it, coming up on her feet. She turned to face Chloe just in time to see something snaking out at her through the air between them. With a crack, the whip snapped against her thigh and it felt like she had been lit on fire. Tisiphone's instincts took hold. No sense in running. The older woman would beat her. Instead, she darted in, closing in on the effective range of the whip. She slid in and drove her foot into Chloe's shin, forcing the woman to her knees. Then she reached in for the woman's dagger, her only hope of equalizing this fight.

Dedication

To my own personal angel: Diana

Chapter 1

Flight from Argos
1074 BCE
The Greek Dark Ages

It was the glow from the burning city that let Alexis pick his way along the rocky hills. One arm hung at his side, barely able to move, dripping blood and seized with pain. With the other hand, he led Myrrine, his wife, silent and docile, over the hills, away from the ruins of Argos and the Sea People who ravaged it. She didn't speak, hadn't made a sound since her screams had driven her throat hoarse. Her eyes kept rooted to the ground, following him without a will of her own. If he couldn't feel her cold flesh against his own, he'd think her a phantom haunting him as he fled his city like a coward. At least cowards were alive, and she was alive with him. She'd recover from the shock. She had to.

At the peak of the hill, he stopped, tired and lightheaded. "I need to rest a moment. Bind my arm. Can you help me?" He turned to his wife, but she already had her back to him, looking back from where they had come.

From here, the view of Argos was unimpaired. The city...*their* city...glowed and flickered like a fire pit, hundreds of fires pulsing and throbbing. Embers of flame rose into the night sky like souls unto the heavens. The wind carried the sounds of the city even across this divide. The screams, cries, pleas for mercy, they all still reached his ears. A thousand all at once, coming together in a great cacophony, and yet it still seemed like he could understand each lamentation, recognize the individual voices of his neighbors, his friends, as they gave up their death cries.

Myrrine couldn't hear him, seeming mesmerized by the sight of it. Perhaps this hadn't been the best spot for a rest, but he feared he'd pass out if he didn't get his arm bound soon. He was on his own, though. It took him ten, fifteen minutes, much longer than if he'd had her help to cut a sufficient swath of cloth from his cloak with his bronze dagger and tie it around his arm with his good hand. Around and around his bicep he wound it until he was reasonably sure it had staunched the worst of the bleeding. He stuck his dagger back in his belt and stood, swaying just a bit as he did. They had to keep moving.

"Myrrine, we need to keep going. Can you walk with me?"

She turned slightly at the sound of her name, her face in profile to him, a silhouette against the inferno of their former lives. She said nothing in reply.

"Can you walk with me?" he asked again, letting just a hint of force into his voice. Never once in their marriage had he ever given her reason to fear him, and he almost regretted that now.

Nonetheless, she turned this time to face him and nodded slightly. Thank the gods! She returned to him, at least a little. She stretched out her hand, and he held it, guiding her down the far side of the hill. Here they would lose the guiding radiance cast by burning Argos, leaving them only with the moon and stars for light. But as the blaze receded behind the hill, so too did the sounds of slaughter abate. It was worth it.

****

They walked for hours and yet the night never seemed to end. Their pace was little better than a turtle, between Myrrine's stupor and his blood loss. At any moment he feared the sound of riders behind them, the Sea People Wrathknights astride their nightmares, hooves wreathed in flames, eyes burning with blood lust. They never came though. The carcass of Argos must have been too plump pickings to bother searching the hills for the few surviving refugees.

At last, after an eternity of walking, they came to a dwelling on the edge of the forest. A good sturdy house of stone, with a wooden roof, it was of good size. Alexis would have thought it the house of a rich man, were it not out here in the middle of nothing. Fire flickered within, visible through the open stone windows. It reminded him instantly of Argos burning, of course, but he couldn't afford to let it get to him. Fire meant warmth, and possibly food, two things of which they had none at the moment. Nor money to pay for it either. Alexis could only hope the gods would deliver him to the kindness of strangers.

Pulling Myrrine behind him, he went to the door. He raised his fist to knock and hesitated, swallowing hard. He murmured a little prayer to Artemis, the patron goddess of his family, and knocked.

From within he heard a scraping sound, the sound of a chair upon stone, or perhaps a knife being drawn. His good hand went to his dagger. In a moment the door opened, and a massive bulk eclipsed the light from within.

The figure before Alexis wore a cloak so bulky it was difficult to make out much else. Alexis looked from one hand of this creature to the other and found no weapon in either. This gave him some comfort. The hands were gnarled and twisted, the skin wrinkled, yet still vaguely feminine. A crone. This impression was given credence by the long strands of grey hair which strayed out of the great hood that otherwise cast the crone's face in darkness. The hag loomed in the doorway to her house, silent.

Unarmed though she was, Alexis took a step back, nearly stumbling over his wife. "I...I am sorry to disturb you so late. I would not do so unless our situation were dire. I am Alexis and this is my wife, Myrrine."

Myrrine said nothing.

The old woman's head swiveled from Alexis to his wife, then back. Suddenly, she sucked in a long stream of air. Her breath seemed to whistle and groan down her nostrils as if through a long, dank cave. At least she stopped with a much shorter exhale. "Argos burns then?" she asked, her voice like the wings of a thousand bats.

Alexis wondered if they might be better off taking their chances with the Wrathknights. "It does. It is the Sea People."

"Isn't it always?" the crone observed with a sound between a hacking cough and a chuckle.

That wasn't true, of course. From beyond the mountains came the Empire of the North, acting as anvil to the Sea People's hammer, with poor Greece caught in the middle. True, the Empire preferred slaves whereas the Sea People preferred corpses, but Alexis saw little reason to prefer one to the other. Still, he didn't see fit to correct her. "We have no food, nor money," he told her instead.

"And I have both those things. You have that blade, I see. Would you use it to take what you need from an old woman?"

The very thought horrified him, and he drew himself up, feeling his face flush red. "By Artemis' name, I'll do nothing of the sort. Desperate we may be, but this night has seen enough savagery. I might beg for the sake of my wife, but I'll not have my core humanity insulted. If you've no charity for two souls in their hour of need, I'll grant you good night."

"Charity," the crone repeated with a laugh. "Fine. Come in. I've food for you, and shelter, perhaps some coin besides I have little need of. But do not mistake what I offer as charity. Nothing in this life comes without a price." She stepped aside, beckoning them to enter.

From within, Alexis could see a pot boiling over a fire, the scent of stew thick in his nostrils. Smoke rose through an open hole in the ceiling. A jug waited on a low table, whether of wine or water, it did not matter. From the door, he could see this room was merely the first of several. Truly, this witch was wealthy to have such a home with multiple rooms. He frowned at her mention of cost, but what choice did they truly have? He led his wife into the crone's home.

Within, it was warm. Praise the gods for that! Alexis looked around, not sure what he expected to find. There were no skulls, no magical beasts, no bubbling cauldron, if one didn't mind the pot of stew. Despite its size, little else stood out about the house as different from any other Greek home. Two wooden doors led to adjoining rooms, but both were closed. This main room was taken up by the fire pit for cooking, and the low table, around which a few straw mats were placed. What furniture there was consisted of shaky wooden things, and the few random pieces of culinary were clay pots or cups. The woman might have made most of this herself, some time ago too by the looks of most of it. No decorations in the place, but only the rich had such adornments.

The old woman clumsily fussed with some of the clay bowls and cups, arranging them for Alexis and his wife. She poured water from the jug into each of their cups. "Sit then. Might as well make yourselves comfortable." She looked back at them. "Alexis you said your name was? What happened to your arm?"

He looked down at it. His makeshift bandage had soaked through. Gods, what a sight he must make. He tried to wiggle the fingers and was greatly relieved when they moved, though they felt a mixture of tingling and pain. "When the Sea People landed, I got Myrrine straight away, and we ran for it. One of the beasts caught up with us, though, and I had to run him through with my dagger. He got me good, though, he did."

She moved closer, inspecting his bicep. Up close now, he could see into the dark recesses of her hood. The crone wore a mask on her face, the kind actors sometimes wore. Clay, the edges of the lips pulled down into a perpetual frown of sadness. He frowned.

"Looks terrible," she cackled. "So, you ran when they came?" He bristled at the comment, although it was true. Before he could protest, she added. "Wise man. None who fight the hordes from the sea manage to live to tell of it. It is said they eat their kills. Cannibals."

He'd heard that too. Rapists, murderers, and cannibals. Thousands of them, monsters from the ocean.

The crone shifted her gaze to Myrrine who shrunk back from the scrutiny. "And what's wrong with her?" She pointed a long bony finger at his wife, who recoiled from it like it was a snake.

"Shock," he explained. "She hasn't said a word since we fled."

"Mmm," the hag responded. "I can make a poultice for your arm. No sense in you getting rot in the flesh and dying."

"You're a witch, then? You can heal with magic?"

"If that's what you wish to call it, then I suppose I can do it. Magic, though. Merely what mortals call that which they don't understand." She started to move off.

"Wait! If you can do something for my wife? Make her better?"

"Mmm." The withered hag returned her gaze to the cowering Myrrine. She watched the younger woman for a moment. Then she raised her hand and slapped Myrrine solidly across the cheek.

Alexis' eyelids shot up in horror, almost thinking his wife might shatter into a thousand pieces from the blow.

Instead, Myrrine took a step forward toward the crone. "Oww!" she exclaimed, angrily, color returning to her cheeks. "Why did you do that, you old bitch?"

The hag cackled and turned to Alexis. "There. She is fixed."

"That wasn't what I meant you to do!" he protested, still appalled, yet thankful to see his wife's spirit returned to her.

"What you want is not always what will be of most benefit to you," the old woman insisted. She motioned toward the mats. "Sit. The stew will be ready soon, and I'll prepare your poultice in the meantime."

Myrrine's eyes widened. "Gods, Alexis, your arm!"

"It will be fine," he insisted. "Sit, we must eat."

Myrrine sat on one of the mats, watching him with worried eyes. "Alexis, what are we to do? We've got nothing."

"We've got each other."

"Alexis, all those people in Argos…"

He chewed his lip and looked away.

The old hag tottered back over to them some minutes later, a foul-smelling cloth in one hand. "Lift what remains of your sleeve."

Alexis did as she requested, ignoring the gasp from Myrrine when she fully saw his wound. His nose wrinkled at the stench of the poultice the eldritch woman had made. "By the gods, it smells foul. What is in it?"

"Nothing that you'd care to know of." She slapped it on the wound, and it burned as if she'd taken fire to the wound.

He winced. "Shouldn't the wound be stitched?"

"If you think you know better than me, by all means, heal yourself." She tottered back over to the low table, apparently done with her ministrations to his wound. She began to pour a bowl of stew for each of them. "You'll keep that on until morning. It will bind the wound. You'll have an unfortunate scar, but I don't imagine you care much about that. You're a soldier, aren't you?"

Alexis gritted his teeth. "I am a bronzesmith. I have not soldiered in many years." He felt his face flush with blood. "I did not owe Argos my life, only Myrrine. I die only for her." He looked over at his wife.

The woman cackled at his answer. "You continue to defend yourself from insults I have not made. I told you already you were wise to run."

Alexis clenched the muscles in his arms, no matter how it hurt his wound. Intended or not, the woman's words stung. But they were the truth, he had run. Protecting Myrrine had been his only care. The whole city could burn if he could keep Myrrine alive and that is what he had done.

"What should we call you?" Myrrine asked, changing their discussion.

The crone barked a short laugh. "Now we have an excellent question. I am known by many names, but I would prefer it if you would call me Koredyne."

"Thank you, Koredyne. For taking us in during our time of need," Myrrine said.

Alexis tried the stew and found it quite agreeable. Meat in it, no less. The woman must be rich.

Koredyne watched his wife for a moment, silent. Finally, she said, her voice quieter, "I do only that what must be done. In hopes it may make some small difference."

A sound from one of the back rooms distracted him, like a cat mewling. That the old hag would have a cat surprised him not at all. Fit the image somehow. Koredyne ignored the sound.

"What is that?" Myrrine asked, more interested than he. "Is that a child?"

Alexis frowned, thinking it still a cat. With a moment of listening, he suspected Myrrine might be right, it could be an infant perhaps, hungry. Koredyne shrugged, taking little interest. "A baby. No concern of yours."

Alexis stopped chewing, a chunk of meat between his teeth. "Tell me," he mumbled through his full mouth, "that's not what this stew is made of."

"Alexis!" Myrrine protested, but the witch only laughed.

"I may have done many things," the hag chuckled, "but I have yet to make stew from babies."

"Is the child...yours?" Myrrine asked.

"That would take a miracle of the gods, wouldn't it? No, as you might surmise, my fields have gone fallow long ago. The child is not of my lineage. She is like you, a victim of war, come to take shelter with old, mad Koredyne." She regarded Myrrine with interest. "Would you like to see her?"

Alexis raised an eyebrow, but Myrrine was on her feet at once, the stew forgotten. "Of course. The poor thing!"

With a sigh, Alexis stood and followed his wife and Koredyne into the adjoining room, a sparse place, small and cold. In the center, a small swaddling bed occupied by a female infant, perhaps one year of age. The bed was decorated with images of leering demons, entirely inappropriate for a child. Already long black hair hung from the child's head, and she was plump and pink, healthy by all appearances. Her eyes were the color of silver. She turned to them as they entered, crying with hunger.

Myrrine went to her at once and picked her up without being invited to do so. The little girl clung to her instinctively. "You poor dear! She's hungry. Do you have any proper food for a child? At least she is old enough perhaps not to need her mother's milk."

"I have nothing but stew," Koredyne answered, a hint of amusement in her voice.

"Alexis, try giving her some of your stew then. No meat, just the broth. And be sure it's cool before you give it to her."

So much for enjoying his dinner, then. With his wife's direction, he spooned broth to the girl, who accepted it eagerly enough. Myrrine bounced the girl gently in her arms between swallows. Alexis looked over at Koredyne with a frown. Somehow, he knew where this was going. Koredyne had lain a clever trap of sorts, just not the sort he might have expected.

Even behind her mask, the woman visibly grinned. "Her name is Tisiphone."

"Tisiphone," Myrrine repeated. "It sounds so beautiful."

"Does it not?" asked Koredyne. "It is in the language of the Dorians."

"The Empire?" Myrrine gasped. "Her parents are of the Empire to the North?"

Koredyne's grin faded even behind the mask, leaving only the clay frown. "Her parentage is complex and unimportant at this particular moment. Suffice to say she has no one, other than having been left to my care. Unfortunately, I have little way with children, nor much care for them. She is destined for a life of suffering, I fear."

"We could take her with us!" Myrrine suggested at once. "We could care for her. We could love her as our own!"

Alexis set his jaw. "I believe that was what was intended all along."

Koredyne laughed softly. "Nothing comes without a price. Still, it is nothing I could or would force upon you. The decision is yours. You are still welcome to my hospitality, whatever you might choose."

Alexis looked back to his wife, who cuddled the now quiet girl close to her. Both sets of eyes were upon him. Myrrine made a little motion with her head to say "go on" making her intention clear.

They'd left so many behind in Argos. Friends, neighbors, customers. Most would be dead before morning rose. And they'd done nothing to save them. Indeed, Alexis had pushed Myrrine to flee as soon as the attack was known, before Argos even had a chance to try to defend itself. Now they were given a chance to save one life.

He grumbled a little and looked back to Myrrine. "Very well, it appears the decision is already made."

Koredyne nodded, seeming pleased. "She will be better with you than with me. Although before your word binds you, you must agree to one more thing. You must agree to teach her your trade."

Alexis' mouth hung in disbelief. "Bronzesmithing? For a girl?"

Koredyne rolled her eyes, the orbs visible behind the mask. "No, you fool. War. You are to teach her the trade of war."

Alexis rubbed his head. This was worse than bronzesmithing.

"She will not thank you for it either. It will make her an outcast among her peers, wherever you may settle. But every day you must teach her the art of killing. You will not have fulfilled your vow unless she is capable of killing a grown man by the time she is fourteen."

"Are you mad? A fourteen-year-old girl?" He looked over at his wife. Though she clung to the child, he could see the crone's words had unsettled her as much as he. "Even if I were to agree to try, a fourteen-year-old girl cannot kill a grown man!"

"Do you not yourself venerate the huntress Artemis? A woman may not be as strong as a man, but that does not mean she cannot kill."

"With words or with poison, perhaps. And Artemis is a goddess!"

"I think you will find our Tisiphone remarkably capable. Although equally unwilling. She will need to sacrifice much happiness, but you are to remain firm. Daily, she must train to kill, whether she cares to or not."

"Why?" Alexis asked, voice strained.

"That counsel I choose not to share with you. If you are willing to raise Tisiphone as your own, it comes with this condition. And I will hold you to your vow."

He looked back to his wife for guidance. She said nothing but watched him with urgency. She made no move to put the little girl down.

"Very well, I swear it," he nearly spat at Koredyne.

"Good, I am pleased." She turned her back to them. "Let us return to the stew then. We can talk of more pleasant things. And you can get to know your daughter."

****

Alexis woke with the sun the next morning, thinking for a moment it had all been a dream. The burning of Argos, Koredyne, Tisiphone. When he accidentally rolled onto his bad arm and it didn't split with pain, he thought it might have been the case. But when he looked over to his wife, sleeping on a mat on the floor, the little girl curled in her arms, he knew it was no dream. They were still in Koredyne's home. And they'd become parents to a girl they knew nothing of.

Alexis sat up and looked down at his wounded arm. He peeled back the poultice carefully. An angry red line still stretched across his bicep where he'd been slashed. But the skin was already sealed shut, forming new scar tissue. It wasn't possible. No wound healed so fast. No poultice could be so good.

He looked around. No sign of the old woman. "Koredyne," he called.

"Shhh…" his wife murmured. "You'll wake Tisiphone."

"We'll need to move anyway," he insisted. "We're not nearly far enough away from those bastard Sea People. Koredyne!"

No sign of the witch. She did not answer. On the low table near them was a bundle tied up for traveling. Looking inside it he found bread, figs, olives, and strips of dried meat, as well as a sealed gourd with wine. Also within was a small purse with a few dozen silver coins. A year's wages, easily. "By the gods…" he exclaimed.

Searching the house took little time, but Koredyne was not to be found. Gone in the night. There would be no more answers to his myriad of questions.

Outside, he waited while Myrrine got herself and Tisiphone ready to travel. In the distance, he could see a column of smoke rising into the sky. Their former lives. Myrrine joined him a minute later, Tisiphone in a makeshift sling over her shoulder, snug against his wife's chest. The little girl smiled and waved her clumsy arms around like she was on the greatest adventure. Perhaps she was.

"So, I am meant to make you a warrior," he said aloud to the girl.

She merely cooed at him in reply.

Myrrine smiled. "She will be like one of the Amazons."

"It is not right," he grumbled. "She will be hated and reviled for it. She will hate me for forcing it upon her." But he sighed. "Yet I have given my vow. For your sake."

She touched his arm. "I know. Thank you. She'll not hate you. We both thank you." She took his hand in her own. Together they stepped forward toward an altogether new and different life from the one they left behind in ashes.

Chapter 2

The End At the Beginning

Tisiphone sailed through the air, feeling for a moment like a bird on the wing. Then the ground rushed up to meet her and she earned a clobbered chin and a mouthful of dirt.

"You're trying to match me for strength!" her father scolded her from behind, no doubt smiling at her. The thought of him grinning infuriated her. "I've got a hundred pounds and about a foot of height on you."

Tisiphone pushed herself up and spat the dirt from her mouth. "If only you ate less, you wouldn't have such an advantage…" she grumbled.

"What's that, daughter?"

"Nothing, Father," she responded louder this time. With a long exhale to calm herself she struggled to her feet. She brushed her hands, then tried futilely to sweep the grime from her tan leather dress. After a day working in the bronze smithy, and an evening of combat with her father, it was a foolish feminine gesture. She licked her lower teeth, which ached a bit from her collision with the ground. That would be just fantastic to break her teeth. Rolling around in the dirt with her father, she had enough trouble getting boys to take her seriously.

She looked up and around. It was an integral part

of her daily humiliation that her father's smithy was in the center of town, and the small clearing in which they sparred was just behind it, only a thin wooden fence ringing it. Usually, on any given day, a handful of townspeople could be counted on to take comfort from their own grueling day to watch her get pummeled by her father. Sometimes, particularly now she was older, and he was getting older still, she got the jump on him. But he was good, very good, and those moments were rare.

This afternoon, a trio of teenage boys watched them without expression or words. At least they knew not to make catcalls; for as much as this was a humiliation for her, her father guarded her honor carefully. More than one vocal fool had soon found her father's boot up his backside. Even if her father wasn't so quick to defend her, she could take any of those boys down herself, singly at least. None of them wanted to risk their own embarrassment at being beaten by a girl. Later, they'd talk and make jokes, but thank Artemis she didn't need to hear it.

Her father was grinning. He enjoyed this. Thought of it as a kind of bonding time. Maybe she would too, if it hadn't ruined her life. He was sympathetic about her concerns but unwavering in his insistence. Apparently, he had promised some stupid witch.

Today they focused on unarmed combat, which was the worst. He was right—his size and strength gave him all the advantages, and he was clever and dexterous too.

"There are some powdery, womanly men in the world," her father instructed, "but even when you're fully grown, which you almost are, you'll never match the strength of a soldier. Men have more strength in their upper body, it's just the way of it. Don't try to match that. Learn to use a man's strength and his momentum against him." He smiled wider and pulled his fingers toward himself, inviting her to attack.

Warily, she approached him again, and got her fists up before her as he'd taught her. Gods, she wished they were training with blades. She was good with them, could almost hold her own against him. She danced and weaved, circling him, looking for an opening. No point in trying to pull the helpless female routine. He'd go harder on her if she gave up.

He darted in with a roundhouse punch toward her head. She ducked, got inside his swing, and drove her fist into his throat. He gagged at the hit, and she spun to the right and drove her other hand into his kidney. Thriving off this moment of success in her attack, she dug one heel into his shins and moved up to fire a jab for his temple when she spotted his fist moving in like a shooting star.

Stars were what she next saw, along with that feeling of sailing through space that had become altogether too familiar through the years. At least this time, she'd hit the ground on her back and didn't need to worry about her teeth. Instead, her father's hand wrapped around her forearm, and she skidded to a kneeling position rather than falling outright.

"Are you all right?" he asked. "I may not have pulled that punch enough." He put his arm around her to steady her as she knelt and rubbed her forehead where he had hit her.

"That punch was pulled?" she hissed. She blinked a few times to get her bearings.

"Do you know what you did wrong?" he asked.

She fixated narrowed eyes on him and said nothing.

"You maintained your attack too long. You got in two solid hits, which was already risky. But you stayed inside my range to get more. It was inevitable I'd eventually connect. Women have the advantage of dexterity, smaller size, and intelligence. Use them. Get inside, strike, then get back out again. Wear your opponent down. Be patient."

She sighed. "I don't suppose we could have a rest, Father?"

"Yes, of course," He leaned in and kissed her forehead. "Perhaps we've done enough for today. I've been pushing you a little harder of late."

"Really? I hadn't noticed. Or perhaps being beaten about the head and neck so often has simply caused me to forget." Irritation burned in her. He had been hard on her lately, at least in training. Outside of it, Alexis might have been a fluffy bear. He never took a fist at her or her mother in anger, and rarely raised his voice. His love for his family poured out of him like water. But when they got into this ring, he could drive her like he was breaking a horse. Particularly during the last year. She'd been thirteen, just recently turned fourteen. Visibly become a woman, a beautiful one if her mother could be considered an objective source. That wouldn't last if her father managed to knock out her teeth.

Her father didn't reply. Usually, he had some nostrum for her when he detected her irritation. She looked up and found he wasn't paying attention to her at all, rather watching the passerby in the village. An old woman tottered by, face hidden in a black cloak.

Her father watched her intently. The woman paid them no mind, and Tisiphone could see no good reason for her father's interest.

"Father!" she whined, her voice calculated to pierce his thoughts.

He turned to her, looking like he'd forgotten about her. "Oh, uh…go inside with your mother. She'll need help mending clothes."

"Mending clothes?" She looked at him as if he'd gone mad. Tisiphone's days were spent battering pieces of hot metal into daggers and tools. Her evenings were spent training in combat. Between that, eat and sleep. Never once had she been instructed how to help her mother around the house.

"Do as I say, Tizzy!" He already had moved toward the fence, hopped it, and begun to follow the old woman.

She did nothing of the sort, of course. Whatever had her father bothered was clearly more interesting than fixing boots, even if she knew how to do it. She waited until her father was just out of view, then hopped the fence herself.

Whatever his skills as a soldier, her father was no spy. Tracking him was as easy as hunting a black bear in new snow. He showed no idea he knew she was following him either. His own skills as a tracker clearly lacked, however, and after several minutes he began doubling back on himself, looking more and more confused and frustrated. Rather amazingly, he'd lost the old woman.

Tisiphone frowned, the little bit of excitement slipping through her fingers. She'd find a way to ask her father about the woman, although she'd have to approach him carefully. If he was reluctant to tell her, she'd have to be subtle in her approach.

As she was thinking this through, a slight movement caught her eye. A black cape, hunched back, tottering movement. The old woman her father was following, wobbling off in an entirely different direction, unbeknownst to her father.

Tisiphone pursed her lips. She should tell him. But what would be more fun would be to follow the old woman herself, try to figure out what was so interesting about her. The obvious course thus chosen, Tisiphone set to following her quarry.

Tisiphone had better luck than her father, and never lost sight of her prey. Granted, the old woman was hardly a wily hare, and seemed to make no obvious effort to evade Tisiphone's efforts. Tisiphone assumed her spying went unobserved.

The woman made her way out of town, away from the buildings. Finally, she approached a little deer trail leading into the woods and continued without looking back. Her dark shawl quickly blended into the shadows. Tisiphone would have to hurry, lest she lose the woman as well in the end.

Exactly what she was planning to do, Tisiphone wasn't sure. She thought maybe the woman must be a witch… an old woman living in the woods, what else could she be? Just confirming that by finding her house would be exciting. So, she picked up her pace and plunged between the trees.

"You track better than your father," a shaky woman's voice observed just as Tisiphone broke through the tree line.

Tisiphone screamed briefly in surprise, although

they were too far now from the village for anyone to hear. Tisiphone stopped running, for the old woman was here, sitting on a log, waiting for her. Through the woman's hood, Tisiphone could see the crone's face was hidden by a dramatic mask, the lips curled down in a frown.

"I know who you are!" Tisiphone stated defiantly. Recognizing the mask from the stories her parents had told her, she thought she should have guessed all along. No wonder her father had been interested in an old woman!

"Do you?" the hag inquired with a cock of her neck.

"You're Koredyne, the old witch who gave me to my parents. They told me about your mask." That the old woman had led her out here on purpose wasn't lost on Tisiphone.

"Yes, it is true. I am pleased they have been open with you about the circumstances of your adoption. That makes things easier. I am pleased also to find that you look well. Tell me, have you been happy these last thirteen years?"

Since they were apparently going to chat, Tisiphone found a stump and rested. Her body still ached from the training with her father and relaxing in the shade felt good. "The last thirteen years. Maybe, I guess so. Although having to play soldier with my father every day has pretty much ruined my life. I have you to thank for that?"

"You do, but your father was right to obey me." Koredyne's eyes rolled a bit in the sockets of the mask, looking her up and down. "Have Alexis and Myrrine treated you well, shown you love?"

"Most often I forget I am not their daughter."

"Good. I chose well with them, then. It was important for you to know love in your formative years."

"Are you my mother, then?"

Koredyne laughed, the sound like grinding rocks against the shell of a clam. "By the gods, no! You would not have come into this world looking so beautiful if you'd come from my womb, I can assure you that. Nor would you care much for the discipline I would inflict on you were you my child."

"Then who? Who are my parents? And why did they abandon me to the care of a witch?" Tisiphone stood and approached Koredyne to emphasize the urgency of her questions. She'd thought on this matter from time to time as a child, but less than she might have. Alexis and Myrrine had been warm, loving parents, despite the training, and she knew they didn't have the answer. So there had been little point musing about the unknowable. Now that Koredyne was here though, things changed. That the suppressed desire to know had been so strong surprised her in its urgency. "They were of the Empire of the North, weren't they? That's why I have a Dorian name."

Koredyne didn't shrink from her approach at all, waving her off like an irritating fly. "I'll not tell you."

"Why?" Tisiphone demanded.

"Because the knowledge would alter your behavior and your course in a direction not at all agreeable to your welfare, and more importantly, not at all agreeable to my interests."

"Are they important people in the Empire? Are they gods?" Tisiphone's imagination began to leap in every direction imaginable.

"Sit down, you foolish girl, before your tongue gets you into more trouble than you could imagine! I see Alexis and Myrrine have taught you neither patience nor prudence. My decision is made, and you'll just have to learn to live with it for now."

Chastened and frustrated, Tisiphone resumed her position on the tree stump. "Why are you here, then, if not to tell me what I want to know?"

Koredyne regarded her quietly for a long time, not answering. Finally, her voice weary, she said, "There will be time, long stretches of time, in which you find it difficult to believe, but I do what I can to make your path easier. I will come to you at times of transition in your life. Your birth, your adoption by Alexis and Myrrine…"

"And now?"

"And now," Koredyne confirmed quietly.

"Are you taking me away from my parents, then?" Her heart felt as if it shifted in her chest. She half thought to take a branch to the old woman, to put an end to such talk.

The old eyes watched her for a moment from behind the mask. "It is not for me to decide. Only to guide in what little ways I can. Alexis and Myrrine have provided you with what was necessary. Love. Stability. Alexis' skills as a warrior. But he has come to the end of what he can teach you."

"There is no finer soldier than my father!" Tisiphone protested. "There is still much for me to learn from him about how to fight!"

"It is not that you must learn how to fight, but that you must learn how to kill."

"So…you've taken me from my birth parents. Now you'll take me from my adopted parents so that I might become a killer? Why? For what possible purpose?"

Koredyne stood. "The purpose is not my own, child." Her voice was not unkind, although it seemed a strain for the old crone to adopt a tone of empathy. "There is little more for me to offer. Only to tell you that you must not give up, no matter how difficult things become for you." The old woman stood, wobbly and unsure. She pointed one long crooked finger back the way they'd come. "You should make your way home to your parents. A storm comes."

Indeed, upon the horizon, dark clouds threatened, growing and swirling together. Outer rings of white and grey quickly gave way to an inner core of black, which snuffed out what remained of the late daylight.

Tisiphone opened her mouth and then closed again. Koredyne turned, intent on the deeper recesses of the forest. Finally, Tisiphone stamped her foot against the ground. "Is that it, then? Do you just show up once every thirteen years to ruin my life?"

Koredyne stopped and turned ever so slightly back. "I've given you the chance to say goodbye." As the first peal of thunder reached their ears, she turned and trundled on.

****

Tisiphone did not make it home before the rain. It came down sudden and hard, and by the time she burst through their home doorway, she was soaked to the bone. As she sprinted back, she gave thought to what she would tell her parents, whether she should tell them the truth about meeting Koredyne, or whether it was kinder to keep the meeting from them. But as soon as she saw them, saw the look on their faces, she could see they already knew.

Her mother rushed to embrace her at once, not minding her wet clothes. "Tizzy, we were worried for you." She stroked Tisiphone's wet hair.

Her father moved close but did not join the embrace. Lines seemed to have appeared on his face that had not been there hours before. "So, you found her then. What did she tell you?"

Myrrine pulled back a bit and stroked her face like she was a child.

"She…" Tisiphone's teeth clattered, and she told herself it was from the damp and the cold. Lightning flashed, illuminating their hovel better than the small oil lamp ever could. "She told me she's taking me away from you. Can she do that?"

Alexis shook his head, but it was not convincing. "She's too young," he said to his wife, "she's just a child. She's not ready to be apart from us."

Surprisingly, Myrrine demurred. "We knew this day would come. Koredyne made it so Tisiphone could have no life here, being worked every day like a boy." She turned to her daughter. "I knew Koredyne would come for you one day. I don't know what she wants with you, but I know you will make us both proud. We could not have wanted more in a daughter."

The finality in Myrrine's words frightened her as much as Koredyne's. Koredyne might have been little more than a mad old woman, but her mother was intent on following her instructions.

"Mother?" she protested, with a feeling like a frightened bird was caged within her chest.

Matching tears ran down Myrrine's cheek as she

held her daughter out at arm's length. "We'll make the finest dinner tonight. We'll eat like kings and tyrants. We'll spare no expense, won't we, Alexis?"

Alexis nodded but remained quiet otherwise.

A goodbye feast. Just like that, the couple who raised her from infancy was going to turn her back over to the mad crone. True, she'd always known the circumstances of her adoption. There had always been an undercurrent of the idea that circumstances might change. But they never had, until now, and she couldn't imagine a world beyond the stability of the only family she'd ever known. Why wouldn't they fight for her now? Didn't they love her as much as she did them?

Although from the hollowness of Alexis' expression and his silence the rest of the night, as well as the contrasting maniacal giddiness with which Myrrine prepared their dinner, Tisiphone could tell they were hurting as much as she. She had no right to be angry with them. They'd opened up their home to her these last thirteen years, made her their daughter. Whatever happened to her, whatever the old hag made her do, someday she'd come back and make it up to her parents. She quietly vowed this to herself and to Artemis.

She dried herself at the fire once the initial shock wore off. The worst of the thunderstorm outside receded, becoming a dull rumble, though never going away entirely. Endlessly, the rain came down outside, and lightning would flicker through their open windows.

The dinner Myrrine made for them, with Tisiphone and even Alexis helping as best they could, was certainly the finest she'd ever had. They had milk to drink and cheese, and bread and fresh vegetables, even some meat. Perhaps not quite a king's feast, but the most expansive and, perhaps even foolishly expensive dinner their family had ever managed. Myrrine spoke the most, speaking for them all, speaking of happy times together.

After dinner, they kept the fire going, and Myrrine did Tisiphone's hair, combing it until it was silky. It felt good, all this attention her mother gave her. If only she could stop thinking that this would be the last time they'd ever have this opportunity.

Alexis, for his part, remained quiet and kept his distance for most of the night. Only when at last she bedded down did he lean over and kiss her like he used to do when she was little. "Good night, Tizzy," was all he said.

In the dark, it seemed sleep would never come. Her heart pounded too much, her eyes always needing to be wiped of the looming tears. At last, she caught herself nodding off, a few minutes at a time, tendrils of a dream lurking on the periphery. It would be best to sleep. Perhaps the next day would not be so different. Perhaps Koredyne would not come after all. She prayed to Artemis that Koredyne would not come.

Eventually, she slept. And Artemis answered her prayers for Koredyne did not come the next day. What did come was worse.

Chapter 3

War Horses

Tisiphone awoke to the sound of horses. The steady drumming of hooves against the ground at first made her think of thunder. And indeed, lightning shone through the open slit of a window nearest her bed. But then thunder, real thunder, rang out and drowned out the sound of hooves for just a moment. So it was real horses and lots of them from the sound of it. But no one in town was rich enough to own a horse.

Then a woman's scream punctuated the night. Tisiphone sat bolt upright in bed, fully awake now. What, by Hades, was going on?

She swung her feet over her makeshift bed and slipped into a shift. "Papa!" she called out into the dark.

She felt her father's hands on her shoulders at once. "Stay here, Tizzy, and keep watch over your mother. I'm going to see what's happening." She felt a blade, a thick-bladed short sword, pressed into her hand.

She saw her father had a spear in his hand. Although weaponry made up only a sliver of their sales in blacksmithing, they were never without a blade.

Her father turned and left the house before she could respond.

She felt her mother's hand on her arm. "It will be

all right," her mother assured her. "Let your father take care of it."

The thunder of hooves went behind their home, several horses together. Men's voices were raised, shouting, then the clang of metal on metal. Another voice, screaming.

Dear gods, they were under attack! She pulled her arm from her mother's grasp.

"Tisiphone, no!" Myrrine called. The tone in her voice was unmistakable. She was afraid, not for herself, but for her daughter.

For all the effort her father had put into training her, she'd hardly hide inside their home like a coward when her father needed her. Together, fighting side by side, they'd be unstoppable. "Stay here, Mother. And bar the door when I go. I won't stray far and will keep watch to make sure you're safe."

"No!" Myrrine insisted, but Tisiphone had made up her mind. She flung the door to their home wide, surveying the night beyond.

Rain poured down, its onslaught unrelenting. Along with the dark, this made it hard to understand what was happening to their town. There were men and some women out everywhere, running to and fro, some screaming. Among them rode men on horses, several dozen at least. Wrathknights, she thought at first, but no, these were ordinary horses, and the men who rode them looked normal enough as well.

She could not see her father. He'd already moved off too far in the rain. She took a few steps beyond her house, keeping to the shadows, blade clutched tightly in her hand. She stepped on something that felt soft under her foot, not a rock. Looking down, she found she'd stepped on a girl's hand. The girl, no older than herself, lay motionless in the mud. The shaft of an arrow protruded from the girl's back. Tisiphone had no idea who it might be and decided against rolling the girl over to see her face. She'd never seen a dead body before, never even attended a funeral. It seemed madness to think this girl had been shot down so randomly just a few steps beyond her own door.

"Papa!" she shouted, but her voice barely carried to her own ears.

A rider emerged from the darkness. He drew up his horse when he spotted her. She couldn't see his face, obscured as it was by a steel helmet. One hand held a short sword, the other a net. He began to swing the net over his head, driving his knees into the sides of the horse. The animal snorted and charged.

Tisiphone got low to the ground. Enough of her training with her father kicked in that she didn't freeze. She moved in closer to the horse's path rather than running away as the rider would expect. It would make it harder for him to net her, although, of course, she risked being run down by the horse. She kept her eyes on the rider, watching for the net.

As the horse came close, she swung her sword for its legs. Only for a second did she hesitate, feeling bad for the animal. It was her or it, though. Hitting the thing's legs was like striking solid rock. The blow knocked the sword from her hands, and her arm bones felt like they had shattered.

The horse shrieked in agony. Its front legs went out from under it, and it rolled head over haunches. The rider flew from his saddle and landed with a thud, net and sword lost.

The horse struggled to its feet, front legs bleeding. Off it cantered, apparently done with the affairs of humans for now. Its rider too began to get to his feet. At that moment, though, her father dashed from the shadows and drove his spear through the rider's chest.

Tisiphone smiled when she saw him. He smiled a little at her as well, although she could see the strain and fear on his face.

She recovered her sword from where it had fallen. Around them, in the dark, she could still hear the sounds of slaughter, of fear, of fury. She felt confident though, ready to fight beside her father, not afraid to kill if need be. Together, they would defend their house, her mother.

Behind her father, a rider came into view, then a second. The first was male, heavily armored with a helmet adorned with ram's horns, thick and curling back on themselves. He surveyed the scene passively for a moment, spear in one hand, a club in the other. He seemed older than the rider who had charged her, less impetuous. Behind him, a woman, unarmored, black dress soaked from the rain. Her hair was braided back behind her ears. She might have been in her mid-thirties, a cold beauty just beginning to give way to age. She grinned, surveying the scene. That look frightened Tisiphone and sapped her confidence more than did the man with the horns.

Tisiphone was right to assess the situation so. The woman waved her hands in the air and immediately Tisiphone's body was wracked with crippling pain. Tisiphone dropped her sword and went down to her knees. Her hands went to her head to try to stop the crushing pain in her skull. So, the woman was a witch!

Her father went down too.

"Papa!" Tisiphone shouted. It wasn't fair! They fought like cowards.

With her father incapacitated, the rider kicked his horse forward. He raised his spear, and leaned in toward Alexis.

Tisiphone tried to stand, tried to get the sword from the ground. The pain had her all but paralyzed. She was helpless. Helpless to do anything but watch. Tears stung her eyes. Tears of frustration and panic.

Her father raised his hands as the ram rider bore down on him. The spear flared, the tip reflecting a lightning bolt. It pinned her struggling father to the ground.

"Papa!" she screamed again, feeling her heart split in two. It couldn't be. Her father couldn't be struck down, just like that.

The rider continued past her father, galloping toward her now, club raised high. There was nothing she could do. The pain would not let up. Her fingers curled into claws. Her vision became murky, eyes stinging with tears. She managed only to duck a little as the club came down, to lessen the blow against the back of her skull. She barely noticed the strike, given how her head already felt split with pain.

Still, she fell to the ground, barely able to keep her face out of the mud. She turned her head, watching the rider as he stopped and wheeled around, raising the club once more. Only, as her vision failed, did she realize she was losing consciousness. Her last thought was that she would see her father again soon at the River Styx.

****

It seemed an eternity passed before consciousness

returned. Her first thought was worry she'd not be able to pay Charon the Ferryman without the customary coins placed in her mouth. Only she could not hear the rushing of the waves on the Styx, couldn't smell its fetid waters. Instead, gentle drops of rain landed on her upturned face, and she could feel fingers gently running through her long hair.

She opened her eyes, an action which rewarded her with a scorching pain. Her head felt like it had been split open from the blow she'd taken to her skull.

"Papa," she whispered.

Silence.

As her eyes adjusted, she saw the face of a middle-aged woman looking down at her. Not her mother, though. She recognized the woman from the village, but her bruised brain refused to recall the woman's name.

She closed her eyes to ease some of the strain from staring into the sky, overcast though it was.

Gentle fingers traced along her forehead. "Come to slowly, Tizzy. You have a bad crack to your head."

Tisiphone became aware that whatever platform held them, lurched back and forth. Around them, she could hear a multitude of sounds. The patter of a gentle rain, the sound of horses, men's voices, and closer, those of women and girls whispering or crying softly. She opened her eyes again, blinking past the pain. Surrounding them were wooden bars. A cattle cart. "We're slaves now," she whispered.

"Yes, Tizzy," the woman nodded. "They came in the night and killed the men and the old. The women and children they are taking for themselves or to sell."

Sea people? No, they never took slaves, she recalled. Slave lords then, fellow Greeks who would sell them to the Empire of the North for profit. "My father is dead," she stated aloud. Hearing the words made it real for her. "What of my mother?"

The woman paused for just a second before resuming the gentle caresses of Tisiphone's hair. "Dead as well. I saw it myself. When you were brought low, your mother came from your house and stood over you, protecting you. The slaver with the ram's horns…I hear it said his name is Kriluss. He struck her down. She died so that you might be spared. She loved you very much."

Tisiphone felt a needle of ice puncture her heart. Her mother was dead as well. Her fault. She should have stayed to protect Myrrine as her father had ordered.

Tisiphone moved her head slightly to look about the cart. It was filled with women and girls, a few barely toddlers, mostly teens and in their twenties. Few were as old as the woman caring for her. Many wept or clung to one another. Despite the wellspring of grief within her chest, Tisiphone refused to cry. The bastards who had taken them wouldn't get that satisfaction from her. She swallowed hard and breathed in deeply several times. Finally, she looked back up at the woman. "I don't remember your name."

"I am Iokaste. We didn't know each other well. We had no reason to. You were always with your father, working or fighting."

Tisiphone forced herself up onto her arms, though it made her feel dizzy and nauseated. From this position, she could see better. Theirs was one of a dozen or so carts, some filled with females, others with boys and youths. Perhaps three dozen horsemen rode alongside, a motley crew of warriors with spears and bows. The slave lords. At the head of their column, she could see the man with the ram's horns. She ground her teeth at the sight of him, but there was nothing she could do. "How long have I been unconscious?"

"It's midday," Iokaste said.

"I need to pee."

"They'll hardly stop for you. We've been using the back corner for what we need to do. Fortunately, it's raining."

Tisiphone crawled to the appointed spot and made fast work of relieving herself. Somehow, she knew this would be just the first of many humiliations. Finished, she returned to sit next to Iokaste once again, the closest she now had to a friend. Squinting, she looked upward. Through the clouds, she could see the slightest hint of an orb, but it was almost directly overhead. Midday, as Iokaste had told her. "Do you know which way we are headed?"

"North, I believe."

"Toward the Empire." It made sense. The Empire of the North was the chief market for slaves in Greece. The Sea People had no use for anything but death, and those few free Greek states that remained would not trade in their fellow countrymen. She looked down at her hands. A lot of good years of training with fists and sword had done for her in the end.

"With your beauty, you'll be sold as a concubine, most likely," Iokaste commented.

Tisiphone's jaw dropped and her stomach lurched at the thought of it.

"Comparatively, it's not so bad," Iokaste assured her. "They'll be less likely to whip a woman they take to bed. If you are clever, you might get your master to fall in love with you. You could live a comfortable life among the Dorians. They speak our language, worship our gods…but, no. I can see living the life of a harlot, no matter how comfortable, is not for you."

The idea of being some slimy male bastard's sexual plaything sickened her. It was the opposite of every value her parents had instilled in her. She preferred to die than to meet such a fate as that. Iokaste was right, though. Women and girls with any beauty would be most valuable if sold into sexual slavery. How could she get out of it? Flee? Take her own life? Perhaps that witch could stop her from doing anything of value.

As if she had been called, the witch rode into view at just that moment. Her braids were now done into loops around her head and she was, by far, the most ornately adorned of the slavers. Somehow, the humid weather seemed to affect her very little. The trade of these slavers must have been lucrative indeed to be able to afford one such as her. The witch smiled in an almost motherly fashion when she saw Tisiphone was awake. "Ah, I see our sprightly girl is awake."

Tisiphone clenched her jaw. This woman had killed her father. Had it not been for her, Alexis could have defeated Kriluss, she had no doubt. Her eyes bored into the woman, but the sorceress seemed to take no mind.

"What is your name, girl?"

Tisiphone's lips pressed together tighter.

The witch only smiled more. "Still spry. Good. There are some men who will pay extra for the privilege of breaking a girl's spirit." Her eyes scanned the rest of the girls and women in the cart with less enthusiasm. "No matter, I already know your name, Tisiphone."

How did she know? Had she plucked it from her mind when she'd been cutting it apart with pain the night before? Or stolen it from her dreams while she was unconscious.

The woman laughed, guessing her thoughts for sure this time. "Your surrogate mother there previously told me." She motioned toward Iokaste, who blushed with shame.

Tisiphone narrowed her eyes at Iokaste for a moment but forgave her quickly. What could the woman do against these slavers and their witch?

"I am Nyx of Euboea." Her grin returned. "I should like you to know my name."

"Why?" Tisiphone spat the word.

Nyx paused as if considering her answer. Her smile faltered for a moment and the host of emotions that played across the sorceress' face confused Tisiphone. Then the hesitation was gone, and that wicked smirk resumed its normal place. "Because you are going to make me a lot of money." With a laugh, Nyx kicked her heels into her horse's flanks and rode away to take her place by Kriluss' side.

****

Their travels to the North continued for three days. During this time, the sky remained grey, and the rain continued. Although this kept them damp, it provided water when the slavers gave them none, and kept them and their cart blessedly clean. No food was given to them and one young girl, injured during the raid, died during the trip. Her body was simply pulled from the cart and thrown to the side of the dirt road before the dreary caravan carried on.

Kriluss paid them no mind during the journey, barely bothering to look at his prizes. Nyx liked to ride up and down the line of prisoners, lauding it over them. She never spoke directly to Tisiphone again, although she watched Tisiphone often with an amused smile. Iokaste played her role as a surrogate mother for the cart of girls and women, comforting the frightened little ones in particular. Tisiphone was glad she was here, although the presence of so maternal a figure made her miss Myrrine all the more.

The countryside was mainly barren and rocky as they passed between the peaks of tall mountains. Only a handful of other travelers did they see, as well as an occasional patrol of soldiers. Tisiphone learned quickly to identify the Empire's men, shields emblazoned with the image of an ever-watchful eye.

On the third day, the terrain flattened, and they passed through a region of meadows. Blooming flowers and butterflies became the norm, a twisted irony for this horrid journey. Finally, the sun pierced the clouds, although this threatened them with baking temperatures and an end to their water. Fortunately, the caravan rode into an expanded clearing where several such caravans converged, divesting and sorting their cargo.

Tisiphone first noticed it by the stench of human detritus, the smell of death and decay. This roused her from a moment of lethargy and self-pity. She turned to the bars, gripping them in her hands. They passed one body on the side of the road, then a second, both of them thin, malnourished. Starvation hadn't been the cause of death though, as each had been slit across the neck. Too poor quality to sell as slaves.

Now they rolled into the midst of the slaver camp. A few dozen carts such as her own were arranged in rows, disgorging their human cargo. The slaves, barely dressed and looking about with great fear, were kept tied together. Perhaps several hundred slaves were herded by a few score slavers. Most of the slaves were women and children, very few older adults and no fighting-aged men. The slavers were all burly men and a few women, unclean, scarred, and motley in their armor and weapons. They delighted in cruelty, shoving and beating the slaves with evident glee and looming over the women with lascivious intent. Perhaps her father would have done her a service to have knocked out her teeth. Or perhaps these brutes wouldn't even care.

While their cart still rolled, they passed by another cart from the village. Males, mostly boys and a few teens. Tisiphone recognized some of them, including the trio of teenage boys who had watched her father throw her about on their last day together. They seemed a pitiful and weak lot now, shivering and huddling together. She must not look much more impressive to them.

Kriluss had already dismounted his horse and began to inspect his prizes. At the point of a spear, the boys were herded out of the cart. The first youth was small and spindly, barely twelve.

"Mines," Kriluss grunted.

The next youth, a taller, older, more muscular fellow was next.

"Agriculture," Kriluss decreed.

And so it went for the boys. Mines. Agriculture.

Agriculture. Mines. The occasional domestic. Only when the last male exited the cart did the routine change.

Tisiphone's own cart had stopped by then, giving her and the other girls the full show. The last male was an elderly man, perhaps sixty years old. Medium height and build, he had just enough remnants of musculature that one of the slavers must have thought he'd pass muster. Tisiphone recognized him from town but didn't know him well. Abas was his name, she thought.

"Oh, by the gods, what's this?" Kriluss exclaimed. "Did one of our horses have to drag this old thing for three days?"

Abas' face fell further than it already had. His color went ashen.

"Who's responsible for this cart?" Kriluss demanded. She could see his face now clearly. Fifty years old perhaps, skin like leather, a bristly patch of white for a beard, scars crisscrossing his cheeks. That face held nothing of love or compassion.

A slaver hustled forward, a young lad, wiry, but not so imposing as Kriluss. "It was I, sir. This man is older, yes, but see his physique. Surely, he could put in a few good years in the fields."

"We'll never be able to sell such a flabby old thing. No one wants elderly." He drew his short sword and struck the wiry youth with the flat of the blade. The youth held up his hands to shield the blow but did not run or draw his weapon. None of the other slavers moved to help him, nor showed much concern. Kriluss struck him again and again, each blow a solid wet thump. Only when the youth was left prone, bloodied, and moaning with pain did Kriluss let up.

41

Abas stood proud, never speaking, never begging, nor crying out. Even when Kriluss drew his blade across the man's neck, sending his life spurting out in a thick gush of blood. Kriluss wiped his blade on Abas' spasming body, then replaced it in its scabbard.

"Aside from that last, not a bad haul. Let's see what we've got from the women." He moved over to Tisiphone's cart, inspecting them as one might a herd of cattle.

The door to their cart was opened and spears began to prod them out. Iokaste was one of the first. Kriluss looked her over skeptically for a moment and Tisiphone feared she'd suffer the same fate as Abas. He rubbed his chin for a moment but eventually decided, "Domestic."

Nyx came and stood by Kriluss, watching the decision-making with obvious interest, although she said nothing.

The older women and plainer girls were usually designated as either agriculture or domestic. The pretty women and girls, even some deplorably young girls, were given the ruling "Pleasure." Tisiphone felt her stomach turn. Somehow, someday, this man would die at her hand.

As luck would have it, Tisiphone was last off the cart. Kriluss appraised her, looking her up and down like a piece of meat. Tisiphone ran over the ways she might kill him through her head. He wouldn't expect her to leap on him, jam her thumbs in his eye sockets. True, she'd be killed soon after, but better that than be this pig's slave. She looked over at Nyx, who regarded her with an even glare and a slight grin. Nyx already guessed her thoughts, perhaps read them straight from her mind, that much was clear. She'd not be able to take two steps toward Kriluss without the witch paralyzing her with pain as she'd done before.

"An unusually fine specimen in this one. Fetch a fine price for her. Pleasure, of course." He turned away from her, losing interest. Not a flicker of recognition from him that he'd killed her father and mother, clubbed her over the head. A vein throbbed in her head.

Slavers moved toward her, rope in their hands.

"If I might, Kriluss, I'd like to escort this one personally to the buyer's cart," Nyx said, never taking her eyes off Tisiphone.

"Yes, yes, whatever you like, so long as we get the coin." Kriluss waved her off, and moved to inspect the next cart of slaves.

Nyx slid up next to her, as close as an affectionate cat. She smelled of jasmine. She shooed away the slavers with their rope and slid her arm through the crook of Tisiphone's elbow. It was like embracing a snake, but Tisiphone endured it. This was not the moment to strike, and she knew it, knew somehow she'd get her moment if she just bided her time. Still, she couldn't stop herself from tensing up, a wave of ice spreading from the spot Nyx touched her, up her shoulder and to the rest of her body.

"Kriluss is not very imaginative," Nyx cooed, her words like oil. "All he can see in you is your face and your body and imagine you spending your life rutting as a sex slave. But I don't think a woman who can hold a sword as you can would make a very good concubine at all. Look at those others…" Nyx pointed toward the group of girls who'd be designated 'pleasure', now being roped together and lead away, as it happened, in the opposite direction Nyx lead her. "Half of them will be dead within a year. Many of the rest will be beaten or maltreated. A few might actually prosper as beloved mates of kindly masters, although they'll have to sell their identities to achieve such a measure of comfort."

Tisiphone fixed her with a hard stare. "Why do you help them, then? As a woman yourself."

"Because I'm a woman, I'm supposed to care about the fate of all other women? It doesn't work for men. Men kill each other with such regularity I am surprised there are any left. Why should we expect women to embrace some misguided uniform solidarity? You've missed my point entirely. I would have imagined you smarter. Pity."

Tisiphone clenched her jaw. "Then what is your point?"

"You wouldn't last a week as a sex slave. Even if some man were fool enough to buy you, you'd kill him or he'd kill you before you ever got to rutting. Either way, you'd end up dumped in a ditch soon enough. I don't find that amusing at all."

"Amusing," Tisiphone spat the word.

"Amusing, yes. I think it would be much more amusing to see how you fare down a different path." Nyx brought her to a cart guarded not by slavers but by two soldiers who held shields decorated with the ever-watchful eye. The Empire. Not just private citizens within the Empire, but the Empire itself. Nyx led her to the open door of the cart and motioned her to get on.

"And what path is that?" Never taking her eye off Nyx, Tisiphone climbed onto the cart.

"One for which you were always intended." Nyx's smile ebbed with those words, as she regarded

Tisiphone with great seriousness.

Tisiphone frowned, tired of talking with this evil woman. "I don't know how or when, but I will kill you for killing my mother and father." The soldiers shut the cage behind her, and she was left glaring at Nyx through it.

"Countless girls have told me the same thing, and I've never seen one of them return. Still," she added thoughtfully, "you just might be different. It is a roll of the bones I am willing to take. Good luck, Tisiphone." She waggled her fingers as the cart lurched into motion, horses taking her even further toward the north.

Tisiphone hoped the hatred pouring out of her eyes would be enough to kill Nyx. The gods did not imbue her with such power, and Nyx remained watching, mocking, until the cart brought them out of view. Only then did Tisiphone turn to see her fellow slaves. They were not the pretty young pleasure slaves she had expected. Rather, they were a mixture of older women, plain girls, and some boys. Domestic slaves, Iokaste among them. Nyx had put her on the wrong cart. But why?

Chapter 4

Slave Lords

They traveled further to the north. Now that they were purchased property, they were treated with somewhat greater care, given water and stale bread for food. The cart even stopped every few hours to allow the slaves to walk and relieve themselves, although the males and females were each roped together in groups. The Empire's soldiers generally refrained from taunting them, though neither were they particularly friendly.

The slaves kept quiet. Tisiphone could read the defeat and resignation in their eyes, their downcast gazes. Even the males had no fight in them. Barely slaves for half a week and already they were little more than livestock. Even Iokaste seemed resolved to her fate. Tisiphone frowned in frustration when she looked at them. Yet she was no better off than they, stuck in the same cage and just as miserable for it.

She turned around, grasped the wooden bars in her hand, and watched the countryside pass by. Hills populated the terrain now, with mountains looming in the distance on all sides. She could smell the faintest hint of water, perhaps seawater as well. "Excuse me, soldier!" she boldly called to one of the troops as he rode near. "Where are you taking us?"

He turned, his face barely visible through the facial

plates on his helmet. Still, she could see he smiled a little at her. "Iolcus, the capitol city of the Empire." His accent was thick, Dorian. Tisiphone marveled how the Dorians worked so hard to emulate a culture they helped destroy. "King Diadarian himself has bought and paid for you lot."

"We'll work in the palace, then? Does the King treat his slaves well?" She pressed her luck. The soldier seemed chatty, perhaps having nothing better to do himself.

"Well, if I may say, you personally are most fortunate to have avoided being put on auction as a pleasure slave. I'm not sure how you avoided it, looking like you do. King Diadarian is said to be dedicated to his wife, Queen Zinovia. He does not take his slaves to his bedchamber. It is said he has some…infirmities that limit his enthusiasm for the pleasures of the flesh." From the slight note of compassion and the lack of mockery in the man's voice, Tisiphone guessed these infirmities went beyond simply male ineptitude to something far more horrid.

The soldier continued. "Most likely you'll find yourself working in the kitchens or laundering the household garments."

Tisiphone grunted, disgusted. "I don't know how to do those things even if I wished to!"

"I suggest you learn, and quickly. It's hardly too late for the palace to sell you for a pleasure slave. Why if I had the coin, I might buy you myself. There's no shame in a soldier taking a slave for a wife, particularly one as beautiful as yourself. And you'd find I treat you with far more kindness than some."

She frowned. "I'd be too much of a handful for

you."

He laughed. "I don't doubt it. You assume I prefer a wife who is passive simply because I'd consider buying you for a slave. You'll find the Dorians prefer their women with a bit of fire in them."

She knew better than to let this conversation continue down this particular path. "What of King Diadarian. You say he is ill?"

The soldier paused for a moment, but apparently decided to answer her. "Has been for as long as I can remember. Few see him in person, and those that do say that his skin is wasted, his visage disgusting. Queen Zinovia most commonly appears for him publicly. She is well adored by the Empire."

"I see. Thank you." She sat back down, turning away from the soldier. "Hmm."

"You shouldn't speak to the soldiers so casually," Iokaste quietly chided her. "Slaves who speak to their betters so will certainly be punished. You were lucky with that one."

"Betters," Tisiphone repeated, nearly spitting the word. "These barbarians from the north."

"From your name, you may be Dorian yourself, Tisiphone," Iokaste reminded her.

There was little to do in response to that but to sulk. Her mind went back to her parents, dead, their bodies not even properly buried. Her grief was deep, but she refused to let her captors see it. It would be something personal she'd carry with her.

This leg of the journey did not last as long as the previous one. Just two days of travel and the capital city gradually came into view. Tisiphone gazed with amazement upon it. Buildings and houses radiated out in concentric circles from a central palace. Some of these billowed pillars of smoke into the air and she wondered if those might be blacksmiths. It comforted her to think so. The palace itself was a huge, square stone building. She wouldn't have called it beautiful, more fortress than home, but it was grand in its own way. The city sat nestled within a bay between a ring of protective hills and blue-green water stretched off to the horizon. Tisiphone inhaled the scent of ocean air for the first time. So this was the capital city of Iolcus. With the bay behind it, it seemed surprisingly beautiful.

Until one got up close. Most of the houses and buildings ringing the palace proved to be ramshackle, dirty, poorly constructed dwellings, smaller on average than her own home back in the village. The people were small, thin, dirty, somehow lifeless. Obviously, incredibly poor the majority of them. They watched the slave cart pass by, and it was uncertain who pitied who more. The city stank as well, fetid, in fact. Horse manure and what Tisiphone suspected was human offal slathered across much of the streets. She couldn't imagine why anyone gave up village life to live in a place such as this.

"They are as wretched as we," Iokaste observed, thinking the same.

Tisiphone only nodded. Closer to the palace, the houses improved, their denizens clearly wealthier, well-dressed, and attended by slaves. Though not palace slaves, Tisiphone watched them for some signs of what life must be like for them. As a whole, they seemed clean and well fed, though their eagerness to please their masters was tinged with the aura of endless fear. These Dorians must like to believe their slaves loved them.

They then passed through the stone palisade. Here, soldiers and courtiers milled in equal amounts, the courtyard a frenzy of activity. Tisiphone could not imagine how such activity was organized.

Tall buildings of white stone loomed over them. Women watched the courtyard from several windows. Soldiers' wives perhaps, or wives and daughters of administrators. One of them might very well be the queen, for all Tisiphone knew.

Their cart moved around toward the back of these buildings, an area out of the way of the main entrance. They stopped and the gate opened for them. Soldiers stood to either side of the cart, shepherding them, though they did not feel the need to prod the slaves with spears as the slave lords had done. Aside from the soldiers, several other men waited for them. Themselves dressed in the robes of slaves, nonetheless, carrying a lash in their belt.

Overseers, Tisiphone guessed at once. Privileged slaves entrusted to watch over the rest. A clever system, she thought. She knew too she'd hate these men. It would be the only way the system worked.

One of these men stepped forward. He was of average height, muscular, vaguely handsome except that he carried himself without grace, with a confidence borne out of cruelty. He grinned at the new slaves, but his grin held no warmth. "Welcome to Iolcus. I am Scerpidicus, your overseer. You have all been hired to work in the kitchens. So long as you do as I or the other overseers say, your time here will not be unduly burdensome." He whapped the slaves with his lash as they exited the cart, although it was more a gesture for the moment, no real force behind it.

Kitchens, ugh. Well, what kind of dream duty had she been expecting as a slave? With her talent for cooking, she'd accidently poison the entire palace and be able to make her escape.

Scerpidicus's gaze fell on Tisiphone and drank her in with mixed surprise and desire. He didn't bother to hide his lasciviousness like most men did. His lash whipped mildly against her upper arm and she resisted the urge to tear it from his hands and jam it down his throat. He fell into place behind them as the slaves were escorted into the building.

Once inside, the palace was dark, intermittently lit by windows and oil lamps. The slaves were isolated in the basements. Quickly, they were assigned cells in which to sleep. Tisiphone was given a cubicle with Iokaste, the only other slave to whom she felt any attachment. The cells were hardly bigger than a storeroom but designed to sleep four slaves. Only a tiny slit of a window allowed a glimmer of light to shine through. Slaves slept on slats of stone carved into the walls, with only a single thin blanket for those chilly nights. They shared a single wooden bowl for their bodily needs and were given no wash basin. Surprisingly, the cells didn't stink as bad as she would have imagined, and she guessed they were washed down frequently.

Once their living quarters were assigned, immediately they were driven to the kitchens. Here they were made to wash their hands and arms before attending to the palace's gastronomic needs. What followed was endless hours of cutting, slicing, heating, carrying, carving, cooking, mixing, mashing, and everything else imaginable with food. At this point, the overseers used their lashes and harsh words more freely. The lashes were not thick enough to cause welts or serious injury like a whip, but their blows stung. Having no background of skill upon which to fall, Tisiphone found herself the target of the lash more than the rest. She endured it through gritted teeth, keeping anger and suffering within.

A single older soldier watched the kitchens. He was the only man with an actual weapon, a lone soldier to guard dozens of slaves within the boundaries of the kitchens. None thought to challenge him and, in truth, he did nothing to harm or interfere with the slaves' work. Indeed, some of the slaves would bring him food and he would smile at them kindly. His name was Spiro, Tisiphone later learned, and she saw more compassion in him than the slave overseers. On several occasions, other soldiers would come through the kitchens, often pilfering food.

At first, she thought she need only press through whatever service they were currently worrying over before they might have some break during which to rest. As hours stretched past, the expected rest never came. The people of the palace must have insatiable appetites, she speculated, for the backbreaking work continued long into the night. By then, her hands were raw, her nerves frayed, her pride wounded, and her back aching from countless strikes of the lash.

Finally, they cleaned the kitchens, and they dismissed everyone to their cells. Scerpidicus and the other overseers herded them back, although they were easier, lazier with their lashes now.

"For those who are new," Scerpidicus called, "get

your sleep. In six hours we begin again."

Not a single person moaned, in fear of a lash or two.

Tisiphone fell in beside Iokaste, joints aching, eyelids heavy. "By the gods, is every day to be like this one?"

"The first will be the worst. We'll grow accustomed to it, child."

"It's not so bad, really," said a voice from behind them. Scerpidicus. "The men who work in the copper or silver mines have it much worse. At least in the kitchens you never will go hungry. We overseers are to prevent theft of the food, of course, but we're inclined to be relaxed on the issue, particularly for those we favor."

Tisiphone slumped her shoulders and sighed. "So, it's to be like that, then?" Iokaste hovered near her protectively, but let her do the talking.

Scerpidicus chuckled. "We merely have the opportunity to make each other's lives easier. Or more difficult. Think on it." He moved past them, on to his chamber, which, as overseer, he had to himself. Tisiphone watched him with narrowed eyes.

"Pay him no mind," Iokaste advised and tugged Tisiphone back to their cell.

Spiro, the soldier, was replaced by a younger trooper who locked them in their cells and remained watch over them through the night. Tisiphone reclined on her stone palette, using the blanket as a cushion for now. When the weather turned cold, she'd have to reconsider how best to use the blanket. She ground her teeth. That kind of thinking was foolish. She'd not be here so long, she vowed. Either escaped or dead. More likely the latter.

She considered Scerpidicus' comments, though. He'd prove to be a problem, she was sure of that. As the dominant overseer, his taking a shine to her would make things impossible for her. Even if he wouldn't resort to force to get what he wanted, he had enough power at his hands to coerce the other slaves to do as he pleased. He wasn't the ultimate authority in the room, though. Perhaps if there was a way she could circumvent him, she might turn Scerpidicus to her advantage.

****

It seemed she'd barely nodded off when the young soldier began yelling for them to awake. Soon the overseers were at it, as well. The lash helped convince even the heavy sleepers to get moving. Tisiphone rolled out of her crevice and began putting on her simple shoes. Sleep still settled in her eyes, and she attended to her dressing mechanically.

The sting of the lash against her shoulder startled her to full alertness. She stood up straight, angry, and swiveled to meet the aggressor. "What was that for?" It was one of the other overseers, not Scerpidicus, but there was no doubt where the incentive came from.

"Be faster about getting ready," the overseer grunted back, not much impressed by her fury. One hand toyed with his lash, at the ready to thrash if she disobeyed.

Tisiphone balled her hands into fists and shot a look at Scerpidicus, busy shepherding his own cluster of slaves. He flashed her a little grin.

"It's a shame," Iokaste frowned. "Slaves themselves, but how quickly they turn on the rest of us.

Selfish bastards."

"Iokaste, working in a kitchen or not, I can't cook at all. Do you have any actual skills with cooking?"

"Well, yes, of course. I cooked for my husband and boys for years before…" she trailed off. That unfinished sentence needed no explanation. Tisiphone lived through the tragic ordeal herself.

They were ushered out into the hall now, on their way to wash before getting to the kitchens. Tisiphone paused, a wave of sadness coming over her at even a slight reminder of how things had once been. "Do you think you could cook something? Something small on the side, without it distracting from your work otherwise?"

"I suppose I could. What did you have in mind?"

Honey and cinnamon were what Tisiphone had in mind. Not that she'd know what to do with them, but Iokaste would. Cinnamon, in particular, was rare and expensive, and Tisiphone had more heard of it than experienced it. Here in the palatial kitchens, it was plentiful, however. Enough that a small amount would not be missed.

Tisiphone felt like she were the ringmaster of an elaborate conspiracy as she and Iokaste collected small amounts of ingredients throughout the morning while carrying out their normal work. Eggs, cinnamon, lemon, honey, flour, clove. Scerpidicus watched her closely throughout. Though his motive was lustful rather than suspicious, it still made it tough for her. At one point, she felt him brush up against her, his hand across her buttocks, but when she turned on him, he merely mocked her.

At last, Iokaste finished it. A small cinnamon cake,

lightly glazed with lemon and honey. It smelled wonderful, a luxury of the sort her family could never afford. Eating it now would be a minor rebellion, but it wasn't for her, of course.

Iokaste, Artemis bless her, made a production of burning herself and dropping a pan of eggs. This earned her harsh words and lashings, but served to make sure the attention was not on Tisiphone. With Scerpidicus and his bastard friends distracted, Tisiphone quickly walked to approach Spiro.

The old man seemed half-asleep...well, maybe more. His head was bent forward, his torso tottering as his muscle tone began to ebb.

"Sir?" she said, and touched his shoulder.

He jerked to alertness. "What's that? Oh, good morning, young girl." He smiled at her, his grin lacking some of its teeth.

"I brought you something." She held out the precious little cake. "I thought you might be hungry."

"Did you?" His eyes lit up with delight. "It smells wonderful. Did you make it?"

"My friend Iokaste made it, although it was my idea."

The old soldier bit down into the cake. Tisiphone felt her pulse race while watching him. His eyebrows went up, and he groaned in pleasure, and she knew she had him. "Sweetheart," he said, "this is fantastic. You're a wonderful cook."

"It was my friend Iokaste who cooked it," she reminded him, pointing back toward the ovens. When she did, she caught a glimpse of Scerpidicus. He roamed among the slaves as he normally did but occasionally glanced her way. Those glances were short but dark. It wasn't lost on him what she was doing.

She nibbled on her lip a little. She'd have to play this carefully.

Spiro inhaled the little cake. "Wonderful, just wonderful. If you ever need anything, if those overseers work you too hard, you just let me know. I don't shirk from reminding them who's really in charge here."

Tisiphone rewarded him with a broad, warm smile. They spoke for a while, twenty minutes perhaps, of his childhood and hers, before he became aware of the time and gently sent her back to her duties. She liked him. And hope that he liked her back. It was crucial that he did.

****

Scerpidicus kept his distance from Tisiphone the rest of that day. Even when the working day was over, he didn't speak to her, made no mention of her play with Spiro. But once the guard changed, his lash spoke for him. He didn't specifically say he punished her for her play with Spiro, but he didn't need to. Nonetheless, he made no attempt for her favors this night. A few minutes of the lash before being locked in her cell were worth avoiding his sexual advances.

Perhaps he'd tire of her. She doubted that, though. She'd challenged his authority. The other slaves would know what had happened. He wouldn't be able to let the issue lie. His status as overseer would depend on him crushing her. It wouldn't be long either.

If he did whatever he'd do at night, she wouldn't stand a chance. She had to provoke him when she had Spiro near. And hope that her meager effort to charm the old man would do the trick. She felt a pang of guilt at manipulating the old soldier, but this was life and death.

That night, she heard Iokaste whisper, "Are you sure this will work?"

"No," she whispered back. "But it's too late now to worry about it. I won't be raped by that fiend." Fortunately, Iokaste's role in the plot hadn't been revealed to Scerpidicus. She hoped to keep her friend out of it if things went bad.

"I'll pray for you. To Artemis, I will pray."

The Goddess of virginity. Suitable. Tisiphone drew in a long breath. "Good night, Iokaste."

****

The next day, she woke and dressed quickly, giving Scerpidicus and his goons no excuse for the lash. Spiro already shuffled to and fro, keeping an eye on things. He smiled at her slightly, and she was spared the lash from the overseers.

Tisiphone and Iokaste were not fools. Another cinnamon cake was in the mix before the morning was hardly underway. Tisiphone had no skills with an oven, but she began fantasizing about more and more elaborate treats for Spiro. Treats she had no idea how to make but imagined Iokaste could, or could at least learn. They could be more open about it with time too, although that would have to progress carefully. She was making nothing less than a power play. It needed to be sustained, but not unduly obvious to Spiro, nor entirely blatant to Scerpidicus. If he lost all authority with the slaves, he'd become desperate. She needed only to convince him to leave her alone. Once his attention was off of her, she could plan how to escape from this hole.

Nonetheless, given she had Spiro's tacit approval, her efforts to collect the ingredients for his cake were less clandestine than the previous day. This proved to be a mistake. Just as she was measuring out the correct amount of precious cinnamon someone bumped her hard from behind. A cup of the prized spice spilled everywhere. "Ugh!" Tisiphone cried. "Be careful!" She turned to confront the clumsy oaf. Scerpidicus, of course. She should have known.

"Look what you've done, slave!" he cried, pointing toward the lost cinnamon. He raised his lash. Tisiphone had just enough time to raise her arm to protect her face. The cords of the lash stung like bees against her flesh. Scerpidicus put all his strength into it.

She cried out and instinctively cringed as Scerpidicus raised the lash again, his face like that of a wild animal.

"Scerpidicus!" a male voice cried. Spiro.

The lash came down against Tisiphone's arm and shoulder again. In another setting, she'd wrench the thing from his hands and drive it in his eye socket. He was strong enough, but she judged him clumsy and unskilled. Now was not the time though. Better to play the harmless victim.

"Scerpidicus!" Spiro demanded.

The lashes ceased. Tisiphone dared to look out from behind her defending and now reddened arm. Spiro lurched his body forward, through the mass of huddled and quiet slaves, toward Scerpidicus and Tisiphone. Scerpidicus stood tall, the lash dangling in one hand. His face was red, and he sputtered at first as Spiro arrived. "She dropped a good measure of valuable spice, Sir. I sought only to discipline her."

An older woman near them spoke without being asked. "He pushed her. It was his fault."

59

Christopher J. Ferguson

Scerpidicus' face went crimson. His knuckles turned white on the lash. For a slave to speak against the word of an overseer was dangerous. Tisiphone looked to see how Spiro would react.

The old man frowned at Scerpidicus. "So you are at fault, and would not only blame this poor child, but give her the lash that would rightly be for you."

Scerpidicus opened his mouth but seemed to find no words.

Spiro got right in Scerpidicus' face. "We give you the privilege of overseer in order to prevent trouble, not to stir it up. If you forget that, you can rejoin the ranks of ordinary slaves."

Scerpidicus closed his mouth and nodded.

Tisiphone watched it all without speaking. Spiro looked down at her. He didn't change his expression, didn't give her anymore than a cursory look, but he didn't have to. He gave Scerpidicus a last cold look and moved back to his chair, shouting, "Everyone, back to work, unless you wish to taste the lash I wield." He put his hand on his sword for good measure.

Scerpidicus glanced at her barely a second. It was enough to chill her heart. She guessed he'd set this up on purpose, to test how ready Spiro would be to defend her. But he'd overdone it, managed to squash his own authority. The other slave speaking up for her had made that clear to all. No slave would speak against an overseer in the prime of his authority. Now Scerpidicus' very role as overseer had been threatened.

Here she'd been thinking she'd have to be careful and play her courtship of Spiro carefully, and Scerpidicus had gone and been an oaf and brought it to a critical level. Damn him. And damn herself, she

60

shouldn't have been so open about collecting the ingredients.

Still, Iokaste made the cake for her and she brought it to Spiro, although she waited until there was much commotion over serving supper for the palace and she could do so discretely. Spiro swooned over it and complimented her. He winked at her as he ate. "And don't you worry. You're not the first girl that scoundrel has manhandled. If he gives you any problem, just let me know."

She smiled and thanked him. But later, when herded back to their cells, she knew it wouldn't be so simple. Not one of the overseers laid a lash on her, kept their distance, in fact. Across the throng of slaves she caught Scerpidicus' glance, his teeth clenched shut, eyes nearly bloodshot with rage. And she knew their clash would come crashing down on them, and soon.

Chapter 5

Rape and Murder

Tisiphone forced herself to sleep. She could spend all night worrying, going over and over events and fears until morning came. But there would be no use to that. Whatever was coming, she needed to conserve her strength for it.

As usual, it seemed her eyes barely closed before the overseers were shouting them awake once more. How they seemed to be up so early and without complaint she couldn't imagine. Some of these slaves had been at this work for decades. Tisiphone couldn't imagine a life like this, day after day of the same dreary soul-crushing work. Maybe no one was truly born for the life of a slave, but certainly, she wasn't. She needed to get Scerpidicus off her back and with Spiro in her favor, she'd have some room to consider an escape. An escape to exactly what she had no clue, but dying free would be better than a life like this.

As with the morning before, the overseers largely kept their distance from her. She dared to hope perhaps the confrontation from the day before had been more positive than she could have hoped. Scerpidicus ignored her entirely, as if she were a ghost.

And so the morning began as relaxed as one could expect it to be for a slave working eighteen hours straight under the lash to make food for elites who they would never lay eyes on. Still, she felt a flicker of hope. She and Iokaste considered how to up the ante a bit with Spiro today, to stay in his good graces. That was the key, of course, Spiro. Not exactly in the prime of health, Tisiphone guessed. If his heart suddenly stopped, her main defense would be lost and she'd be at Scerpidicus' mercy. Realizing that, she felt a pang of panic…what if Scerpidicus poisoned him? She couldn't rule out the possibility. Spiro obviously wasn't the most careful about taking food from the slaves. Surely there'd be something in the kitchens that might serve as poison. She'd have to get the better of Scerpidicus before he hatched such a scheme of his own.

In the meantime, persist with the current plan. Iokaste hatched on an idea for a fruit pie as a switch from cinnamon. Less danger of spilling an expensive spice. So at Iokaste's direction, she went looking for the proper ingredients. Slave or not, she'd become used to pressing her luck a bit, coming and going through the kitchens as if she were more than a lowly slave; as if she aspired to something more. In search of the fruits, she went to a storage locker where they could be kept cool and dry.

The noise from the kitchens receded in here. Only a small window offered light by which she could see. She took a moment to glance outside, to see the ocean and the sun, and realized this window would be the only way she could see either until she escaped. She might climb out now, other than the guards patrolling, who would certainly spot her for a slave. With a sigh, she turned back to the crates of fruits…olives, wild strawberries, dates. She tried to decide upon the sweetest options.

Then hands gripped her wrists and wrenched them hard behind her back. She screamed instinctively, but the storage locker door slammed shut at the same time.

Tisiphone jumped at the sound and turned her head. There stood Scerpidicus. He leered at her like a demon would, his face a horrid mixture of glee and rage. Behind her, one of his fellow overseers kept her arms in his tight grasp, preventing her from moving. She couldn't see the man well, but from the feel of the man against her, she knew he was tall and his grip on her wrists were like iron bands.

Her heart felt like it had expanded, trying to break out of her chest. Her first thought, though, was to wonder how stupid Scerpidicus could be. Spiro was right outside. If Scerpidicus hurt her…

"Are you mad?" she screamed at Scerpidicus. With the door closed, no one would be able to hear her.

He sauntered forward, unable to wipe the grin from his face. It never made him look truly happy. Even in his moment of triumph, pain, and humiliation mixed freely with his satisfaction. She guessed he'd been a broken man long before she'd come across him, his position as overseer the only way for him to vent his frustrations. And now she'd threatened to take it away from him.

"Going to run to Spiro, are you?" Scerpidicus growled. He inched toward her, clearly savoring the moment.

She kept her mouth shut, knowing the consequences if she dared say anything. The tall overseer had her arms pinned behind her back, his own body pressed tight against her own. She could feel his chin just over her head. Her feet were still free, of course. She pulled against his restraining arms just to see how tight he had her against him.

"Pretty quiet now," Scerpidicus observed. "You know, you're right, though. Beating you would be madness. You'd just run to your Spiro, and he'd have done with us. What we're going to do to you, though, you're not going to want to tell him about. You will not want to tell anyone about it."

Tisiphone swallowed hard. That was their game, then. To shame her womanhood, take away her virtue. Scerpidicus was right...maybe the Dorians had laws against rape, her own people had. But it didn't always matter. People were always quick to blame the woman involved. In the eyes of many, she would be forever tainted.

Scerpidicus slithered toward her like a snake. "I don't even like this sort of thing. I take no pride in it, no joy. But I'm not going back to being just another slave." He shook his head back and forth, the grin draining from his lips. "I may not have much, but I've got the lash, and I'll die before I let it go."

Standing a few feet from her, he seemed to hesitate, looking her up and down. "Do you know what I was before I became a slave?"

She shook her head, still not trusting herself to speak. There were plenty of words to be spoken, but not now.

"A blacksmith's apprentice. Just like you."

How in Hades did he know?

He laughed, apparently guessing her reaction. "Calluses on your hands, but you can't cook worth dirt. Good boots with wooden soles means your family had some income, and you needed to protect your feet from shards of metal." He pursed his lips for a moment. "Slavers killed my parents and took me when I was a boy. Same as you, right?"

The memory, so recent, came flooding back. She felt tears stinging her eyes, threatening to spill over the lashes. Damn him, if he got her to cry…still, she nodded her head.

"I'm sorry for that," and from the look on her face, she believed it. She could see a kernel left of humanity in the blackened soul Scerpidicus had become under the slavery of the Dorians. Years in these kitchens had made him into what he now was. "I'm sorry for what I must do, too. I am. But I won't let go of what little power I've managed to take."

He moved forward, and reached for her dress.

As he moved closer, she kicked her legs off the ground, using the man behind her as a brace for her back. She drove off the ground with her right foot and brought her left foot up and smashed it into Scerpidicus' nose.

Tisiphone caught only a glimpse of surprise on his face before her foot obscured it. Under the hard sole of her boot, she felt his nose crunch like a fruit. He cried out and staggered back.

As her weight came down, she drove both boots into the shins of the man who held her. He cried out and, as she hoped, released his grip on her wrists. She turned quickly and thrust the heel of her palm into the side of his head. He went down on one knee with a grunt.

Then she turned back to Scerpidicus. He still blocked her path to the door. A tremor of fear ran through her for a split second. He pulled his hands away from his nose, covered in blood, and glared at her. "You broke my nose, you…" She drove her foot into his groin before he could complete the sentence.

As he screamed, she moved past him, toward the door, out to safety. She managed to pull it open. Outside, a dozen or so nearby slaves turned and gawked at her in surprise. She darted out the door, but as she crossed the threshold, felt a hand on her ankle. Whomever the hand belonged to pulled hard, and she lost her balance, skidding hard into one of the tables with a crash. She looked up to see a bloody Scerpidicus and his collaborator bearing down on her. She stood quick and grabbed a kitchen knife from the table with which to defend herself.

"Stop this at once!" a voice called loudly. Spiro. The gaping slaves parted before him like water as he lumbered forward, his sword drawn. His frown turned to surprise when he saw her. "Tisiphone? What is going on?"

Scerpidicus and the other overseer careened into view then, but skidded to a halt upon seeing Spiro.

From upstairs, heavy footfalls and clanking metal could be heard. More soldiers, come to investigate the commotion no doubt. Soon, they rushed into view, four men who filed behind Spiro, swords drawn.

"Scerpidicus, what is the meaning of this?" Spiro demanded.

"She struck an overseer!" Scerpidicus cried, indignant. "Both of us." Scerpidicus' face was purple, even where blood did not coat it. Fluid from his ruined nose flowed freely down his shirt. His friend had a developing bruise on the side of his head but, unlike

Scerpidicus, had gone ashen.

"They tried to rape me! I merely defended myself!"

"That's not true. We caught her stealing from the storage locker. Fruits, no doubt, for a pie." And no doubt for Spiro, that much didn't need to be said. So Scerpidicus had found his advantage. Even a common soldier guarding the slaves wasn't intended to partake of the King's precious stores.

Iokaste rushed to Tisiphone's side, taking the knife from her hand, and holding her protectively. "If she says he tried to rape her, then it is true!" she proclaimed. Many of the other slaves, particularly the women, nodded their heads. Though opinions mattered little, it cheered Tisiphone to see so many who knew her barely at all take to her defense.

Spiro's face turned to stone. "Scerpidicus, just yesterday I warned you that it was for an overseer to stop trouble, not create it!"

Scerpidicus sputtered, "And so I meant to do! It does not matter. She struck an overseer, and we all know the penalty for that!"

Tisiphone, of course, did not, but from the gasps and murmurs from the slaves, she could very well guess.

Spiro went silent, glaring at Scerpidicus with naked rage.

Iokaste ran her hand over Tisiphone's hair, looking about wildly. "We are slaves. But does that mean a woman cannot defend herself from other slaves?"

Spiro's lips puckered like he'd just bit into a lemon. "Do you mean to tell me, Scerpidicus, that this young girl half your size managed to best both you and your fellow overseer?" Spiro's eyes traveled over to her, and met her gaze. There was something unreadable in his look.

Scerpidicus hesitated. Spiro had caught him with a riposte. He could not escape now without great humiliation. After a moment, he forged ahead. "She surprised us when we confronted her. She is wily, and strong!" Several of the younger soldiers openly laughed at that. Scerpidicus' companion looked as if he wished to dissolve into the wall. "She struck an overseer, and she must die!" Scerpidicus insisted.

Spiro did not laugh. He fixed Tisiphone with a long, hard, appraising look. "Is it true? You physically beat both these men?"

"I sought only to defend myself," Tisiphone implored quietly.

"The overseer is weak, but what he says is true," proclaimed one of the younger soldiers. "The penalty for striking an overseer is death."

That sent a shock wave of murmurs and protests through the slaves.

Iokaste yelled, "No!"

"Silence!" Spiro demanded, and he got what he asked for. He considered Tisiphone for a long while, then drew in a long, harried breath with a shake of his head. "There is nothing I can do. The law is clear."

Tisiphone felt the breath go out of her. She stood there behind a veil of silence and numbness.

"Wait!" called Iokaste. "Among the Dorians, is it not custom that a parent may accept the penalty meant for her child, a guardian for her ward?"

Tisiphone turned and stared at her. "Iokaste, what are you doing?"

Spiro looked at Iokaste for a long moment and his

expression changed to something like…relief? "It is true what you say. It is law within the Empire that a guardian may accept the penalty for her ward."

"Then I take the penalty meant for Tisiphone. She is my ward!"

"Wait, Iokaste, no!" Tisiphone clutched at the woman's clothing. "You can't do this. It's my mistake, not yours."

"Very well," decided Spiro.

"No, good Spiro," Tisiphone beseeched the man who would have been her guardian. "The crime is mine. Do not give it to another. I have only just met this woman. She is not my guardian."

Spiro fixed her a look like stone. "You told me yourself she was your companion who aided you in the kitchens." And with that declaration, Tisiphone realized her plan had worked too well. Spiro wanted her alive. At the cost of Iokaste. Spiro motioned to one of the soldiers. "Take the older woman away."

"No, oh, Artemis, no!" Tisiphone clutched harder at Iokaste's robes. "Take it back. I can't bear to be responsible for your death. Don't do this!" Tears streamed openly down her cheeks now, and she made no effort to hide them.

Iokaste took Tisiphone's face in her hands and spoke softly. "Shhh, child, it is all right. I have no life here in the kitchens—my family was taken from me. You are my family now, and I give what little I have for you. It is the way it must be. Protest no more. Don't let them see weakness in you. Be strong, and honor well what I do. Promise me that?"

Her eyes stung with regret and rage, but Tisiphone nodded. It took all of her will not to scream at the injustice of it. Her heartbeat thumped against her chest as though about to explode. This was all her fault, all her doing. Promise or not, she could not help herself but be reduced to blubbering when Iokaste was wrenched from her grasp and led from the room.

Spiro then turned to the overseers. First, to the one whose name she had never learned, he ordered, "Hand over your lash. You are stripped of your rank." The man did as told, and looked relieved to have gotten off with only that as punishment. Spiro then beckoned two of the other soldiers. "As for Scerpidicus, take him to the dungeons."

"Wait, what?" Scerpidicus screamed. "I have done nothing. It is she that is at fault!"

"I warned you, Scerpidicus," Spiro intoned as the young man was hauled from the kitchens. To the last soldier, Spiro asked, "Maintain my post for a while, won't you?" Then he knelt and put his arm around Tisiphone while she quivered on the floor. "Tisiphone, you can't stay here. I would have you come with me."

Her mind begged for this to be a dream. The inevitable loss of a kind woman had rendered her speechless for a moment, but eventually managed to nod understanding. Spiro took her arm gently. Distantly, she was aware of eyes on her as she passed. But she didn't care. Didn't care either where Spiro led her. He spoke as he guided her, but her mind slipped beyond hearing him. He led her upstairs, that much she would remember, that was all. Beyond that, she could sense nothing but her own grief and her guilt.

He brought her to a bedroom, small and spare, but far better than what she'd had in the kitchens. He led her to the bed and sat her down gently. He spoke to her again and she nodded her head though she did not hear him. Then he left with a last worried look at her.

Substantial light seeped into the room by a window close by, but she did not go to it, for fear it might look out on the very field where Iokaste would be killed. She hoped only that Scerpidicus might die a death a thousand times more horrible than the woman who had given her life for Tisiphone's. She did not move from the bed, did nothing but quiver, and occasionally wipe the tears from her face, lost as she was in her thoughts.

At some point, a slave girl came to the room bringing food and water, but these Tisiphone did not touch. Eventually, merciful exhaustion overcame her, and she slept, though her dreams were haunted by the spirits of the dead.

****

Her dreams morphed into an earthquake that rent asunder her village. A great crack appeared in the earth, swallowing whole buildings, animals, people. Around her, villagers screamed and ran for cover, though wherever they ran more cracks appeared, the earth itself seeming to shake itself apart. She spun around looking for her family, the only source of safety she knew. There they were! Not far away, calling her name. A moment of hope blossomed in her, and she raised one hand to them. Then the earth broke open underneath their feet and into the abyss of steam and magma they plummeted. Tisiphone screamed.

Her eyes fluttered open. The world still shook, but it was no earthquake but rather hands on her shoulder, gently shaking her awake. She spun suddenly, coming to full alertness, and swatted the hands away, skittering away from them.

"Easy, girl." It was Spiro. "It's just me."

Tisiphone looked about, getting her bearings. Light streamed in through the open window. Morning. Memories flooded back in rapid succession. The assault on her village, her enslavement, Scerpidicus and… "Iokaste?" she whispered.

Spiro shook his head. "That's done, girl."

Tisiphone buried her hands in her hair and balled them into fists.

"She was very brave to the last," Spiro told her, his words soft. "You've got to honor her sacrifice."

Tisiphone looked up at that. She'd never let Iokaste's death be in vain, but she had no idea what Spiro was talking about.

He held out his hand, palm down as one would to a nervous animal. "Whoever sold you to the palace for the kitchens made a big mistake. You don't belong as a domestic slave."

Tisiphone remembered Nyx, how she'd diverted Tisiphone from the ranks of the pleasure slaves. "I think she knew exactly what she was doing." Although why Nyx had bothered was unclear. Certainly, the kitchens had proven to be their own special hell, but Tisiphone doubted the life of a pleasure slave would have been any more to her liking. What had it been for, just to add the guilt of Iokaste's death to her burden? Although how could Nyx have ever foreseen that?

 Spiro paused for a moment, not understanding her reference. Then he pressed on. "I've arranged something for you. A way out of this, at least. But I need you to make your mind into steel for me, to be strong. Can you do that?"

Tisiphone furrowed her brows, but nodded all the

Christopher J. Ferguson

same. What choice did she have?

Spiro pushed a basin her way. "Here. Wash. Eat and drink too. When you're ready, come out into the next room. There's someone you need to meet." With that, he stood and left her.

The puzzle of it was hardly enough to wipe away her misery, but she did as instructed. She washed and ate the simple food and water. Then, hesitantly, but curious what Spiro had done, she pulled open the door and moved into the next room.

She'd been in such a haze the day before she didn't remember it. But it was a much larger room than the bedroom she'd been kept in, with a series of long open windows allowing considerable light to filter in. The walls were of stone, with wooden floor and ceiling. The walls were decorated with mosaics depicting scenes of battle, presumably victories of the Empire of the North. Otherwise, aside from a small table in one corner, the room was unfurnished.

Spiro waited for her in the room, leaning against one wall. Guarding the only other door in the room were two other soldiers in full battle armor. All three, though, appeared in deference to a fourth man, tall and elderly, with balding gray hair and piercing blue eyes. Like the other soldiers, he wore armor as if prepared for war, although his armor was decorated with silver inlays and his tunic of red marked him as an officer. He watched Tisiphone with his arms crossed, one hand rubbing his chin. His mouth twisted in a slight grin at the sight of her. Just next to him stood a fifth man, dirty and bruised. One whom Tisiphone recognized immediately.

"Scerpidicus!" she hissed.

The former overseer looked as bad as she felt—one eye blackened, his lip cracked and swollen. And, of course, his nose was bent and purple. Nonetheless, he was intact, and glared at her with naked loathing.

"I understand you two have met," said the officer, his voice lilting as if on the verge of laughter. "Good Spiro has told me the whole sordid tale. I'm curious to know exactly who you are, though."

Tisiphone wished she could become Medusa, just so she could turn Scerpidicus to stone. She almost missed the officer's question. "I am Tisiphone," she answered simply, brushing away the rudeness from her tone. It would serve no purpose. She was indebted to Spiro and needed to find out what this was all about.

The officer laughed out loud now. "Yes, that much Spiro told me. He also told me that a little girl like you, barely a baby bird in a dress, managed to best not only this hulking oaf but a comrade of his as well at the same time. Is that true?"

She nodded, looking to Spiro for guidance. Spiro only watched her evenly, made no motion, and said nothing. Likewise, Scerpidicus said nothing to interrupt the officer, only continued to glare at her.

The officer chuckled, more softly now. "I'd have to assume you caught him unawares. Spiro says otherwise, says you have real talent. Do you have skill with a blade?"

She nodded again. "My father taught me."

"If that is so, you would be a rare find." His tone lost its laughter, and he gave Spiro a long look as if deciding something. Finally, he turned to the table and retrieved two long military daggers, balancing them in his hands. "I'd like very much for you to prove it."

He took one of the daggers by the tip of the blade and flung it toward Tisiphone's feet. It landed between them with a thunk, penetrating the wooden floor. Tisiphone did not allow herself to jump back from it. Then he turned and launched the other dagger at Scerpidicus' feet, where it similarly embedded itself.

"Here is the deal I am about to offer you," he informed her. "I am going to give you and this oaf a chance to settle your differences, once and for all. Neither I nor Spiro,"—his tone hardened, a warning to the other man— "nor the other soldiers will intervene in any way. If this dirty slave bests you, he may have you however he wants. Kill you, rape you, I don't really care. Similarly, if you best him, you can kill him. Simple as that." He walked around the back of the table, giving them maximum room to fight.

Scerpidicus reached down warily, plucked the dagger from the floor, and hefted it, testing its weight.

Tisiphone looked to Spiro again, and this time he gave her a little nod. She bent her knees and took the dagger. She judged it to be made of good, solid bronze. An iron weapon would be better, she knew, but not all blacksmiths worked with iron yet. The weight was well-balanced, and the blade sharpened.

They'd fight for this officer's amusement. Very well, she welcomed the opportunity to kill Scerpidicus. He'd be the first man she killed. Even the Sea People warrior, whose horse she brought down, had been killed by her father. It didn't bother her to think of it, killing Scerpidicus. He'd earned it. However harsh his own life may have been, he'd only dealt that suffering back out on others.

Scerpidicus hunkered down, keeping his body low

to the ground. His dagger spun a bit in one restless hand. His jaw hung open, thick tongue running along his teeth.

Tisiphone studied him for a moment. He'd dropped his arrogance, which was a pity. Would have been simpler to best him if he played the fool as he'd done the day before. He was wary now, knew what she could do. Still, his advantages were mainly in size and strength. He was untrained, unintelligent.

She moved to the side, keeping a distance between them. Distance was her ally, giving her time to understand his attacks and counter them. That much, her father had taught her well.

Scerpidicus moved first and lunged after her. She danced deftly to the side, parrying his blade with her own. He drew back as one would while trying to catch a snake. He collected his nerve, then lunged again. He was not quick, not skilled, as she judged. She darted beyond his reach, striking against his dagger as much to provide theatrics for their audience as anything else. She had a sense this audition went beyond who killed who.

The old officer and Spiro watched quietly. Spiro chewed on his lip. The officer watched impassively, scratching the side of his head. He wanted a show.

Tisiphone furrowed her brow. She could lead Scerpidicus around in circles for hours, but that would hardly prove satisfying. Fine. She'd have to take chances.

She moved forward slightly, narrowing the distance between them. Presenting herself as an easier, more tempting target. In no time at all, Scerpidicus launched himself at her immediately. His blade drove in toward her left side. She dodged his first strike, slipping to the right. Then he slashed wildly. She ducked, the blade moving harmlessly over her. She skipped back out of reach.

After a moment to catch her breath, she repeated her feint. Scerpidicus responded in the same manner, the same series of lunges and swipes. As ever, she remained frustratingly out of reach, sliding back out of striking distance after the final swipe.

Breathing in deeply, she looked over at Spiro, who watched her back over a balled fist. She thought of her father, who'd taught her everything she knew. How she missed him. She imagined him here with her today, smiling upon her as she sparred with this slave. What would he think of her if she killed him?

She glanced over at Scerpidicus, his hulking and sweating form.

She decided her father would approve.

Another feint, her blade swiping toward his thigh. She dodged his response and moved right. He struck back, clumsy once again. Underneath it she slid. This time, instead of darting away from him, she slipped forward, moving next to him. He glanced down at her, eyes going wide.

She drove the tip of her dagger up, under his exposed arm, and into his armpit. His scream pierced her ears. Yet without doubt, without mercy, she twisted the blade and drove it in further.

Scerpidicus' blade clattered to the floor. His arm swung down and struck her across her shoulder, though it had only weight, not force. She pulled her dagger free and now backed away, retreating to a safe position to evaluate the damage she'd done.

In a moment, she assessed it as devastating. Scerpidicus' right arm hung useless and unmoving. His left hand pressed desperately against the wound under his arm. It did little good as dark blood spread down his shirt, down his leg. He stared at it, eyes and mouth wide.

Once, her father had told her about the secret spots to strike a man. Places where a blow might be unexpected, yet lethal. It seemed her father was correct about this one. An artery ran under that spot, and hitting it right could cause the arm to cease functioning.

Scerpidicus backed up against the wall, looking back and forth between the officer and Spiro as if one of them might save him. He sunk to his knees. He never spoke, even as tears finally came to his eyes. He could only stare open-mouthed as his life's essence began to pool around him.

Tisiphone felt a moment of sadness well in her chest. A flash of pity for the man who would have raped her, would have killed her. She wouldn't have changed her choice to kill him if she could, but she couldn't help but wonder what he would have been if he hadn't been taken as a slave. Would he still have become a monstrosity if he hadn't been treated heinously?

Tisiphone watched him die, silently. She guessed it took a minute before he lost consciousness, bending forward until his head came to rest against the floor, his greasy hair spreading out in the pool of his own blood.

"Well done," the officer said at last. "You are as good, better perhaps, than Spiro suggested."

The compliment meant nothing to her. She tossed her dagger to the floor. "You could have killed him yourself. Why did you have me do it? Because you were curious to know if I could fight?"

"I needed to know if you could kill," he answered her, his voice even.

"Why?"

"I have a particular interest in girls who can fight like men. Who can kill like men."

Tisiphone took a step back, away from him. She looked to Spiro for guidance, but the old soldier merely watched her as if too afraid to participate in the conversation.

The gray officer stepped closer to her. "I'm about to offer you something a slave girl such as yourself will seldom see again in her lifetime."

She looked back at him and narrowed her eyes.

He smiled at her. "A choice."

Chapter 6

Against the Cliff

Tisiphone stared at the old soldier for a long time. Finally, she repeated his words. "A choice?" She didn't know if she cared for any choice the Empire would give her. Nonetheless, something tugged at her mind. Intrigue consumed her.

The man nodded. "First, I should introduce myself. I am Abeiron and I train elite soldiers for the Empire. I do offer you a choice, a divergence of possible paths. Consider them wisely."

Tisiphone remained quiet, letting him fill the silence as she considered.

"I have a friend, a good man," he continued. "He is advanced in years, his wife is dead, his children grown. He is a man of means, gentle in demeanor. I would be pleased to see him have good company in his remaining years."

"A sex slave," Tisiphone translated with a growl.

"Yes," Abeiron acknowledged. "I should point out that my friend is old enough I imagine his appetites are fewer than once they were. I can offer no guarantees, of course, but he is kindly at heart, far more than most men. I would imagine it probable he might grant you freedom upon his death, perhaps some small portion of his estate, as well. It would be the best chance you had

81

at regaining your freedom. For the small sacrifice of making an old man happy."

Tisiphone wrinkled her nose. "What's my other choice?"

"Well, that's a bit more to the point." He stepped forward and retrieved her dagger from the floor and replaced it on the table. "I wanted to see it for myself that you could fight as well as Spiro promised. You might have been lucky once, even against two men. But you've got skill, nascent to be sure. Enough to get the better of an ignorant, albeit strong, slave."

Tisiphone shifted her gaze to Spiro, who remained silent, lips pressed tightly together. He glanced at her quickly in return, but gave her no indication of his thoughts.

"The Empire has a modest need for female soldiers," Abeiron continued. "Elite soldiers to function as scouts, infiltrators, spies if necessary. We have a training ground above the city against the cliffs. I am always on the lookout for girls with natural talent. Of course, it is considered unseemly for Dorian women to engage in men's activities, thus slave girls are my only resort."

"A slave soldier," Tisiphone tossed the idea around in her head, found it less disagreeable than a sex slave to be sure.

Abeiron nodded. "Despite your status as a slave, there would be considerable opportunities for honor, even fame. Chloe, the woman who trains the girls now, made her name as one of the founders of a group we called the Amazons, women warriors who were easily equal to the finest warriors in all of Greece. Any one of them a match for a wrath knight. Slave or not, there's not a hoplite who doesn't respect her. You could be like her." He stepped even closer to her. "But I'll not lie to you. The road of a soldier is hard. You can expect to be whipped in training, deprived of sleep, food, comfort, driven to extremes your body was never meant to endure."

Her mind turned that over and over. Finally, it dawned on her there was no simple path of escape for her. One did not simply slip away from slavery. She'd been naïve to think she could, and that had cost Iokaste her life. It dawned on her too that somehow this must have been what Nyx had driven her toward. There was no reason for Nyx to divert her from sexual slavery simply to return to the same scenario. How could Nyx have predicted this outcome though, and what purpose did it serve the witch? She hated to think anything she might do would help that evil woman, but what choice did she have? "I choose to be a soldier rather than a whore."

Abeiron crossed his arms. "Choose carefully. There will be no turning back. Once made, you will either become a warrior or a corpse."

Tisiphone met his gaze without fear. "I understand. My decision holds."

Abeiron grinned widely, a sudden change from his craggy and serious face. "Excellent! I'm very pleased with this decision." He approached her and put a heavy hand on her shoulder. "Let me speak openly and say I can imagine you must chafe at your new status as a slave. A girl who is intelligent enough to charm Spiro and fierce enough to kill a man twice her size must surely have her eyes set on looking for any opportunity to escape. Of course, if caught, you would be killed, and there's nothing out there for a penniless girl, regardless. I won't attempt to downplay to you the horrors of life as a slave soldier, but I will draw your attention to the unique opportunity for honor, glory, and even fame deprived of most slaves and indeed even of most freedmen and citizens. Your mentor Chloe should serve as an example for you in all that you could be. Perseverance and fortitude will be the defining features of your success." His hand squeezed the bones of her shoulder. "Come, let us remove you from this castle. Spiro will take you to your new home at the cliffs."

Tisiphone looked to Spiro who smiled at her finally. She sucked in a deep breath. So, they guessed she would be thinking of escape. Somehow it never dawned on her they might have seen through her intents. And Abeiron did have a point. If she escaped…then what? She couldn't go home. The Slave Lords had obliterated her town, killed her parents. She had nothing, nothing but her guile and skill. If she didn't offer that to the Dorians, then to who? The monstrous Sea People who ravaged the coastal lands of Greece? The Slave Lords? Or would she take up banditry? Surely she didn't want to be a slave, not to people whose market for them had led to the destruction of her family. But alternatives were in short supply for the moment.

Spiro took her by cart out of the city, up the tall hill and to the cliffs, where Abeiron's training ground perched over Iolcus and the ocean both. His words to her were encouraging, warning her a bit of the harshness of soldierly training, but ensuring her she could endure. Her efforts with the cinnamon cakes had certainly taken hold; he clearly rooted for her. She let him do most of the talking as her mind twisted on the directions fate had taken her over the past week. She kept looking about, half-expecting Koredyne to waddle out from behind a rock or some bushes and pluck her from this surreal experience. But just as Koredyne had failed to adequately warn her about what the future held in store, the old crone did not save her now. If anything, she had more reasons to thank that evil witch Nyx for the turn in her fortunes as Koredyne. Koredyne who had seen what was coming could have spared her and her parents but had chosen not to.

At last, the cart lurched to a stop. Tisiphone was started from her thoughts. She found herself on a plateau overlooking Iolcus, a plateau which dropped to precarious falls over both the city to the South and the sea to the East. It held a beautiful view, ruined only by the choice to place here not a palace but rather a filthy training ground for soldiers. Not far away, she could see and hear males at training. Dozens of men drilled at shield and spear, the crack of a whip demanding more of them and more still. Here, where they had stopped, though, the area was peaceful. One long rectangular building sat quietly near the sea. This, she supposed, might be a barracks. Next to it, a smaller building with open windows. Ramps were cut into the ground, and these led to a long, deep area like a trench. Wooden fencing on either side made it possible for onlookers to observe the activities within the trench without falling in. A handful of other buildings as well, all nondescript and built of stone or clay. No impressive fortress. This camp seemed as modest as her village and likely to be swept into the sea by even a mild storm.

She looked at Spiro curiously.

"This is it," he confirmed. He looked at her evenly. "I know what you were doing with those little cakes. I don't blame you for it. Showed initiative and planning. I hope only that you'll put it to some good use here."

She considered for a moment, then nodded. "Thank you, Spiro."

"Thank me in a year once you're done with this place."

A woman approached them as they sat in the stationary cart. She was dressed like no woman Tisiphone had seen before, none of the flowing shawls of a well-born woman, or the primitive wrappings of a slave. She wore the tunic of a soldier, which came down only to her mid-thigh, leaving the rest of her legs scandalously exposed. Her legs were well-rounded with muscle, the shins protected by leather guards. Her chest, likewise, was protected by armor made from hardened leather with metal studs. On one hip she wore a thick whip, not one of the mild lashes the overseers used. On the other hip, she wore a dagger. Her hair flowed free and long, tied only with a simple cord to keep the strands from her face. Her hair was dark and curled, as was common among the Dorians.

From the distance, Tisiphone thought the approaching woman must be a paragon of athletic beauty, so trim and muscled was her figure. As she came closer, Tisiphone was disabused of this notion. The woman's face might once have been amongst the most beautiful in the land, so perfect was her chin, and nose and cheekbones. One piercing blue eye took in Tisiphone with a critical look as one might apprise a horse. The other eye was a milky orb, with only a gray hint of iris and pupil behind the cloudy surface. A great horrid slash cut diagonally across the woman's face, from forehead through that damaged eye and down to the jaw. A shock of white went through the woman's hair where the slash met her hairline. The scar remained pink and looked raw despite that Tisiphone guessed it must have healed years before.

A dozen smaller scars marred the woman's hands, arms, and legs, from what Tisiphone could see. A brand was burned into her shoulder, although Tisiphone wasn't close enough to see the pattern. A soldier, through and through. Tisiphone had no doubt this was the vaunted Chloe.

Chloe put her fists on her hips and looked from Tisiphone to Spiro. She spoke to the old soldier boldly and without deference. "What is it we have here?"

Spiro, if anything, sounded deferential to Chloe. "It is Abeiron's wish, madam, that this girl be trained amongst your latest cohort."

"We have a full cohort already and this girl is as thin as an underfed worm. She has potential?"

"She killed a man twice her size in fair combat not three hours ago," Spiro assured.

"Did she?" The piercing blue eye turned to her. Tisiphone made herself hold the woman's gaze but said nothing. The interaction between slave-soldier and free-soldier had not been lost on her. Abeiron had not lied about the potential. A woman and slave treating a veteran soldier like an underling. It amazed her. "I'll see for myself!" Like a claw, Chloe's hand reached out and plucked Tisiphone from the cart, hurling her roughly into the dirt.

Tisiphone's heart lurched with shock. She fell hard, but rolled with it, coming up on her feet. She turned to face Chloe just in time to see something snaking out at her through the air between them. With a crack, the whip snapped against her thigh and it felt like she had been lit on fire. Tisiphone's instincts took hold. No sense in running. The older woman would beat her. Instead, she darted in, closing in on the effective range of the whip. She slid in and drove her foot into Chloe's shin, forcing the woman to her knees. Then she reached in for the woman's dagger, her only hope of equalizing this fight.

Instead, her face met Chloe's fist. The bones of the woman's hand felt like a rock against her cheek. Tisiphone lost her balance, sailing back onto her rump. She struggled to lift herself onto her elbows, but Chloe's weight landed on her stomach and the woman drove her fist into Tisiphone's eye. Tisiphone saw stars and it was all she could do to hold onto consciousness.

Nonetheless, the weight was relieved from her stomach and she heard Chloe say to Spiro, "Not bad, actually. She's got heart and instincts. She may even have given me a bruise. No guarantees she'll survive training, but it's worth making room for her."

Tisiphone shook the cobwebs from her head and managed now to push up onto her elbows. She took stock of herself. Covered with dirt and scrapes from being thrown. The welt on her thigh was already beginning to form. Undoubtedly, the left side of her face would turn purple before long. Quite an introduction. Mentor indeed.

Chloe turned and looked down at her, her expression never changing. Her father would have had an amused grin by this point, but not Chloe. "The next year of your life will feel pretty much like this," she promised.

"She volunteered for this," Spiro observed, "rather than choosing the life of a pleasure slave."

Chloe watched her for a second, but said nothing in reaction. Finally, she asked. "What's your name, girl?"

"Tisiphone," she answered. Then spat dirt from her mouth.

"Dorian name," Chloe replied with a moment's thought. "You'll address me as Captain. If you call me Chloe without being invited to do so, you get the whip. If you speak without being invited or seeking permission first, you get the whip. You'll get the whip for a lot of things, including just when I damned well feel like it. The sooner you make your peace with that, the easier things will go for you. Now get yourself off the ground, and I'll show you to the barracks."

Aching, Tisiphone managed to pull herself up. She didn't bother wiping the dirt from her. Oddly, she didn't feel a swell of resentment over the treatment by Chloe. A slight sense of foreboding, sure, but no resentment. She hoped only that she could handle what was to come, and make Spiro's efforts on her behalf worth it. She turned to look at Spiro one last time as she fell into step beside Chloe. Spiro waved to her, then got the horse into motion and the cart began trundling off.

"So, Tisiphone," Chloe began, her voice even but cordial as if she had not just beaten the younger girl, "how long have you been a slave?"

"Uhh…"—the days ran together already— "A week, I think?"

"Parents are dead?"

"Yes," she said simply, walling herself off from the wellspring of emotion that topic inevitably called up. A

Christopher J. Ferguson

raw nerve that would hurt for some time, if ever to be healed.

"Just as well. Most of the girls are orphans or unwanted. I've found that those who aren't tend to harbor irrational fantasies about their parents coming to rescue them, or escaping to find them. Those are usually the girls who die first. Same with the ones who think some boy is going to fight their way into camp on a horse and carry them away."

As they walked, Tisiphone spotted several soldiers, not trainees, but full-fledged soldiers in bronze armor with spears at guard. Chloe might walk about freely enough, but this was still a slave camp, at least the female portion of it. "I don't have a boy either."

"Good. You won't have much male company over the next year, but if you survive it and honor yourself in combat, you'll find little shortage of male admirers, even if you begin to look like me. Just be sure not to get with child. The Empire doesn't care what you do with your body, but it has no use for pregnant soldiers. They'll beat you until you lose the child." Tisiphone frowned, horrified. "If you survive the year and take a lover, I can tell you some ways to avoid pregnancy."

Tisiphone felt her face grow hot at this frank and unexpected discussion of her future sexual hygiene. Still, she was gratified by talk that assumed she would survive the next year, talk which implied also she would be able to control her sexual decisions even as a slave, so long as she avoided pregnancy. She'd never thought much about children thus far. Perhaps when she was older that requirement to avoid pregnancy would become burdensome. She'd worry about that when the time came.

Chloe guided her to the long stone building. As she'd guessed, it proved to be the barracks. "You sleep here and eat here," Chloe confirmed as they approached the building. "You all rotate duty in the kitchens, which means the food tends to be awful, particularly at first. Since I have to eat it too, and I take the whip to those who leave me gagging, the food tends to improve as the year progresses."

Tisiphone wondered why no trainee had thought to poison this woman, although probably no poison had been created capable of killing as hard a woman as Chloe.

That was oddly comforting.

Chloe opened the door to the barracks. Within it was fairly dark, only a few open slats in the walls letting in light. A simmering of girls' voices immediately hushed into silence as Chloe stood in the doorway. Beds mainly took up the room, twenty of them, each one with a scraggly occupant much like herself. Blondes and brunettes, each clothed in the simple tunic of a slave. They all turned and stared, silent. The oldest might have been sixteen, the youngest barely thirteen.

"As I said," Chloe said, "we already have a full cohort. Twenty beds have already been taken. You'll need to sleep on the floor until a bed is freed up. It shouldn't take long." With those ominous words, Chloe pushed her into the room and left, closing the door as she did.

Tisiphone took a few hesitant steps within as her eyes adjusted to the dim light. The girls within were a disheveled lot, some short, some tall, but thin and wiry. Twenty sets of eyes shone back at her, apprising her as she did them. Eventually, they turned away, returning to their whispered conversations.

"Hey, new girl," hissed a voice from nearby. Tisiphone turned to it and saw a tall, lanky girl sitting atop a thin straw mattress. She couldn't have been much older than Tisiphone, but even sitting down, Tisiphone could see the other girl was much taller. "You don't have to sleep on the floor. We can share."

Kindness among slave soldiers. Who would have guessed? Nonetheless, she was glad for it. She approached closer to her new friend.

"I'm Megaera, but just call me Meg," the girl said, patting a portion of the stiff bed meant for Tisiphone. It was a narrow thing, barely comfortable enough for one under normal circumstances. But better than her hole in the wall in the kitchens. "We'll sleep head to toe. I've done it before." Up close, she could see Meg was no beauty. Her face was asymmetrical, one eye socket slightly larger than the other, and her nose shifted at an angle. She wore shoulder-length brown hair she might have cut herself, and her chin jutted out from her face like a plank. She was thin and lacked a woman's figure, but with visibly rounded muscles in her shoulders and arms. If Meg was as well trained as she was, a physical fight between them would seldom go Tisiphone's way. She could do worse than to make a friend and ally of a girl such as Meg.

"Thank you," she said. "The floor would be more humiliating than uncomfortable."

"Yes, it would." She smiled, and at least her teeth proved to be reasonably straight and healthy. "So, you met Chloe. What do you think?"

Tisiphone plunked down on the mattress. Straw

poked into her flesh, but it felt like heaven after the past few days of sleeping in a cart or on rocks. "I think she's going to kill at least some of us. Particularly if she catches you calling her Chloe."

Meg grinned. "She's not kidding about that, either. Lysistrate over there,"—she waved her hand in the direction of a tall blonde girl, one of the oldest and solidly built, holding court among a bevy of younger admirers— "called her Chloe one time to her face, all innocent like she forgot. I think she meant to test her. Chloe strapped her to a board of wood and whipped her until she wept. Lysistrate held out as long as she could. I think Chloe would have killed her had she not finally cried. It's no idle threat. She's 'Captain' to us." Meg rolled her eyes in the safety of the barracks.

"How long have you all been here?"

"We've been trickling in for a month, I think. I wasn't the first one. They've been assembling a cohort. Chloe keeps us exercising, running a lot, and lifting heavy things, but hasn't started training us until the cohort was complete. We start tomorrow. Looks like you're the last one."

"Any idea what's in store?"

Meg shook her head. "Nothing specific, although everyone keeps thinking it's going to be horrible. Aside from Lysistrate, a half dozen of the girls have already been whipped, and we haven't even started yet." She considered for a moment. "Despite that, I don't think Chloe is so bad."

Tisiphone raised an eyebrow. "You are very forgiving. I got the impression she'd kill any of us who step too far out of line."

"She would. But she wouldn't enjoy it. That's all I

ask."

Tisiphone furrowed her brow and considered that for a moment. She listened and took in all the information that may help her survive.

"Are you an orphan?" Meg asked, interrupting her thoughts.

The question didn't sting so long as she didn't think about it much before answering. "My parents were killed by the Slave Lords."

Meg nodded at the assembled girls in the room. "Most of us are orphans. I don't even remember having parents. Lived on the streets, begging, stealing, fighting, as long as I can remember. A couple of the girls were sold by their families."

Tisiphone winced at that. Horrid as it had been to lose her family violently, she couldn't imagine the pain of being abandoned as a young girl by the people who should protect you would bring on. She looked around at her new peers. They were not a cloistered gaggle of pampered nobility. Rather, they were a straggly, lean crew. Lost children to a girl, but the harshness they had endured had made them tough, brought them to the point of becoming soldiers, saving their lives perhaps. Still, scrappy though they might be, no one would mistake these twenty-one girls for a unit of hardened warriors. She couldn't understand what the Empire would want with girl soldiers.

"How did you get picked for this?" Meg asked.

"I killed a man."

"He tried to rape you?"

Tisiphone narrowed her eyes at Meg. "How did you know?"

Meg's mouth twisted into a half-grin that held no

true mirth. "Same story for a lot of the girls. The Dorians seem to favor girls who can turn the tide on their rapists. Perhaps the Dorians aren't so bad after all."

"They would have let him rape me if I didn't kill him," Tisiphone observed.

There wasn't much to do during the day other than sit around and talk with the other girls. Tisiphone was introduced to them all, although it would take a few repetitions to remember all their names. Some had been waiting as long as a month for the training to start, others were almost as recent as herself. As Meg had stated, they were a hardened lot. Tisiphone herself had enjoyed an upbringing as normal as any of them and better than most. None of them had families waiting for them, and Tisiphone guessed some had far more sinister stories to tell than unlucky orphanhood. As a group, they were wary, nervous of what was to come. Chloe had been less than reticent in informing them that some of them, many of them, would die during training. The Empire only needed small cohorts of women soldiers, not twenty at a time. The Amazons Chloe herself had belonged to and led for a time, had numbered only seven at their peak. None of the girls wanted to die, of course, but for the moment, they shared a sense of solidarity. Chloe had said nothing to indicate that they would directly compete, or that a maximal number of survivals were necessarily mandated. Until then, the girls would work together to ensure as many as possible survived.

Three of the girls were selected to prepare the dinner and left the barracks early. Dinner followed a few hours later. The girls filed, under the guard of two male soldiers, to an adjoining building, squat and ramshackle, but containing what passed for their dining hall. Tisiphone sat with Meg and a small, younger girl named Pandora, barely thirteen. Pandora was blonde, childlike, and maintained an aura of innocence about her absent from most of the girls. Tisiphone liked her very much from the start, but couldn't imagine her as a soldier.

Supper, when it came, consisted of bread, water, and a thin, gravelly broth that contained chunks of unidentified meat and some green leaves, and seemed to have been cooked with sand. It was horrid, but the girls didn't complain about it and ate it dutifully. Remembering what she had said about the food, Tisiphone looked for Chloe, who ate with them, sitting alone at her own table. Indeed, Chloe looked furious, glaring at the three girls who had cooked throughout the meal.

Not surprisingly, after supper, the three girls were taken out and whipped by Chloe herself. Three lashes across the bare back each. Not crippling, but enough they'd sleep on their stomachs the next few nights. The others were forced to watch. Tisiphone flinched with each crack of the whip. Her own thigh had formed into a puffy welt where Chloe had lashed her earlier. This was not going to be an easy year. *If* she lived through it at all.

Tisiphone watched Chloe as she whipped the girls. Her eyes narrowed as she watched every movement, every expression on the woman's damaged face. Chloe was a master with the whip; that much was evident. Not merely as a device of punishment, but the leather came down exactly where Chloe wanted it each time. In her hands, the whip could be a precise instrument of war. Never once did Chloe smile as she whipped the girls. Tisiphone couldn't say she saw regret in the woman's face, but the woman's expression never changed from that of someone doing heavy work. Nothing indicated she enjoyed whipping the girls. That made it better somehow.

Once the punishments were over, Chloe began to coil up her whip. To the group she said, "Let's try for better tomorrow night. As you might imagine, I don't have particular tastes, but I do have some standards. Now get to sleep. Enjoy it. This will be the last night of real sleep you'll have for a year."

The girls began filing away, quietly. A few went to help the victims of the whippings cover themselves and get back to the barracks. Tisiphone turned and began walking to the barracks.

"Wait. New girl." Chloe's voice rang out like a hammer.

Tisiphone's blood drained into her feet. She stopped and turned. By the gods, what had she done?

Chloe regarded her coldly through her one good eye. "Come with me. I want to talk to you."

Chapter 7

Eye of the Beholder

The short walk to Chloe's hut felt like an eternity, each step a mile. Tisiphone followed in silence, staring helplessly at Chloe's long, curled tresses, for the woman never looked back at her. Chloe merely coiled up her whip absently, clipping it to her belt when she was done. She barely held the door open for Tisiphone.

By now, the sun had fallen and only the last hues of orange and pink slipped down beyond the horizon. It was dark within the small house. Chloe struck a flint several times until she could spark up a wick, then put this to a small oil lamp. Merely the possession of such a treasure as an oil lamp would have marked Chloe for very wealthy in the village in which Tisiphone had been raised.

The light cast a faint orange glow across the room. Chloe lived in this simple, one room shelter, her possessions limited to a simple bed with a straw mattress, a chest for what clothes she had, a number of accruements for washing and hygiene, and a table and chair. Upon the table were Chloe's remarkable riches, the oil lamp, and, sitting dangerously next to it, several rolled up parchments and a writing stylus. Scrolls. Tisiphone wrinkled her nose.

Chloe began unstrapping her leather armor, letting

the breastplate fall to the floor. Her tunic underneath bore red stains from the leather. She sat on the edge of the bed and began doing the same with the leather greaves that protected her shins. It seemed almost as if she had forgotten Tisiphone.

Tisiphone opened her mouth, then hesitated. She didn't want to go stumbling into obvious mistakes, inviting intimacy with that leather whip. Tentatively, she asked, "Permission to speak, captain?"

Chloe looked up, her eyes narrow, as if greatly inconvenienced by the girl she'd asked to follow her. At least she didn't reach for the whip. "You may speak."

"You have papyrus," she observed, impressed. She'd only ever heard of it before. Something kings used to write down lists of their riches.

Chloe watched her for a moment. "The Sea People bring it with them. We've been able to capture some stores of it."

"And they give some of it to you?" she exclaimed with wonder, then clamped her mouth closed. She'd as much as proclaimed Chloe, a mere slave, unworthy of such a gift.

Chloe cocked her head slightly to one side and remained silent for a moment. "I can write. Why give it to people who can't?" She stood and unhitched her belt, flinging it, with the whip atop the leather armor. From a distance, just in her tunic, she might have appeared now as any other woman. Tisiphone wasn't fooled by it, though. It wasn't the armor that frightened her. "You'll learn to write too, soon enough."

That took Tisiphone aback.

Chloe smiled. "We're to train you to slaughter. The sword isn't the only tool you can use to kill. The parchment isn't a gift. No one gives me anything I haven't proven I could pay back their investment with interest."

Tisiphone considered that for a moment, absorbed it. Eventually, she felt brave enough to ask. "You wanted to speak to me, captain?"

Chloe sat in her simple wooden chair, near now to the oil lamp. Light flickered across her scarred face. "I noticed you watching me as I whipped your peers tonight."

Tisiphone felt a needle of ice go down her spine. She had watched Chloe closely but didn't think the woman had noticed. She swallowed, trying to stop her mouth from going all dry. "Was I wrong to?"

"Most of the other girls averted their eyes or watched the whipped girls with empathy. You watched me. Why?"

Tisiphone looked away, considered her answer. Probably there was a correct answer, just as probably there were a hundred, a thousand wrong answers. There'd be no easy way to guess what Chloe wanted to hear, so Tisiphone decided to go with the truth. "I wanted to know if you enjoyed it, hurting them."

"And what possible difference would it make, whether I enjoyed harming them or didn't enjoy harming them, as I evidently have no difficulty doing it either way?"

"I suppose understanding it helps me to understand you. And since you will have more influence over me than anyone for the next year, I thought it was important to try to understand you."

"And so, what did you come to decide? Is my stomach all aflutter at the chance to beat young girls?"

"No, I don't think you enjoyed it. I think you'll drive us near to death if you must, because you think it will help those of us who survive you to survive at war." There, it was all out, her brief speculation about her new overseer. Pragmatically but not ideologically cruel.

Chloe worked her jaw back and forth for a moment. Then turned her back to Tisiphone and began unrolling a scroll. "That will be all, new girl. You are dismissed."

Tisiphone stood still for a moment, bewildered. Then, not wanting to risk her fortune, she turned and left, making her way back to the barracks.

****

The barracks was near silent by the time Tisiphone returned. It startled her, the absence of the expected girlish chatter, but she guessed they feared the leather more than they wished to talk. Still, by the time she slid into the cot next to Meg, her head next to the other girl's feet, a low hum of whispers started back up.

Meg nudged her gently. "What did that scarred bitch want with you?"

Tisiphone gasped. "If she whipped Lysistrate for using her name, what would she do to you if she heard you say that?!"

Meg giggled. "Oh, I'm not afraid of her." But she didn't sound like she believed it. "So, go on, what did she do to you?"

"Nothing. She just asked why I was watching her while she whipped the others."

"Oh. What did you tell her?"

"Just that I was trying to figure her out."

"And she didn't beat you for that?" Meg rolled

onto her side. "What have you figured out about our mistress?"

"Not much, really. Just I don't think she takes any pleasure in whipping us."

"She doesn't seem exactly crippled with guilt over it, either."

Tisiphone snorted. "I've only been a slave for seven days maybe, and already have my fill of those who enjoy beating their lessers. I suppose I already find someone who does it only from a sense of duty to be refreshing. How quickly my hopes shrink."

There were no more questions asked. Soon, sleep overtook them. Tisiphone let the darkness consume her. Her dreams, what little she remembered of them, were garbled and fitful. She could recall images of both Koredyne and Nyx, and the feeling that the two witches were pulling her about like a puppet. Not terribly different from reality, it seemed.

Just as she faded out in the darkness, so too she abruptly woke to it. Chloe's voice, yelling for them to wake up with a wooden truncheon banging the edge of their beds. For those particularly heavy sleepers who ignored all this, a crack of the whip had them on their feet.

Groggy eyed with barely time to put on their sandals, the girls assembled outside their barracks. They huddled together, shivering in their tunics for the sky was still dark, and the spring temperature at its lowest ebb before the dawn. Above them, the constellations twinkled, the heroes of old watching them from the celestial home.

Their breath formed on chill air. Tisiphone had no idea how soon it must be before the dawn. It seemed the darkest night when even the most robust revelers must be tucked safely in their bed. A time for gods and monsters. She guessed all of her mornings from this point out would start the same way.

Outside, Chloe paced up the line of them. The woman seemed alert as ever, dressed already in her leather armor. How she managed to wake on her own at such an hour, Tisiphone had no idea.

"Good morning, girls," Chloe said, her one good eye shining in the moonlight. "I hope you enjoyed your last night of extended sleep. Be warned, henceforth you'll be waking at this same hour each morning. I wouldn't stay up all night gossiping if you know what's good for you. Come on, now, look lively. This is the best hour to run."

And run they did. Chloe led them at what seemed a reasonable enough pace at first, until she seemed to go on and on. They left the camp well behind them and it occurred to Tisiphone they could simply scatter into the woods, but none of the girls seemed so brave or perhaps so foolish. Tisiphone had already decided she had nowhere to go, even if she got free. They ran along narrow mountain trails through thick woods, along the seashore, up and down sides of the rocky hills, until the sun not only rose but sat full and hot, high in the sky. Once they were on clear paths, Chloe would drop behind to the back and use the whip to ensure stragglers remained with the group.

Finally, they returned to camp and Chloe led them just aside the blacksmith's forge, where she finally allowed them to stop. Most of the girls immediately collapsed into heaps.

"Fools!" Chloe cried when she saw this. "Walk off

your exhaustion or your bodies will betray you!" And, of course, she was right. Several girls began to vomit, and one passed out entirely and had to be revived before Chloe took her lash to her. Several male soldiers arrived with a bucket of water and the girls took to it like kittens before a bowl of milk.

There were many elbows and growls, but Tisiphone managed to hold her own and get her fill. Once she was sure she'd replaced the fluids she'd lost on the run, she crawled away from the cacophony of her colleagues and crumpled into a clump of soft grass, her chin still wet. Chloe be damned, her legs felt like the stems of dandelions, and she dared not look at the soles of her feet for fear they must be bleeding. Soon Meg joined her in the same cluster of grass.

"She's trying to kill us," Meg whimpered between shuddered breaths.

"She's trying to get us to ask her to kill us," Tisiphone corrected.

"I had no idea running for so long could make your face hurt."

Tisiphone managed to push herself up on her elbows once she'd caught her breath. At least her companions all looked horrible. Only Lysistrate heeded Chloe's advice in full, walking in tight circles, though the blonde girl's face was near purple. The forge distracted Tisiphone's attention. The smith used his bellows to make the thing huff like a dragon, the fire becoming ever hotter.

Tisiphone's stomach pulled into a tight knot. "Why do I think it's no accident we finished off here?"

Soon, they had their answer. Once the girls had recovered enough to be able to focus their attention once more, Chloe stood in their midst and pulled back her tunic and armor to reveal the brand on her shoulder. Inside, a circle about the size of a woman's fist, the image of a dragon with upraised wings, had been seared into scarred flesh. "You are to become soldiers for the empire. You are the Emperor's property. Whatever honors and fame you may find for yourself in his service, you will never forget this. I bear the seal of my compatriots, the Amazons. For you, we have chosen the image of the hydra, for your strength will come from the unity of your many blades."

Meg groaned and settled back in the grass. "By the gods, couldn't she have chosen a brand with fewer heads?"

The smith held up the brand for all the girls to see. It was a surprisingly intricate design to waste on slaves. The image of the hydra with its dragon body and five heads encircled with the circle of steel, no bigger than Chloe's. Beautiful in its way, if only it didn't glow with the white-hot promise of pain.

To say this beautiful image was greeted with less than total enthusiasm by the girls would have been an understatement. Chloe seemed pleased, however, and grinned as she asked, "Who's first?"

Lysistrate, of course, was first, and she took the brand without screaming, although she grunted and grimaced as the circle sizzled into her shoulder. Brave bitch, she set a hard example for the rest of them to follow. Tisiphone was stunned to find her own hand in the air once Lysistrate was done.

Chloe raised her eyebrows. "New girl. I didn't think you had it in you. Very well, take your place."

The smith had set up a tree stump for the girls to sit

on while he applied the brand. The beating of her heart seemed to have become a flutter as she took her seat and pulled her tunic up over her shoulder. She thought to herself, what a bad idea it was to be branded. If caught by the Sea People, there would be no doubt they were the Emperor's soldiers. Although, presumably, that was the point should they try to run away. She wondered how painful branding could possibly be. Yet she'd burned herself accidentally at her father's forge enough times to know it would not be trivial.

The smith used the bellows to fire up the coals once more. The brand was reheated in that furnace. Tisiphone locked her eyes on Meg, who tried to grin back some encouragement. She refused to look as the smith approached her, closed her eyes when she felt a circle of warmth hovering at her shoulder.

Then pain crackled through her arm and torso so intensely she nearly lost consciousness. She clenched her teeth so tightly she thought they might crack, but refused to cry out. She might not be Lysistrate, but she wouldn't give the blonde girl the satisfaction of besting her by much in her stoic response to the branding. If only she could stop her head from swooning. Passing out would hardly be inspiring. It did not help when she could smell her own flesh burning.

But then it was over. Her shoulder still burned with great agony, but at least she braved it out. No one moved to put water on the burn, which she knew was best to avoid a scar, because scarring was the intent. She couldn't make herself look at the brand, nor stop holding her arm just below it as the pressure somehow eased the pain. But she could open her eyes and step away from the stump with only the slightest wobbliness, even if it took all her concentration.

Chloe nodded at her in approval. "Well done."

After the example she unwittingly set with Lysistrate, the other girls began to vie for the honor of going next. Tisiphone pressed her lips together, having learned a lesson from this. It only took one fool to volunteer...Lysistrate...then the rest of them fell into line, eager to endure something they actually did not want. Each wanting to be thought of as brave and strong. In this way, Chloe got all the girls branded without having to hold any of them down.

****

After the brandings were done, Chloe led the assembled to the edge of the cliffs. Here the girls stood, still clutching their burning arms, yet feeling the soothing coolness of the ocean breeze wash over them. Down far below, waves crashed against black rocks, washing over them, before pulling back to reveal a narrow strip of black pebbles. The repetitive sound of the tides calmed the girls and gave them energy.

Until the last few days, Tisiphone had never seen the beach. A turquoise sea stretched to the horizon, churning into foaming waves before crashing against the unwelcoming rocks. She breathed deeply of its salty smells now and felt her hair billow behind her in the strong wind. She thought for a moment it might even be pleasant to live here in the seat of the Empire, in Iolcus, just to partake daily of the ocean. But she had come to Iolcus as a slave and would ever remain one to them.

Chloe stood at the very edge of the cliff, almost recklessly. It seemed that an unlucky shift in the wind would be enough to send her sailing over the edge, but Chloe seemed confident in either her luck or her own ability to fight against nature. "Know this," she said, turning to them. "There is no leaving the life you have entered except by those rocks below. Unlike running, there is no dishonor in it should you find the training too hard to bear. You won't have been the first. If ever you make that choice, you will not be stopped."

They all remained silent as they watched the black rocks below, slick with the currents. Tisiphone wondered how many girls such as herself had chosen to throw themselves to their mercy. She wouldn't join their ranks, she told herself. She would be strong. She would be a soldier. She would avenge the deaths of her parents.

"All right," Chloe said at last. "It is time that you learned to fight."

****

On the first day, they only fought each other with wooden replicas of weapons. Soon these were replaced with bronze blades. Then they fought male slaves who had been promised freedom should they succeed in killing the girls. They felt their weapons cut from flesh and chop bone. Blood, hot and sticky, splashed their faces. They learned to accept this steady stream of killing and death or they died themselves.

Spring became summer, and they trained in the brutal, scorching heat. Sometimes Chloe would allow them a morning to bathe at the bottom of the cliffs rather than run until they nearly dropped. These days were a special treat. They learned also to ride horses, which Tisiphone was fond of. The training, particularly combat with the male slaves, took its toll, however. By the time the first snow fell on their camp, their numbers had dropped to fifteen. Tisiphone had long since acquired her individual bed.

They were taught to fight with short-bladed swords and light weapons. As women, they could never hope to match the physical force of men, so they learned to work around it. Chloe demonstrated how to use men's force and momentum against them, how to strike for the weak spots in armor, how to focus on speed and ingenuity rather than brute force. They learned to use the bow, expensive recurve bows, weapons men shunned as dishonorable. At last, once winter came, Chloe decided those that remained merited suits of light leather armor which matched her own.

The killing of male slaves seemed endless. Gradually, Tisiphone became inured to their suffering. They were given the opportunity for freedom, were killed in combat, with honor. It was enough.

Between it all, they were taught to read and write in the Greek language with the Dorian alphabet, all alphas, gammas, omegas, and other squiggles. They learned the barbarian language of the Sea People, too. Chloe remained a constant presence through it all, a stoic and punishing mother for them. Though she seldom spoke it aloud, Tisiphone could sense her growing pride in her cohort of girls.

So, it seemed it could go on endlessly. Although any day might bring death, the training settled into a kind of predictable routine. If Tisiphone could not say she was happy, she could at least say she was content. It helped to know that what she learned she would one day turn against Kriluss in vengeance for her adoptive parents. She could afford to be patient so long as Chloe's efforts made her stronger. Nyx, too, she would kill, although when she thought of the witch she felt both more ambivalence and dread. She still could not puzzle out the woman's larger schemes in taking an interest in Tisiphone's life. Beyond the training, her friendship with Meg grew, as did her acquaintance with the young girl Pandora, who remarkably was not among the early casualties of the training. Even Lysistrate she managed to tolerate despite that the other girl was her superior at the sword and feats of athletics. In the dead of winter, Tisiphone did not think much about the future.

But, as it does, her fate came to find her.

Chapter 8

Of Letters and Assassin's Blades

If Tisiphone could say one thing positive about the Dorian and Sea People's alphabets, it was that they overlapped considerably and made learning them easier. It helped that they had boiled the spoken sounds down to a few dozen squiggles. Chloe once showed them clay tablet examples of the old language that had been used in Greek Mycenae, long since burned by the Sea People. It looked as if a chicken had walked over wet clay. Trying to learn to read that would have been a nightmare. Nonetheless, Tisiphone struggled with letters. Mathematics she could absorb, and put her atop a horse with a recurve bow and she was matchless. She could even learn to speak the language of the Sea People. But put the letters in front of her, either in Dorian or the Sea People languages, and she seldom failed to embarrass herself. Whether the punishment of Chloe's lash or Lysistrate's snickers was worse, she could not decide.

So, once the other girls settled in for an hour or so of conversation before precious sleep, Tisiphone would remain in their dining hall with the clay tablets, trying to make sense of them. Pandora, the youngest and cleverest of their number, stayed to help her. Tisiphone prayed Artemis would bless the young girl for this kindness she did not need to give. It helped that Pandora was patient and content to repeat lessons in a way that Chloe was not. Usually, it was Tisiphone who grew tired and ended their sessions. So, it was on one particularly cold night in the dead of winter.

"Aaaarrr!" Tisiphone growled, her brain refusing to absorb one particularly difficult passage. She put her fingers in her hair and pulled at the roots. "I just don't understand why this is remotely important. Doesn't the emperor have scribes for this?"

Pandora slid a discarded tablet back in front of Tisiphone. "Some of the letters look similar, so it takes a bit of practice," Pandora explained quietly, ignoring Tisiphone's growls and not rising to the futile bait of arguing the importance of letters. That Chloe would beat them for failure was reason enough to learn. "Just as you have told me to practice with those heavy bows, you must practice with the letters. We all have both strengths and limits." Pandora had only just turned fourteen, yet she seemed infused with subtle maturity that eluded many of the girls years older.

Tisiphone turned and looked at Pandora for a moment with a frown. Then she sighed. "Yes, yes, I know. This will all be of value someday. Perhaps a Wrathknight will one day hold me at sword point, threatening my life unless I can read aloud a passage of his favorite poetry."

Pandora giggled a bit but nudged the tablet again. "Try it one more time, why don't you?"

"I think my skull is going to crack open," Tisiphone replied, irritated at the sound of whining in her own voice. "I'll take my risks with Chloe…" She instinctively looked around to make sure the woman didn't overhear them using her name. Lysistrate still sometimes let it slip in front of their captain, and the reason Lysistrate got whipped most often. Despite her snickers, the older girl was not much better at letters than Tisiphone, but excelled at everything else.

"Okay, if you wish," Pandora said with a nervous tone. "Will you come to bed, then?"

"In a moment. I need some air to calm my frustrations."

Pandora patted her on the shoulder. "It will come to you one day. You'll see."

Tisiphone nodded, then stood and made her way to the door, relishing the feeling as the crisp air hit her skin. She wore the fitted leather armor made for her once she seemed unlikely to die in training. It was not strictly required they wear the armor outside of weapons training, but they had little other heavy attire to help protect them from the cold. Besides, it made them feel like soldiers, which was comforting somehow.

Her feet crunched in frost-coated grass, and her breath formed clouds in the air. Overhead, the stars shone brilliantly in the heavens, and the sound of waves crashing against the rocks brought some comfort. Here, all seemed peaceful and right with the world. No matter what wars might tear apart Greece, the gods would ever watch from the skies above.

Here, alone for a moment and away from her training, her mind could pause to reflect on all that had transpired these past months. Perhaps six months ago she had been safe in her village, with her parents. Certainly, her life had been odd, training at both weaponry and blacksmithing, neither woman's work.

But, it had seemed normal enough to her. Aside from tossing her father around or, more often, being tossed about by him, she'd never harmed anyone. Now, six months later, she'd killed men. Certainly the first had earned it, but the rest, the slaves killed in training, had not. They were as well armed as she, true, and were given a chance at freedom if they killed her, but at this juncture, there could be little doubt that the average slave, even a man, had any chance against her or the other Furies in training. It was slaughter. How could she become so inured to it? Or was that the point, to make her a killing machine, ultimately no better than a Wrathknight? Would they expect her one day to ride down on another little girl's village and pluck her from her dead father's arms?

Tisiphone swore she'd never let it get that far. A slave she might be, but she'd never let the Empire have her soul. Besides, there was still the matter of Kriluss, and the vengeance she must take for her adoptive parents. She had no idea what larger plan the Empire might have for her...or what scheme Koredyne, or Nyx, for that matter. Why did so many strange people seem so interested in her fate? Whatever they wished for her, though, she meant to see Kriluss dead.

A soft crunch from behind broke her from wandering thoughts. Her senses went instantly on alert, although she took care not to move suddenly, to give any indication she'd heard. She sighed loudly, as if still in rumination, but her mind quickly went into gear. The sound was like a footfall on the frozen grass. A careful one, trying to be quiet. Perhaps ten paces behind her.

Had it been one of the girls, they'd have called out to her. It was foolish to play pranks sneaking up on one another unless you wished for a fist in your face at the very least. Perhaps Chloe might be testing her, but even she was usually direct about it and hadn't taken yet to ambushing them. As such, there was little reason to believe anything than that she was under imminent attack.

She reached instinctively for her blade, but, of course, she didn't have one strapped on now. She was close enough to the woods, though, that she might be able to improvise something. A rock or even a branch she could defend herself with momentarily while she raised the alarm. If she could fend off the initial blitz, her attacker would have no hope against a camp of Furies.

She sucked in a deep breath and held it. There…just a few feet away, was a good solid-looking wooden branch, perhaps three fingers in diameter. A little shorter than she'd have preferred, like a wooden dagger, but it would do the job she needed.

Another soft crunch of a foot in the frost.

Tisiphone darted into the woods. Behind her, she heard her pursuer's footfalls break into a run to intercept her. She managed a sidelong glance, saw little more than a shadowy blur moving in fast. As with strength, athletic men tended to have the advantage in raw speed, but she could use that against him. She deviated from her intended course slightly, listening for his steps behind her. Closer they came. She could hear his labored breath now, panting as he came at her. She could almost feel his fingertips as they reached for her tunic. When he reached her, surely he'd draw a blade across her throat.

Then she threw herself to the side, rolled into a ball

through the frost, and directly at the branch she'd spied. Her attacker roared right past her, unable to shift his momentum, and slipped in the frost when he tried. She heard him curse softly. Greek. She had her branch now, and rolled back to a standing position, taking a defensive posture and holding her ground. "Alarm! Alarm!" she screamed.

The man in front of her pulled himself up. Still, he was little more than a shadow, a black cloak hiding him expertly in the night. The flash of starlight off a blade was difficult to miss, however. His head darted from side to side when she called out. He'd blown his best chance, and now had only moments left. As soon as she'd called out, commotion rustled in the Furies' barracks, and the clanking of male sentries could be heard as well.

He darted in toward her, the blade flashing. She anticipated his strike and batted it away with her branch. He was small and lithe, a little taller than she. Fast, like a viper, rather than strong. But he was distracted now, desperate to get in his strike and escape. He moved in again, a little too determined, going directly at her body. She stepped to the side, deflected his dagger, and clunked him across the side of the head for good measure. He slipped once again and fell. He rolled backward out of her reach, though she had little more than the branch to beat him with, and came up standing.

By now, figures were rapidly approaching. The Furies moved from their barracks into the darkness like a horde of ghouls, silent and dark, only the pinpricks of light glinting off their blades to give evidence of their approach. The male sentries were more distant, but louder. The assassin looked at Tisiphone, then at shifting forms in the darkness he knew heralded his own end. She stood ready to meet any further attempts on her life that he made. The man was no fool and knew his opportunity had been lost. He drew his cloak around him and set off at a sprint in the direction opposite the Furies' barracks.

"Over here!" Tisiphone cried, not wanting the fiend to get away.

She needn't have bothered. He'd gotten no more than ten paces before his sprint suddenly stopped and he flipped onto his back with a "Glurk!" He writhed there for some moments, clutching at his throat, and Tisiphone already knew well the sound of a man struggling to breathe through his own blood. In a minute, he was still.

A small, female figure emerged from the dark and kicked the still form with a foot, as if curious whether he was still alive. Tisiphone knew it would be Chloe even before she moved close enough to see. The woman was dressed for sleep, only in her tunic and barefoot, but the sword in her hand had been all she needed.

The Furies, fourteen other girls with swords, bows and daggers, surrounded them just seconds later, then finally several big, armored sentries lumbered into view.

"What is going on?" Chloe demanded. "Who is this man I have slain?"

Tisiphone stepped forward. "Captain, I had been taking some air outside the barracks after studying. I heard him approaching from behind me and managed to defend myself from his attack while raising the alarm."

She tossed her branch back into the undergrowth.

Chloe regarded her evenly as she spoke, her thoughts unreadable. "So, he got all the way into the center of this camp. Do our sentries not patrol regularly anymore?" She turned her gaze on the male soldiers, who only looked down or away. Their commander would no doubt hear of this. Likely as not, they had floggings in their future.

"Do you think he came to rape one of us?" one of the girls asked.

Chloe nudged away the hood from his face. "Coming here to satisfy one's urges would be foolish for any man. No, I think he had other business. Has anyone seen his face before?"

The girls moved in closer to have a look at him. He was hard to see in the darkness, but his face was average, with short facial hair and a scar over his left eye. Tisiphone didn't recall having seen him before, nor did any of the others admit to it. Silence settled over the assembled mass.

Chloe looked away, dismissing them as useless. She began moving quickly, backtracking the assassin's movements, pausing where he and Tisiphone had fought, then moving toward a cluster of rocks and bushes not far from the barracks. The others followed her, watching. At last, she spoke. "There is no frost along the ground here, and much scuffing of the ground. He waited here for some time, watching the girls' barracks. Was Tisiphone the only one to step outside after dark?"

Several girls volunteered that they, too, had stepped out in the hours before Tisiphone, to attend to chores or heed nature's call.

"Then he waited here, possibly for hours, while one girl after another paraded before him," Chloe observed. "Yet he only struck once the new girl was outside. Either she is far more beautiful a target than the rest or…"

Tisiphone bit her lip softly and looked down, aware of the many eyes upon her. She'd been the target all along. This was no random attack, either by a rapist or otherwise. He'd come for her, to kill her.

Chloe's eyes bored into her, somehow making her feel shame to have been the target of such an attack. "The rest of you are dismissed. New girl, I wish to speak with you. Follow me to my quarters. My feet are freezing."

The others broke up with sympathetic looks toward her. The girls returned to their barracks, murmuring, while the male soldiers began to cart off the body. Chloe made haste toward her hut, never looking back to be sure Tisiphone followed. She didn't need to.

Once inside the hut, Chloe lit her oil lamp. No other source of warmth cut through the winter chill, but the presence of two bodies in such a confined space helped some. Chloe sat on the end of her cot and began to rub her feet. Tisiphone stood near the door, remaining quiet, as was expected.

"We typically don't ask many questions of the girls we recruit," Chloe began without looking up. "Most of their stories follow a similar theme. Orphaned or sold, forced to learn to fight to live in a cruel world, many of them the product of unimaginable depravity or violence. We hone that to make them something useful, something more than feral children living on the margins of Dorian society. The life of a slave soldier may be short, but it opens a door to honor most of these girls would not know otherwise."

Tisiphone swallowed and remained silent, curious to discover the conclusion of this discussion.

Chloe now looked up, her eyes cold. "We fought the Sea People in my day as well. It seems they've been crashing along our shores for as long as anyone can remember, destroying all in their path."

Tisiphone clenched her jaw when Chloe referred to 'our shores.' These were not Dorian shores; they were Greek. The Dorians were as much parasites on the former glory of Greece as were the Sea People.

Chloe stood, peering hard at Tisiphone. "You still think yourself a Mycenaean, don't you?" She paused, allowing the question to hang in the air between them, then turned and paced a short path several times in her modest abode. "The Sea People might know well enough from the Amazons that we train women here to fight. I might be willing to believe they'd send an assassin to disrupt our camp, to sow fear into our finest warriors before they are fully honed. But this one didn't come for one of the Furies. He came for you." She stopped and stared at Tisiphone. "And I want to know why."

Tisiphone opened her mouth but found herself without breath. She stammered for some moments ineffectually.

"How did you learn to fight?" Chloe demanded. "Before you came here. Who taught you what you already knew?"

"My father!" Tisiphone instinctively took a step back, but collided with the closed door behind her.

Chloe's eyes narrowed. "A Greek man teaching a

girl to fight. Why?"

Tisiphone's head twirled like a child's spinning toy. She hadn't expected to come under such an interrogation. "He was told to, by Koredyne. I was adopted. Koredyne was a witch who gave me to my adoptive parents on the condition my father trained me. I don't know why."

Chloe frowned. "Is there more?"

Tisiphone swallowed. "Another witch, Nyx…she helped the slave lord Kriluss kill my father. But then…she helped me of a sort. Had me sent here rather than made a pleasure slave. Again, I don't know why."

"Nyx, I know of her," Chloe growled. "I'm a fool not to see you're different from the others. Your soul, too full of hope and purpose, not feral. And here you are with not one but two sorceresses playing with your destiny. That would seem to leave no doubt you were specifically targeted."

"But why? I've done nothing. I'm not even the best of the Furies. That's clearly Lysistrate or Meg."

"You're smarter than they, and a better leader," Chloe said, almost absentmindedly, thinking of other things. She paced back and forth in the small hut.

Tisiphone felt her breath stolen from her chest. Complements from Chloe! And no small ones, either. She guessed Chloe would never have uttered them had she not been so distracted. It was almost worth nearly being assassinated to hear them.

"Whoever is behind this…The Sea People, or someone else…they will not stop at one attempt. Damn. You place all the Furies in jeopardy." Chloe continued to pace.

Tisiphone withered. She should not have expected

the flow of compliments to continue for long. "I will leave then, so as not to endanger the others."

"Don't be a git. The Furies do not abandon one of their own. Have I taught you nothing? Besides, you are a slave. You are not permitted to simply leave." She rubbed her hand along her forehead. "But Furies don't sit idly by and allow their enemies the initiative, either. You say you don't understand why these sorceresses have an interest in you?"

Tisiphone shook her head. "No, neither told me."

"Then we must discover it for ourselves." She paced a few times more, running a hand along the outer edge of her scar at the margins of her hairline. "These accursed witches and their secrets, always meddling in the lives of real humans!" she spat. She stopped her pacing and sighed. "I know of one other of their kind, however. She might be willing to help us."

"Another sorceress?" Tisiphone did not feel instinctively cheered by the prospect of putting her fate in another of their kind.

"Indeed. Although it won't be an easy matter. Last I knew of her, she lived near the village of Astakos, on the western coast. The land near there is not under the control of the Empire, and is frequently raided by the Sea People. And Adrasteia will not give you information for free."

"Nyx and Adrasteia...you know two sorceresses?"

Chloe's good eye narrowing, rounded on Tisiphone. "I said I know *of* Nyx. She is sister to Io, the Mycenaean Queen of Euboea. One of the few remaining kingdoms of that bygone era. Nyx has little to do with the kingdom, however, having struck out on her own among brigands and tyrants. As you have learned all too well. Adrasteia is another matter. None of these witches can be said to be pure of heart, but she and I have history, and that will work to our fortune. Still, she will expect payment to help us."

"I have no money," Tisiphone stated the obvious. Whatever prestige Chloe had, Tisiphone doubted this had translated into riches for her, either.

"She keeps herself apart from civilization, taking gifts of food from the local populace. She has no need for money. The payment she takes from you will be something difficult, something personal."

Tisiphone held Chloe's gaze. She didn't understand what the payment could be, but it sounded ominous. She swallowed, hard.

"I'll go then to Astakos and find this Adrasteia. If she can tell me why I am being hunted…why these witches have meddled so in my fate—"

"You'll not go alone. Take four others with you. It is your choice who will accompany you." Chloe watched her, waiting.

Tisiphone furrowed her brow. She didn't feel good about endangering others, but she'd be crossing considerable territory, some of it potentially under Sea People's control. It made pragmatic sense to travel with a group. "Meg, of course. She is my trusted companion. Lysistrate, as well. She is insufferable, but there is no better sword arm among us. Pandora is our cleverest, even if she's not the best with combat—"

"I wouldn't disregard her talents at war," Chloe interrupted, although the tone of her voice suggested she approved of Tisiphone's choices. "Who is the last?"

Tisiphone thought for a moment. "Hagne. She is from that region of Greece and will know the area."

"Good, you have chosen well." She turned her back to Tisiphone. "I will see that horses and supplies are prepared for your team by morning. Pray to the gods they will guide your path. Get some sleep."

"Yes, thank you." Tisiphone turned and returned outside into the biting wind. Her head reeled. Her life had been odd enough, the last few months such a radical blow to all she had known before. Her parents dead, herself enslaved, then trained as an elite soldier...or assassin, depending on how one looked at it. And now she was hunted, for reasons she could not imagine. But Chloe had given her hope, hope for answers. And they would be traveling across chaotic territory, the prime hunting ground of slavers. Perhaps Kriluss would be there. She would avenge her father's death. She ground her teeth at the thought of Kriluss and Nyx, using black arts to best him unfairly. They'd pay, both of them, no matter Nyx's reason for sending her here to Chloe.

But for now, she needed to tell the others they'd be accompanying her. And sleep, with the hope her dreams would not be haunted.

Chapter 9

Underwater and Over Ground

Riding out of Iolcus, Tisiphone felt an exhilaration flare in her skin. Slave though she might be, she was free of Chloe, free of the training camp, free from the Empire's troops. She had armor and a sword at her hip and a recurve bow across her back. Beneath her, a fine horse. But for her comrades, she might ride for the horizon and never look back. Perhaps somewhere far away would be a land where no one would recognize the brand on her shoulder. A place with no Sea People, no Kriluss and his Slave Lords, no Nyx, no Empire of the North.

A tantalizing thought to make her smile for a moment. But no. Freedom was not in her future. Kriluss needed to die, and that wouldn't happen if she ran away. And she knew it was trickery to think Koredyne or Nyx would simply let her vanish. She had a destiny here, and here she would stay. If the other four gave any thought to running, they didn't give voice to it. Doing so would have been dangerous. A Fury was duty bound to kill any comrade who spoke treason against the Empire and running from their duty would certainly qualify.

They rode hard to the southwest. After a day, they crossed the border of the Empire and the terrain shifted noticeably, the land becoming arid, sickened, exhausted with war and suffering. Here the last of the Mycenaean Greeks tried to scratch out a life, pressed between the Empire and the Sea People. Towns were few and the inhabitants' gaunt, wraith-like creatures robbed of all hope.

Tisiphone had learned her geography well enough. To the east lay the Kingdom of Euboea, ruled by Io, sister to Nyx. There the last of the Mycenaeans rallied what hopes they had of independence from the Dorians and Sea People. To the south and west, the Sea People spread across Greek land like locust. Tisiphone and her comrades hoped to hew just north of their lands, through terrain not yet incorporated into either empire. Through lands chaotic and brutal, full of marauders and brigands and Sea People raiders.

Once they left the Empire, they saw little more than rock and misery, felt only the cold winter winds on their skin, took comfort only in their armor and the closeness to one another. Those villages they saw were mere hovels, carved out of stone and frost.

On the third day, that changed. The jagged outcroppings of rock gave way to rolling hills of forest and field. The air warmed slightly under a brilliant sun, and the desolation of their travels gave way to a good-sized town of perhaps one or two thousand souls. Small clay or stone huts dotted a valley like pox. Through this, their road passed, and as they rode through, the smell of cooking meat greeted them. The town was big enough for a vendor to have set up shop, grilling meat for a price. The Furies had some coins given them for the trip, and coupled with the quality of food they'd suffered the past months, the temptation was too great.

Lysistrate pulled up her horse first. "Do you girls smell that? I barely recognize it—real food." She looked lustily at the small vendor's hut.

The others pulled beside her. The locals looked up at them with suspiciousness, five girls astride horses, bristling with leather armor and weapons.

"The town is Apamea," Hagne told them. "In this region, it is one of the larger towns, as it hasn't much to contend with. The people are simple folk, mainly."

"A town large enough to have a militia," Tisiphone observed, "to keep away the Slave Lords or the Sea People raiders."

Hagne nodded. "It is likely." She was a tall, thin, dark girl, about Tisiphone's age. If she had opinions on much, she kept them to herself, unlike Lysistrate. Hagne's knowledge of the geography of this area had proven invaluable.

Tisiphone swirled her horse around in a circle, scanning around them. The villagers watched, but eventually went about their business. She saw no signs of trouble, not immediately.

"We get food, then we go," Meg offered, a rare moment her opinion was in accord with Lysistrate.

"We're Dorians to them. And girls," Pandora pointed out.

"Armed enough to antagonize them, and female enough not to frighten them." Tisiphone frowned.

"We'll teach them to be frightened of us!" Lysistrate proclaimed, laughing.

"We're not here to fight," Tisiphone reminded them. Tempting though it was to ride through the town as fast as they could, it would cost in morale to forgo the tantalizing food. And Lysistrate had something of a point. To race through as if frightened might actually invite trouble. "We pay for our food, we eat, we leave. No more than twenty minutes."

They dismounted near the hut, tying their horses to a tree. Here, tall pines grew, the evergreens giving shade even in the winter. The village felt warm and alive in contrast to much of what they'd seen crossing through the heartlands of Greece.

A window was cut in the side of the hut so that customers could do business while also allowing the smell of the cooking meat to spread freely through the town. The man who ran the hovel looked at them warily as they approached. Five girls they might be, but the Dorian armor was unmistakable. Not something that would endear them to the locals. The man appeared middle-aged, gray streaking his black beard, his eyes drooping with a time-laden sadness. He said nothing as Tisiphone approached.

"We're not here to cause any problems," Tisiphone told him softly. "We're just hungry, then we're moving on. Look, we can pay." She showed him several of the copper chalkoi pennies they'd been allowed to buy supplies along their journey.

His features softened a bit. "That will work for the five of you."

She smiled and dropped the coins on the window board that functioned as a counter. Such copper coins were a trifle to the coffers of the Empire of the North, but to a man such as this, probably used to bartering with his neighbors, they'd represent a valued payment. "What do you have on offer?" The other girls clustered behind her, eager for hot food.

The man moved inside to where a large bronze pot

brewed over a primitive grill. "Rabbit, squirrel, sometimes chickens," he told her brusquely. It wasn't a list of options. He, no doubt, cooked whatever he or his family managed to hunt or barter for. Fair enough. She doubted any of the girls were picky. He began scooping helpings of the stew into rough clay bowls. These he handed out one by one to the girls.

"Thank you," Tisiphone said once the process was done. Just aside from the hut was a cluster of logs and tree stumps. A place fashioned to sit and eat. The girls made use of it, gathering together to talk while they wolfed down their food. As hoped, the hot meal proved to be an incredible luxury, almost unbelievably good to taste buds long since starved of any joy.

They chattered like the girls they were. If not for the armor and weapons, they might have been a gaggle of teen girls gathered to spend time together. They remained alert, however, eyes scanning the little bowl of forest in which they ate.

Tisiphone kept up the act of smiling and laughing even as the first men appeared on the rim of the bowl, alone or in twos. They tried to be inconspicuous at first, leaning against trees, or otherwise trying to appear as if they belonged. But they were armed, mainly with farm implements, but one or two had bows.

Tisiphone shoveled a mouthful of food, figuring they were about to run out of time to eat, and spoke through it. "I'm counting eight, nine men, mostly young within my field of vision."

Meg nodded, keeping up the act of looking casual. "Same behind you, maybe ten, eleven. No armor, primitive weapons."

Lysistrate snorted, only barely managing to make it

seem like it were part of a cheerful conversation. "We'd cut them down like rabbits." She speared a piece of meat with a small knife and chewed on the flesh nonchalantly.

Tisiphone worked to finish her food. She wasn't going to let these fools steal a meal from her. "Maybe so, but I'd prefer to avoid a fight." They shouldn't have stopped at all, perhaps, but the allure of hot food would have been too much to keep from the girls. And, Dorian armor or not, they'd paid for their food and sought no trouble. "Loosen your weapons, though. I see one archer ahead of me."

"Two behind," Meg responded.

They'd need to go first. From the look of their bows, they'd need a direct hit to pierce even the Furies' leather armor, and these youths didn't look the type to be steady with their aim. But a lucky shot to the face or throat would be devastating. They'd need to go down fast in the event a fight. So, Tisiphone shifted her own recurve bow along her back so she'd be able to pull it free quickly.

The young men were probably militia, meant to keep the village safe from Sea People and Empire raiders. If defense was their main concern, they might be reasoned with.

Once the men reached some kind of critical mass, they gave up any pretense of loitering about and began to converge on the Furies. They held their primitive weapons with menace, surrounding the girls. The Furies went silent, but did not stand.

Two men emerged from the mob, both of them barely in their twenties. Unclean, unruly sorts. Tisiphone peered at them, sizing them up. The larger of the two projected forward like a solid wall of muscle. His chest and arms weren't those of a soldier, toned like a bowstring, but built more like a boulder from a lifetime of bone-breaking labor. He grinned and salivated like a fool, bearing down on the group from behind Lysistrate.

Just left of him, from Tisiphone's perspective, a shorter, but by no means weak blond man, build solid and sure. He watched the Furies with a smile, oozing confidence and bravado. The leader of this motley band of militia, she figured. He didn't quite manage to be handsome, teeth too yellow and crooked, the smile radiating disdain rather than warmth. Around his neck was a metal chain, no small treasure, and dangling from it, a little bronze dolphin. Curious, she thought, for a village so far inland.

"Well, what have we here?" he chortled, enjoying his perceived safety in numbers. "Some Dorian girls have gone for a ride." Unlike his hulking companion, he kept a slight distance from the Furies, watching each of the girls in turn. An axe slung over his shoulder and a dagger was secured in place through his belt. The latter marked him as a fairly wealthy man for a town like this. "You're a long way from the Empire of the North."

"We're just passing through," Tisiphone responded quietly. "The delectable scent of the vendor's food urged us to stop and eat. Now we're finished, we'll be on our way." She shifted in her seat to face this pair.

The blond frowned in a mockery of sadness. "No need to go so soon. We like when pretty girls visit us, don't we, Nikon?"

His titanic friend stopped behind Lysistrate. "We

do, we do. Stay for a bit." He took a strand of Lysistrate's golden hair in his stained fingers, rubbing it between them. Lysistrate's face turned to stone, her jaw set hard.

Tisiphone gave her a warning look. "We can't stay."

"Where are you going in such a hurry?" the blond asked.

Tisiphone paused, considering how best to respond. "I mean no offense, but that is our own business."

The blond chuckled, and Nikon followed suit in what seemed an instinctive mimicry reaction. None of the other militia looked so amused. Tisiphone saw in their faces the usual look of worry of young men forced to become soldiers when it wasn't in their character. There needn't be a fight if not for these two in the lead.

The blond opened his mouth to speak, his expression belying his belief he must have a clever comment planned.

The old man who ran the food stand interrupted him. "Sethos!" he cried, emerging from his hut, and scuttling forward with the jerky movements of the aged. "Leave them be! They are just girls."

"Dorians, old man. The Empire must be running out of men to make soldiers out of little girls." That got a chuckle from most of the militia. It was a good line, managing to minimize whatever threat the Furies might have projected. The militia would be more confident this was a fight they could win and easily. Fools.

"Dorians who pay for their food. More than you can say, brute!" the old man chastised.

"Be gone, old man. I tire of your prattle. Be gone,

or I'll have you removed!"

"You'll do nothing of the sort!" called another male voice from the periphery. A tall man emerged from among the trees, walking between the militia as if they were children. He wore the garb of a hunter and held a good recurve bow in one hand. Wonderful, another bowman, with a quality weapon at that. He seemed a bit older than the militia, perhaps thirty with several days' growth of beard. His form was thin and graceful, and his face was handsome in a rustic way. His countenance commanded respect, although he seemed to be apart from the militia. "What is the meaning of this, Sethos?"

Tisiphone looked over at the other girls. This town didn't have a clear governance structure, she guessed, allowing an assortment of alpha males to struggle for supremacy. Somehow, it was women who always suffered most in such environs. She kept quiet for now, though; discord among the locals could only work to their advantage.

Sethos groaned. "Ah, Galen, your timing is impeccable, as always. You have no authority here. Take the old man and be gone."

Nikon watched Galen's arrival with suspicions, his hand still entwining Lysistrate's hair.

Galen was not to be dissuaded. "Picking on the weak, as usual, I see, Sethos." His eyes scanned the Furies for a moment before turning back to the blond. "Although you may be in for a surprise with this lot."

"Is that so?" Sethos seethed, although Tisiphone could see him give pause.

"Let them go, Sethos," Galen suggested. "There's no benefit to fighting here today."

Tisiphone watched the newcomer carefully, trying to intuit his motivation, his intent. He proved harder to read than most. Their eyes met briefly, but he showed her nothing. Whether he truly meant to be helpful or had other motives, was difficult to discern. Nonetheless, the distraction he caused was enough for her to quietly slip her bow over her shoulder while the militia watched Galen and Sethos talk. Out of the corner of her eye, she saw Meg and Hagne do the same. Lysistrate was caught under Nikon's attention and had no such opportunity, nor did Pandora next to her, who also had her back directly to Sethos. So, three bows at the ready, and three archers to be brought down immediately. Subtly, Tisiphone motioned targets for Meg and Hagne, so their efforts would be coordinated.

Sethos appeared to consider Galen's words. "Let a patrol of Dorians go in our territory? Why, they could simply return with more of their kind, bring the Empire down on us."

Galen countered, "Killing them would more likely do the same."

"Our business has nothing to do with your town," Tisiphone said. "Once we leave, you'll not hear from us again. I swear it by Artemis."

"Yes, the oaths of a Dorian are comforting." He stroked his chin. "Very well. We will allow the Dorian girls to leave. But their horses stay. And their weapons."

Galen shook his head. "That's madness. They'll never agree to that."

Tisiphone frowned. Men, bargaining over their welfare as if they weren't even there.

"Make them give us a kiss," Nikon added

gleefully. "The pretty girls should give us a kiss, so we let them go." His hand in Lysistrate's hair tightened into a fist.

Sethos chuckled. "Nikon is a simple man. But he has a point. Your weapons and horses stay. And I don't think it unreasonable to leave us some of your favors. Nikon deserves his kiss."

"Sethos…think for a moment…" Galen attempted.

Tisiphone had had enough. Blood boiled fiery within her veins. Her eyes locked with Lysistrate. "I agree, actually. Lysistrate, give Nikon your kiss."

The blonde girl grinned, and like a tornado, spun into motion. She twisted in her seat and spun her arm around to drive the small knife into Nikon's cheek. Nikon screamed and fell to one knee, blood squirting in a gush onto Lysistrate's hand.

Tisiphone stood, pulled the recurve bow from her back, and had an arrow notched and fired before the men had even moved. Her target, his face obscured by the distance, fell with a grunt. Next to her, she heard two more arrows whistle away through the air, two more cries in the distance. The militia archers were down.

Pandora drew her short sword and moved into position to defend Tisiphone, Meg, and Hagne from assault by the foot militia. Lysistrate, too, drew her sword so as to finish Nikon, the big wall of a man little more than a bleeding, mewling cur with the knife still in the side of his face.

Tisiphone drew her second arrow and notched it, sighting down on Sethos. Her gaze flashed only momentarily on the rage his face betrayed, centering on the easy target of his broad torso. Hardly two seconds had passed since Lysistrate had stabbed Nikon. These village fools stood no chance. In five seconds, maybe ten, it would be done. They could have brought a hundred such as these, and it would have made no difference.

Sethos had only managed to pull the axe from his shoulder, hefting it with both hands. Tisiphone drew back her bowstring.

"Enough!" Galen stepped between them. His voice echoed through the small valley, the command in it bringing the fighting, if the impending massacre could be called that, to a halt. Even the Furies obeyed it, though with bowstrings drawn and Lysistrate's knife still firmly embedded in the sobbing Nikon's cheek.

Tisiphone tried to aim around Galen. She needed only a sliver of Sethos to hit him. She was a good enough shot to hit even a small target. Galen gave her little chance, though. He held his hands up in the air, no weapon in them. "Would you shoot me down, then?" he asked her, looking straight into her eyes. "I have no weapon drawn and have done you no harm."

"I'm not beyond it," she responded, but felt uncertain. "Take a step toward me and you die, be certain of that." The blood rushing through her told her to shoot him. He might very well be attempting to trick her, to get some advantage.

"Fine, fine. I'm staying right here." He glanced away for a moment, and Tisiphone got an impression of his nervousness. He had nerves of steel to step between them as he'd done. She gave him credit for that. "These boys here, they are nothing but children. They don't understand what you are, what you're capable of. There's no need to do more than you've done."

"We only wanted food, for which we paid. We did not seek this fight."

"I know that, and it's done now. These boys are going to put their weapons down and go home…" Behind him, Sethos grumbled something. Galen glanced over his shoulder. "Sethos, if I step away, you die first." The grumbling stopped.

Not far away, Nikon wept in suffering. Lysistrate had not released her knife from his face. His crying maintained an incredible tension between the two sides. If only the blonde girl had put him out of his misery a moment earlier.

Tisiphone scanned the battlefield. Over a dozen men remained, standing uncertainly; weapons in their hands they must have now realized were all but useless to them. Three of their comrades lay on the ground. "They put their weapons down," Tisiphone demanded, "and they go home. You too, Galen."

"It's fine, it's fine." He reached gingerly over his shoulder and removed his bow, placing it on the ground next to him. His quiver of arrows followed. Tisiphone watched him carefully, waiting for a trick. None came. He was a man of his word.

The other men surrounding them put down their weapons as well, not even waiting for Sethos' command. Most drifted away immediately. With a scowl that spoke volumes, Sethos dropped his axe. "Let Nikon go," he demanded.

"There, it's done," Galen assured. "There's just the three of us now and unarmed, hardly a match for you five. Let Nikon go. He's a bastard but no threat to you now."

Tisiphone considered for a moment, then nodded at

Lysistrate. The blonde frowned, evidently disappointed, but pulled her knife free with a wet slurp. Nikon collapsed into a ball, his hands desperately trying to hold in the blood that flowed down his neck and into the dirt beneath him. Sethos went to him and pulled him to his feet. He looked back on the Furies with naked hatred, then led his sobbing behemoth of a friend away.

"Must you keep your arrow trained on me?" Galen asked once they were gone. "I sought only to avoid bloodshed."

"We leave, once you are gone," Tisiphone replied. "Until then, we have no reason to trust you."

Galen sighed and looked her up and down. "It is a pity the Empire would transform such a precious young girl into a cold-hearted killer."

Her jaw tightened. "Better cold-hearted killers than the other options that awaited us. Is there something you wish to say to us, or do you have only condescension?"

He visibly flinched before her words. "No. Apparently, my words are misplaced. I would advise you only to ride hard and swiftly away from here. Men with wounded pride can be trusted to see them avenged." He nudged his bow with his foot. "And if you saw fit, I'd prefer you left me my bow. I see you have recurve bows of your own, and it would be difficult for me to replace mine."

"We are not thieves," Tisiphone sneered.

"Very well. I wish you good fortune, Dorian warriors." He gave her a little smile, then turned his back to them and walked away calmly. Tisiphone kept her bow drawn until he had disappeared over the edge of the depression.

Once he had, Lysistrate snorted. "Looks like Tisiphone has a boyfriend." The blonde girl sheathed her sword and wiped down the blade of the small knife.

Tisiphone's jaw dropped, and only the greatest of patience kept her from putting the notched arrow through her fellow Fury. Through gritted teeth, she commanded, "Mount up. We'd best be away from here."

The others chuckled a bit but did as she asked. Meg patted her on the shoulder on the way back to the horses. "Don't mind her. I bet Chloe has it in her mind that you'll be leading the Furies for good. Lysistrate will give you a hard time for years over that."

Tisiphone shook her head but said nothing.

Meg pulled herself up and onto her horse. "So will we continue to Astakos, then?"

Tisiphone nodded. "Yes. I still have an appointment with my own fate."

Chapter 10

Joy Formidable

A day later, they reached the western coast, the scent of sea air strong and welcoming after so long in the barren midlands. A long plateau ended and dipped down to the coast. The five girls stopped to admire the view for some moments. Down below, parallel to the waves, the village of Astakos stretched before them. It was little more than a hovel of mud huts, with primitive fishing boats casting out onto the sea.

They rode along swiftly. Five Dorians sweeping down on another Greek village, but there was nothing to be done for it. No signs of militia in this town. Too small for much of an organized defense, perhaps. They approached the first adult they could find, a middle-aged woman salting fish outside her home. She regarded their approach warily, understandably so.

"Good day." Tisiphone held her hand out to demonstrate she meant no harm. "We're trying to find Adrasteia."

The woman paused in her work and squinted up at the girls. "I'd ask what five girls would want with one such as she, but from the look of you, I'd guess fate has already had its way with you." She looked down for a moment, then looked Tisiphone in the eye. "Stick to the coast heading north. You'll find a small temple not far

140

up. We leave our offerings and requests for intercession with the gods there. You'll not find it so easy to speak with her, though, if that's what you seek."

"I know," Tisiphone nodded to her, and turned her horse around.

The temple waited only a short ride up the coast, mere minutes of travel at a canter. The wind off of the ocean was refreshing and crisp, although the waves seemed always to hold the menacing potential of Sea People's boats. The temple itself was simple enough; small, round, little more than a series of thirteen columns supporting a stone roof. The marble flooring was cracked, the entire structure overgrown with weeds and in disrepair. It overlooked a crag of rocks against which the ocean waves crashed violently.

The Furies dismounted, tying their horses to a small tree. They set about investigating the structure they had traveled so far to see.

"Not much of a temple," Lysistrate grumbled. "Where is this Adrasteia of yours?"

"You expected her to be sitting on a bench, patiently waiting for us?" Meg asked, shooting her a look.

"It would be nice."

"The cracks," Pandora interrupted after a moment, "they break through the ground. There's a chamber below us. Come look." Along the base of the temple, the cracks were wide enough in parts to fit an arm through. Peering within, they could see light flickering off the stone walls, but it was too dark to discern much else.

"The cracks are wide enough that the locals might pass food or offerings through," Hagne observed. "This temple has probably been here since the time of the Mycenaeans. The rural people prefer their local gods. Perhaps they view this sorceress of yours as a deity, or at least as an oracle for a deity."

"Possibly." Tisiphone bent down to peer into the crack. "Adrasteia!" she called into it. "I must speak with you!" Her voice echoed into the darkness but received no reply.

"This is embarrassing," Lysistrate muttered.

"Do you have any better ideas?" Meg rounded on Lysistrate, coming to Tisiphone's defense.

"Well, if there's a sorceress in there, there must be some way to get in, unless you think she magically shooed herself in through the crack." Lysistrate frowned, placing her hands on her hips.

"We didn't spot anything coming in," Hagne said. "The nearest hills are at least a hippikon inland. That's the only place for a cave entrance, and that would make for one massive series of underground caverns." She pointed to the hills off in the distance.

They all went quiet for a moment. Lysistrate kicked a rock into the waves and moved to stand near the overhang, letting herself get sprayed. Then she turned back to the others. "The water here is deep, right to the edge of the rock."

Tisiphone stood. "You think the entrance to the caverns is underwater?"

The others joined Lysistrate at the bank, all staring into the unwelcoming ocean. A jump of only a few feet would bring them down into the swirling darkness. Lysistrate was correct, though. The water looked to be deep here. How deep—it was difficult to tell.

"In the cold water of winter, you won't have long

to search for the cave," Pandora said. "Even if you find it, without a fire to warm you, you'll die of frost before long."

"I see little choice," Tisiphone replied. She began removing her bow and belt.

"Don't be absurd," Lysistrate scoffed at her. "Raised by a blacksmith with not an ocean in sight? You'll flounder around uselessly until the waves pull you under. I was raised in a fishing village. Give me a rope. I'll find your cave, then use the rope to guide you."

Tisiphone felt a stab of irritation that she couldn't do this without help. But she nodded at Lysistrate. Her suggestion was pragmatic.

"And get a fire burning brightly," Lysistrate ordered, taking charge for the moment. "Pandora is right. We'll need warmth when we return from the sea." She began undressing, stripping nude for the swim.

The others collected wood for the fire. Fortunately, there were enough dried and dead trees nearby to make for an easy task. Soon, they had a fire roaring. Even in their armor, it felt good in the chill air.

Lysistrate kept a robe about her until it was time. Once ready, she tied it to a tree, then slipped out of her robe. Without hesitation, she plunged into the water. Her scream rose immediately. "By the gods, it's cold!" Then she slipped under, the rope becoming taut as she swam. The others could see nothing but the black, roiling waves below them. They stood silently as the waves crashed against the rock.

"Do you think she'll be able to find the cave?" Hagne asked. No one answered her. "Do you think she'll survive long in that water?" she persisted.

Meg merely looked at her and shrugged.

The seconds seemed to stretch into minutes, or worse. But the rope remained taut and shook at times. Tisiphone took that to be a good sign. Then, finally, Lysistrate burst to the surface, gulping air. The crashing waves pushed her to the rock face, and the others reached out, grabbed her, and pulled her violently shaking form onto land. They had to all but carry her to the fire where she shook so badly Tisiphone thought she might just come apart.

Through chattering teeth, Lysistrate managed, "Cave. Down, ten pygons maybe. Tied…rope…to rock. Follow it. Don't know…how far in cave."

"Thank you, Lysistrate," Tisiphone said. She stood and began removing her own clothes.

"It will be dark soon," Pandora observed. "It might be best to wait for morning?"

Tisiphone shook her head. "I want to be on our way by dawn. Judging by Lysistrate, I won't be in any shape for riding after coming out of that water."

"There won't be a fire waiting in the cave," Pandora noted. "Assuming it goes through to where Adrasteia waits. If she waits."

"We've come this far. There is little point in turning away now." As she stripped off her leather armor, winds pierced through her cloth shift. Even before she was fully nude, Tisiphone began to realize just how unpleasant this experience was going to be. Finally, she stood naked, already shivering before the expanse of swirling black waves. "This is going to be horrible," she muttered.

"W-w-worse than you c-can imagine," Lysistrate confirmed. "Just k-keep to the r-rope."

Meg stood by her and touched her shoulder. "Don't push your luck. We don't know the cave Lysistrate found leads for sure to anything useful. We don't even know Adrasteia is anything but a myth. We need you alive, whatever else." She smirked. "Chloe will skin us if we go back to Iolcus without you."

Tisiphone rolled her eyes.

Meg laughed. "It's true. She's not exactly one for expressing it the way human beings would, but you're her favorite. Surely you know she's preparing you to lead the Furies?"

Tisiphone looked at Meg for a long time, absorbing those words. Is that what Chloe was doing? Sure, she'd put Tisiphone in charge of this little expedition, but she'd figured that had as much to do with it being personal for Tisiphone as opposed to the others. And she couldn't say her leadership had been flawless. Going into that town for a hot meal had been a mistake. A mistake that had gotten men killed who hadn't needed to die, and which would only inflame relations between the Empire and the unconquered towns in the wastelands. And whatever Meg might say, if they came back from this empty-handed, Chloe was sure to give her hell.

Meg patted her bare shoulder with a smile. "Good luck. I'll be here waiting for you."

Tisiphone stared down into the water. As the waves hit the rocks, they cast up a spray of icy droplets, giving her a taste of the discomfort that awaited her. She flinched each time they hit. The gusty breeze whipped her hair around her face. There was no point trying to convince herself that a perfect moment would come; that it was possible to mentally prepare herself for what awaited. After a few seconds, the impulse hit her and she dove in.

It felt as if she had plunged into fire. Every fleck of her skin erupted in searing agony that drove deep into her bones. Her muscles seized up, and she opened her mouth to scream, horrid tasting saltwater rushing in. By the gods, she never imagined anything could feel so cold. She opened her eyes, though they stung from the cold and the dark. The ocean was pure blackness, and the currents tossed her body to and fro. Never having seen the ocean until her time in Iolcus, she struggled to make her arms and legs move, to break the surface.

Finally, she sprung forth, back into precious air, and gulped it wildly. The current immediately slammed her against the rocks, and she felt her shoulder scrape against the jagged edges and the slimy surface.

"Tizzy!" someone cried, Meg maybe, or Pandora. She could barely hear over the churning water.

She groped around in the dark, searching for the rope Lysistrate had left for her.

"Here, here!" another voice shouted. Then the rope was in her hands. Still the waves tried to pull her back under or crush her against the stones, but with the rope in her hands, she managed to keep anchored, at least for now. The rope didn't keep the heat from leeching from her body, though. She wouldn't last long.

Blinking the stinging salt water from her eyes, she gulped deeply, filling her lungs as much as she could. Then she dipped under, pulling herself down with her hands until she was inverted. What light was left above didn't seem to penetrate here, and save for the rope, there was nothing but cold, impenetrable darkness. It was a testament to Lysistrate's skills that she'd been able to find a cave entrance in this. Tisiphone would never have managed it on her own.

She pulled herself deeper and deeper along the rope. It felt like descending into pure suffering. The journey seemed endless, and Tisiphone began to wonder if her arms would cramp from the cold before she reached the cave. At last, the rope angled into the mouth of a cave.

Here, Lysistrate had tied off the rope against a column of rock. Tisiphone had further still to go. How far, she had no idea. She pushed off into the darkness, feeling her way along the slick rock with her hands. Her lungs began to strain, and with that, panic threatened. Down here, in the cave, she couldn't just float back up to the surface. Either this passage brought her to the subterranean cavern, or she'd die down here.

At last, her hands found the surface of the water and she splashed up against a gravelly incline. Her trembling hands hauled her body out of the water, and she sucked in deep breaths. Once out of the water, her body began to shake violently and she could do little more than curl into a ball, desperately trying to keep her exposed flesh warm.

The chamber she found herself in was dark and dank, the sea water lapping and surging against her toes. What little light illuminated the place came from cracks in the surface above. She could see little more than the contours of a rough natural cavern that might or might not continue into the dark.

"Adrasteia!" she called, though her voice came forth weak and hoarse. She tried again, with little more success. Even if the sigil were somewhere in this place, she might never hear Tisiphone.

Only on that score, Tisiphone was wrong. As she spoke the name a third time, a fire roared to life, only feet from the girl. The flames emerged from a circle in the rock, the flames flickering between orange, yellow and green, a most unnatural sight. Tisiphone had no call to be picky, however, and crawled immediately toward the flames. Their warmth bathed her, and penetrated deep into her freezing skin, warming her blood, and soothing her shaking form. Tisiphone could not claim to be fully warm, but at least she did not feel on the edge of freezing to death.

"Thank you," she whispered, but there was no reply.

The fire cast a dim light across the chamber, and she could now see it was perhaps forty feet in circumference, and twenty feet high. There were no adornments, no sign the chamber was lived in aside from this supernatural fire. The flickering illumination revealed a shadowy recess toward the back wall, a tunnel leading further into the rock. For now, though, Tisiphone could only rock herself, letting the fire thaw her fully.

"Why have you come to me?" a voice at last asked like a murmur in her ear.

Tisiphone jumped and turned to face the speaker, but found only empty air. She looked around, confused, for a moment. The voice had been like dry leaves crumbling; vaguely feminine, but not remotely human.

"Adrasteia?" she whispered, unsettled.

"The same," rustled the voice again, now at the other ear. She could almost feel the breath against the back of her neck. She did not turn this time but could not resist peering out of the corner of her eye. Still, she saw nothing but an empty cavern.

"I am Tisiphone," she said, a bit more boldly. It suddenly occurred to her that explaining her situation would be rather complex. "Chloe of Iolcus sent me to you. She said you might help me."

"Chloe of Iolcus," the voice repeated with the grating sound that might have been a chuckle. "And does she think herself of Iolcus?"

Tisiphone furrowed her brow, confused.

The voice continued, though. "I know of you now. I should have known it would be Chloe who would send you to me. She saved my life once, but I have forgiven her for that."

Tisiphone turned her back to the fire so at least she would be freed of the sensation Adrasteia was always behind her, wherever she might actually be. "Chloe said you might be able to give me information. She said you would require payment, something difficult and personal. But all that I had has been taken from me. I don't know what I could offer you."

Her words were met with only silence for a long minute and Tisiphone wondered if she had offended the witch, or if her voice had even been only the delusion of a half-frozen mind. But finally, the harsh rasp replied, softly, even sadly, if it were possible for such a voice to sound so, "She would say that of me, for once I asked of her a dear price." Silence again for several long seconds. "I could ask from you a promise that would take away your goodness without you even being aware. But I've come to tire of such things. It is sufficient that you know I could do such a thing. Do you believe that?"

Tisiphone nodded. "I believe it."

"Very well. Let us just say that a moment will come when you will repay me what I do for you today. But, and I become soft with age, I will allow fate to decide when that moment has come. Do you agree to this?"

Tisiphone thought for a moment to see the trick in it, but really, what position was she in to argue, even if there were? "I agree to your terms."

"Then ask your questions."

Tisiphone thought for a moment. "You know who I am, don't you? You said you should have known Chloe would be the one to send me. You knew I would seek you out."

"It was highly probable this day would come. I know you very well, indeed, in some ways better than you know yourself. Better even than Koredyne, who is assigned as your guardian."

"She...what?" Tisiphone managed to keep her jaw from hanging open too long. "Well, she hasn't done a very good job!"

Silence from the darkness.

All right. Tisiphone clenched her jaw. So many questions all at once, it was difficult to know which to choose. She stuck with the one right in front of her for the moment. "Who, exactly, is Koredyne? Is she my mother?"

More raspy sounds come in bursts, undeniably chuckling this time. "By the gods, no. Even Demeter could get no more blood from that particular stone. But I suggest you begin with the question that sent you here."

Tisiphone drew her knees into her chest, as much annoyed as cold. "Fine. I've been training with Chloe to be a slave soldier for the empire," —she rubbed her brand as she spoke.— "Someone tried to have me assassinated. Between Koredyne, Nyx, and now, apparently, you, everyone seems to know what is going on with my life except me. I want to know who is trying to have me killed and why."

"That is the question I was tasked to answer for you…"

"Tasked, by whom?"

"Silence, child, let me answer. The man who wishes you dead is named Bael. He is the Overlord of the Sea People. Your line crosses with his and only one continues on. Which line continues is not yet determined. He seeks to make it sure that it is his own."

"Bael." She churned the sound of the name around in her mind, finding it sounded rough and foreign. To her, the Sea People had always just been the Sea People, an anonymous horde from distant lands. To hear the name given to their leader was almost jarring. Despite their months of education, their tutors had not specifically spoken it. A spark caught in her mind. "Is he…"

"Before you waste precious air on foolish notions," the voice hissed in her ear," he is not your father. You are not connected in any way aside from that dictated by fate. One of you lives, one of you dies."

"But why me? Why do our lines cross if we have nothing between us?"

"So it has been decided by fate."

"And so I'm supposed to kill this Bael?"

"If you wish to live, it would seem most prudent," the voice whispered, moving to her opposite ear. Adrasteia seemed almost taunting.

"And this is why I was taken from my natural parents? So that Alexis might train me to fight?"

"That, and so you would be difficult for Bael to find you, though he himself, only a young man at the time of your birth and not yet Overlord. Koredyne did well to find you your adoptive parents."

Tisiphone thought of Myrrine and Alexis, the memories seeming increasingly distant. How she had grumbled about having to fight her much stronger and faster father over and over. Now they seemed such pleasant images. "And did they have to die? Was that determined by fate as well?"

Tisiphone felt something move through the air; even the fire flickered slightly. A moment of silence passed and when Adrasteia spoke again, her voice seemed further away, almost inaudible. "I have been tasked with the integrity of your bloodline for many generations. Now that I no longer move beyond this cave, I have passed that task to Koredyne. But neither she nor I foresaw Kriluss' path crossing your own. Not until it was too late. Fate perhaps, or random chance, but now I can see it is the path that made the most sense." Adrasteia's voice carried just a hint of sadness.

Tisiphone, too, felt a wave of grief pass over her at the thought of her parents dead. Particularly that fate might have decreed their death so that she might train under the Empire, for surely that was what Adrasteia implied. It was her fault then. "And becoming a Fury, that was part of the plan too?"

"That, as you know, was Nyx's intervention. Not ours."

"Does she conspire with you, too?"

"No," Adrasteia answered simply, perhaps missing

the accusation in Tisiphone's tone. "She minds her own webs. Whatever her purpose may be, it has benefited you thus far. And, for what it may be worth, I am certain she is not in league with Bael. Even her partnership with Kriluss is one of convenience, and little emotion exists between them." A moment of silence passed. Then Adrasteia asked, her voice closer now, "You are trying to decide whether Nyx is your enemy?"

"She helped kill my parents."

"She has aided in the death of many. Though she is sister to Io, Queen of Euboea, she keeps her own council. Whether she is enemy or ally to your cause will be for you to discern."

She pulled her arms close around her and furrowed her brow in the direction she thought Adrasteia might be. "Is *she* my birth mother?"

She felt more than heard Adrasteia withdraw once more. "The issue of your parentage is not the question I was tasked to answer for you. Neither I nor Koredyne are permitted to speak of it, to what I imagine must be your frustration. I have already said too much in saying Bael is not your father. I will not play the game of elimination with you."

"Why are you not permitted to say?" Frustration was only the beginning of it.

"For Koredyne and I, it simply is part of the pact we swore. But I imagine the larger motive was to prevent you from running straight to your biological parents should they still live, which would be entirely against the point of hiding you in the first place."

"But if Bael knows who I am now, what does it matter? Now that I am with the Furies, I am obviously no longer in hiding. What harm in knowing my parents now?"

"Sending you to Iolcus was a risk on Nyx's part. I believe, whatever her motives, she selected the best path possible for you. Although among the Furies, it is true, you could not evade Bael's spies for long. But as I have said, my tongue is bound for this question. If you suspect Nyx may be your mother, you might seek her out and ask her yourself."

Tisiphone went silent, mentally digesting the notion that Nyx might be her mother. It would make some sense why Nyx had suddenly helped her after being part of the enslavement of her village and the murder of her adoptive parents. Nyx had certainly recognized Tisiphone as this person bound by fate to Bael, that much was now evident. Whether Nyx's involvement was some twisted remnant or motherly love or something else was yet to be discovered. The idea of Nyx, murderer of Alexis and Myrrine, as her biological mother sat in her stomach like a stone. "So, either I seek out Nyx or go kill Bael."

The whispering voice made a sound like the wind blowing through leaves. Chuckling, Tisiphone guessed. "Nyx is more likely to find you than you her. And you will find an army of Sea People between you and Bael. You are fortunate there is also an army of Dorians between him and you. Then again, is not infiltration and assassination part of what the Furies are trained to do?"

It was, in part at least, although they'd not yet carried out such a mission outside of training. This journey to Adrasteia had not been remotely stealthy, too lumbering, if anything.

"I have told you all that I can," said the harsh

whisper. "Now be gone. I must rest." To emphasize the point, the green-tinted fire went out, plunging the chamber into chill and darkness.

"Thank you, Adrasteia," Tisiphone said to the darkness. She stood, trembling, and faced the dark lapping pool that provided her only exit.

"And remember," said the whisper, distant now, barely audible. "You will have a favor one day to return to me."

Tisiphone turned back to the cavern but sensed she was now alone, Adrasteia having withdrawn entirely to whatever recesses she inhabited within. There was nothing to do now but to plunge back into the killing cold of the sea.

Chapter 11

Of Nightmares and Empty Dreams

A day of riding and recovery behind her, Tisiphone sat beside an early evening campfire amidst her comrades, thinking and thinking deeply. They'd traveled to the North after Tisiphone spent a night recovering from the cold water, eager not to backtrack through hostile territory. North would bring them into the Empire faster, even if the terrain were less hospitable. As the night got cold, Tisiphone was reminded of her time in the horrid ocean. She shivered, thankful to be near the flames. She considered, as she had during the day's ride, how much the effort had gotten her.

"We should ride straight south," Lysistrate advised, uninvited and not for the first time. "Find this Overlord Bael and kill him. That would solve more than just Tisiphone's problems. Get rid of the Sea People for good. Keep Greece for the Greeks!" By which she meant Dorians.

"I have to think the Empire must have thought of killing Bael by now," Meg observed with a smile of amusement. "If it were that easily done as said, someone would have done it by now."

"We don't even know where to find him," Hagne added.

"Isn't this what we do?" Lysistrate sounded exasperated. "Were we not trained to locate and infiltrate and, if need be, assassinate?"

"Lysistrate," Hagne retorted, "we managed to defeat a gang of villagers. That doesn't mean we're prepared to bring down the Sea People horde single-handedly."

Meg and Pandora giggled as Lysistrate could do little more than huff and protest. Tisiphone managed to smile at it all, although she kept out of the discussions. Meg sat beside her after a while. "Finding Adrasteia hasn't brought you much peace."

Tisiphone's smile faded. "No, it hasn't."

"Most of us have no idea what our destiny might be, or if we even have one."

Tisiphone leaned into Meg so that their arms touched. "You're quite right. It's not that, though. I'm frustrated that Adrasteia and Koredyne know my parentage but refuse to tell me. I don't know why it bothers me so. It never did before. Now I want to understand where I came from, and why they gave me up."

"From what Adrasteia told you, it sounds as if there was little choice."

"What if my mother was someone like Nyx? Gods, my father might very well be someone like Kriluss. At least it's not Bael."

"Your mother would be a woman now between thirty and perhaps fifty? This Nyx of yours, she was of the right age, wasn't she? But then again, so are countless other women. The Queen Zinovia herself, for instance." Meg got a mischievous smile on her face. "Maybe you are secretly a princess of the Empire!

Today slave, tomorrow ruling the Empire of the North with an iron hand!"

Tisiphone rolled her eyes. "If you're not even going to take this seriously…"

"Why not? If you have this destiny that brings your path in line with the Overlord of the Sea People, you can't possibly be merely from common stock. You must have…something extraordinary in your blood."

"Perhaps my father is Zeus or Apollo."

"And your mother is the moon." She smiled. "Yes, why not?"

"Girls," Pandora's voice called, interrupting them. "A rider approaches."

Conversation ceased, and they reached for weapons. Five bows drew down on a horse and rider as they appeared on the road in the dusk. A man atop a common steed, riding hard. She recognized the rider at once. Galen, the man who had tried to intercede on their behalf among the militia of that Mycenaean town. What on earth was he doing here?

Tisiphone waved off the other girls and stepped out of cover. "Galen!" she called, waving to him. It could be no coincidence he followed them.

Galen reigned in his horse as Tisiphone stepped forward to greet him. He looked down at Tisiphone from atop his mount, then to where the others waited with bows still drawn. "Dorian, it is good that we meet again."

"I may be a Dorian slave, but that doesn't make me a Dorian. What are you doing here? Answer quickly, before my friends shoot you down."

Galen leaped off his horse, taking it by the reins. "I've come to warn you. You are in grave danger."

She sighed. "Let me guess—Sethos and Nikon have gotten up to mischief. And how did you find us?"

Galen watched as the other girls came out of cover, although most of them kept arrows notched, their faces wary. "You haven't yet perfected the art of traveling without leaving a trace. Five horses on the road, it's difficult. Certainly from one such as myself. You are right, though, it is Sethos and Nikon and some of the others. I tried to reason with them, but their points of pride were wounded, to be bested so soundly by young girls."

"They picked the fight, not us," snorted Lysistrate, drawing closer.

"It's not so simple as that," Galen responded. "Many of the towns in the lands between the Empire of the North and the Sea People...they live on borrowed time, waiting on death from the south or enslavement from the north. Too far from Euboea to seek common cause with the Ionians, the followers of Io, they are on their own. The Sea People do not yet have the numbers to surge north against the Empire, but they bide their time and, in the meantime, send emissaries to the villages, making them promises of peace..."

"The bronze dolphin." Tisiphone remembered the chain around Sethos' neck. "The militia was in league with the Sea People. That's why they attacked us without provocation."

"Dorian soldiers, slave or free, riding into any town in the unclaimed lands would stoke fear. In one seduced by the Sea People bloodshed was inevitable."

"Will the Sea People really let them live?" Pandora asked.

Galen shook his head. "They make promises until

159

they grow stronger. And thus, they keep the unclaimed lands as a buffer between them and the Empire while they overrun the Ionians. Once they do, they will turn north and slaughter all in their path as always they do. But the people in the villages have nothing to cling to but false hope." He tied his horse to a tree, close to their own. "I've tried to speak to them, to get them to end their misguided allegiances to the Sea People, but they are too far from us for us to offer them any comfort."

"You work for Queen Io," Tisiphone guessed.

Galen nodded. "I do. And I regret to say I've done her little good in these lands. They are lost to us. It is only a matter of time until they fall forever; either enslaved by the Empire or obliterated."

Tisiphone recoiled slightly whenever he mentioned the Empire, instinctively sickened at her own role in fighting for it. "Why help us, then? And what is it that Sethos and Nikon have done."

"Lesser of two evils, I suppose. And as you say, you are slaves of the Empire yourself. And it is an opportunity for me to do something of worth." He looked over the assortment of girls before him. An onlooker might have thought him their mentor or uncle, although the sight of them all in armor would have put anyone off. "Sethos and Nikos have gone to the Sea People. They've gone to one of the Wrathknights who keeps watch on the unclaimed lands. I got away once I knew their intent. But they will be behind me, riding for you in force."

Tisiphone clenched her jaw. "I should have realized...that dolphin Sethos wore. It marked him as their creature."

Galen nodded.

"How many are they who follow us?"

"Wrathknights typically travel with seven lesser warriors. Sethos and Nikos will be with them, as well. Perhaps several others from the village."

"So maybe ten to fifteen." Tisiphone thought for a moment. "We must presume the Wrathknights may be out to get me specifically and could follow us into the borders of the Empire to bring back my head. I don't see much benefit in trying to outride them."

"I agree." Lysistrate stepped forward. "Let us fight them right here."

"They'll only be coming for me—"

"We'll not abandon you," Meg interrupted, "so don't insult us by even suggesting it."

Pandora and Hagne each nodded in turn, agreeing.

Tisiphone felt heartened, although she would have expected no less. They might still be in training, but their ethos would not permit them to run frightened, even from a Wrathknight. She looked to Galen. "What of you?"

He smiled, white teeth almost shining in the dusk light. "I've not ridden a long way just to let you young women die. I'm a decent aim with a bow, and can swing a sword, too, if I must."

"Can we trust that one?" Meg questioned openly.

Tisiphone regarded Galen for a moment. "I think there's only one way for us to find out." She surveyed the terrain near where they'd stopped. They'd picked it because of its relative defensibility. High ground with a good view of the road in both directions. Rock outcroppings for cover. The ensuing darkness would be to their benefit as well. "This is as good a place to fight as any. If we can ambush them, we'll neutralize their numbers."

"Fifteen against us five...six..." Lysistrate eyed Galen sideways. "They're not bringing enough to make it a fair fight as it is."

"Since when did Chloe ever teach us to fight fair?" Meg observed.

Lysistrate just laughed at that.

"They'll be tracking our horses," Tisiphone said. "Hagne, can you run our horses up the road, a hippikon or so? Tie them up, except circle one back off the road. We'll keep you on horseback with your bow."

Hagne nodded, and moved off for the horses, gathering them up to lead off.

"If they're trying to ride us down, they'll be going at a gallop. Lyz, get your rope. We'll use the outcroppings to tie it across the road. Hopefully, they won't spot it in the dark."

"That'll be a waste of some good horses," Meg observed, although nothing in her tone indicated disapproval.

"Meg and Galen, along with Hagne on horse, will shoot them down with bows. Lyz, Pandora, and I will move in with swords and finish those who are cast from their horses. If we keep our heads and support each other, we'll be able to take advantage of the chaos."

Galen smiled at her. "A tactical commander at such a precious age."

Tisiphone frowned. "If you've a better idea..."

"On the contrary, I'm rather impressed. Perhaps I am unneeded, after all. But have any of you ever seen a Wrathknight?"

They all shook their heads.

Pandora spoke up, "We've heard they are

monstrous, and that their horses kick up fire wherever they step."

Galen laughed, although only lightly. "Much is said about the Wrathknights, not all of it true, of course, although they are formidable opponents. They are not monsters, but boys identified at birth as coming from the strongest stock. They are ritually bound and mutilated to take on the appearance of demons, but do not be distracted—they are only men. As for the Nightmares, legend has it that the Wrathknights make diabolical deals with demonic agents to gain these mounts. It is true the Nightmares make fire as they gallop, although how they do it, whether some trick or true evil, I do not know."

"Monsters or men, we'll bring one down tonight," Tisiphone vowed.

They set to work on their plan. Lysistrate's rope stretched across the path, securing it among the rocky outcroppings lining either side. It took some time to find the best places to secure the rope; sharp edges might cause it to shred rather than trip riders. They needed openings through solid rock so the rope wouldn't slip free. They used some of their water to make mud from the dry dirt and rubbed this along the rope to make it harder to see. The rest they rubbed on their own hands and faces. Then they settled in to wait in silence.

Minutes stretched into hours. Tisiphone began to wonder if Galen had underestimated the time it would take the Wrathknight and his entourage to catch them. Or if the Wrathknight might have camped for the night down the road, leaving them foolishly waiting. She began even to construct wild notions that Galen might have betrayed them, being sent ahead to delay the Furies until the Wrathknight could catch up, although that made little sense.

Eventually, though, hoof beats sounded in the distance, riders coming strong. Galen had been right after all. Tisiphone peered over the mass of stone that concealed her. She saw them come into view, shadows mainly in the dark, a horde of them, difficult to count. They rode in a tight pack, and furiously. Only the Wrathknight she could make out, toward the center of the cluster. It was true what they said about them. His mount, the Nightmare, struck sparks as its feet pounded down against the earth. The path here was dirt, not stone, so she could think of no way the dark horse could do that without the aid of some evil magic.

Tisiphone's heart pounded thinking about what was to come. They were facing down a Wrathknight and his entourage, not merely some band of villagers. This would be their first real test.

The first riders bore down, ignorant of what awaited them from what Tisiphone could see. Her mind raced with everything that could go wrong. The rope could break, or the knots slip. The stone itself might break rather than hold the rope. Or the riders might spot the rope or one of them. The ambush might turn into a massacre.

Then the first rider hit the rope. Tisiphone had to resist closing her eyes. The horse's scream piercing the night was the first indication the trap was successful. Its front legs buckled and its head and chest hit the ground, its hindquarters rising above it in a slow, bone-crunching somersault. The rider ejected from the saddle, spinning through the air like a falling star, his spear tumbling away. He hit the ground like a rock, tumbling awkwardly, arms and legs flailing.

In quick succession, the second and third riders hit the rope as well. The sound of hooves became drowned out by the screaming of horses and men, the snapping of bones, and the grinding of flesh against dirt and stone.

The Wrathknight followed fourth, but he had the warning and reflexes to react. Tisiphone saw him pull on the reins and the Nightmare leaped into the air, four fiery trails blazing through the air over Tisiphone as the horse avoided the rope. It came crashing down on one of the wounded beasts, nearly slipped on the thing's wriggling form, and managed to right itself, wheeling about. The other riders pulled their horses up short, but this made them excellent targets for arrows. She heard them whistling through the air, the flicking sound as they struck flesh, more screams.

That was the last moment of the battle that held any coherence in her memory. She moved forward, stealing out from behind her hiding place, intent on facing the Wrathknight. Quickly, in the mayhem, she lost track of Lysistrate and Pandora, both of whom ought to be to her right. The Wrathknight proved an elusive target as well, disappearing into the void. She'd catch glances of sparks among the fray and move toward them, only to find he'd moved on again.

She hurried around an injured horse, moving toward the cluster of riders, using the rocks and the dark to remain hidden. She kept away from the horse's kicking legs and found the rider, crawling along the ground for cover, one leg twisted unnaturally. She drove her sword down against the back of his neck, hacking deep into bone and flesh and dropping him instantly.

She stepped over the rope into the larger mix of horses and riders, still trying to recover from their confusion and regroup. Another rider picked himself off the ground, one hand holding the shaft of an arrow that protruded from between his ribs. She stepped forward and slashed her blade across his throat before he even saw her. He'd worn a mail coat over black leather armor. One of the Wrathknight's entourage. None of the villager militia could afford such protection.

She heard the clanging of metal against metal between the mass of horses and men. Her comrades in battle. She thought to join Pandora in particular, the younger girl the weakest of them in physical combat, but couldn't locate her.

Another of the Wrathknight's comrades stepped in front of her. Stripped of his horse, his teeth gnashed with rage. He swung a jagged bladed sword at her with one hand, then stepped and drove a club at her head. Tisiphone danced back, bending lithely at the waist to allow the sword blade to arc over her, then glided to the side as the soldier charged. With both hands, she drove her sword up and into his gut, using his own momentum to drive his weight down on the blade. As she did, another blade came in high from behind him, hacking deep into his neck. Blood splashed her, and she spat it from her lips.

He fell, and she moved into the empty space. Pandora waited on the other side, heaving with effort, but unharmed.

"Where is Lysistrate?" she demanded. She twisted her position so they were near back to back, defending one another. They seemed to be the eye in a storm of chaos. Movement and pain and dust swirled on the edge of their vision, but for the moment, no one attacked.

"I lost her!" Pandora shouted back. "She went hunting some of those villagers trying to escape on foot."

Tisiphone shook her head, angry at the other girl for breaking ranks. Together, the three of them could have cut through the ranks of these barbarians. Still, she didn't worry too much about Lysistrate's fate. The girl could take care of herself, particularly against a couple of worthless militia.

From the dark and dust, a figure loomed. Tisiphone spotted it only from the sparks struck along the ground. The Nightmare emerged from the maelstrom like a demon, the Wrathknight looming atop her, sword raised high. She couldn't see him well in the darkness, but his head looked misshapen, elongated in the back like the blade of a hatchet. Astride his demon mount, he seemed like a monster. But that's what the Furies were trained to do: kill monsters.

He drove his sword down, but Tisiphone saw it coming. She grabbed Pandora by the shoulder and pulled her down, dropping her own sword in the process. The Nightmare thundered by them, and the ground shuddered under the thing's hooves. After several lengths, it stopped and turned.

"A spear!" Tisiphone demanded. "One of these bastards must have had a spear!"

The Nightmare pawed the ground, then charged them again.

"Here!" Pandora cried and held out a blood-spattered spear.

Tisiphone helped Pandora grip it. They'd been trained to fight with light blades and bows. Thrusting spears were a man's weapon, but now this one would come in handy. "Drive the butt of the thing into the ground."

Sparks showered as the Nightmare tore down on them.

Their four hands and two bodies kept the spear angled up at the horse's chest. They could only hope the darkness and dust prevented the Wrathknight from seeing what they were doing.

"This is going to hurt," Pandora muttered.

"Why do you think I let you be in front?" Tisiphone started to grin, but then the Nightmare hit them like a wall of force. The spear flew apart in Tisiphone's hands. Her face slammed against the soft flesh of the horse, but the thing's weight reverberated through her. Vision failed her, and she felt herself soaring through the air. Her head rattled and, in the midst of her flight, she hoped she wouldn't hit the ground too hard. She thought she heard a scream, whether of the horse, Pandora, or even herself perhaps, she couldn't be sure.

Then she hit the ground. Her bones jarred and her jaw ground painfully against dirt. She rolled over several times, letting the momentum ebb, and thankfully, no limbs felt broken. Not far away, she heard something heavy fall with a thud. Even as she spat soil from her mouth, she couldn't help but grin. That had to have been a horse.

She pushed herself up onto all fours, and with effort, managed to stand. Wobbly, but she did it. She reached for her belt and pulled her dagger from its sheath. Better than nothing. "Pandora?" she called. She couldn't see much of anything. Sounds of battle continued, but they seemed far off now. "Pandora?" she tried again.

Then a form moved into her view. Not Pandora. Looming over her, at least three times her own weight, the Wrathknight frowned down at her. Perhaps it was his helmet, but his head did look malformed, elongated in the back, and inhuman. His teeth were filed to points. His nose had been cut away so his face resembled a glaring skull. He'd been made to be a monster, probably from when he was a young child. For just a flash, she felt oddly bad for him.

Then he grunted angrily, and her empathy drained away. In one hand, he held a thick sword of some exotic design. In the other, he held a wooden shield decorated like the face of a leering demon, as if he needed the help. He was covered from neck to foot in expensive mail, armored better than even most Dorian heavy infantry. And she, in leather armor with a dagger. This was going to put Chloe's training to the test, Tisiphone mused.

Then, like a bull, he lunged forward, the thick blade arcing down for her skull. She could see he was prepared for her to run and flee. It wouldn't do to retreat. There was only one thing to do. With a whispered prayer to Artemis, Tisiphone dove directly into his path.

Chapter 12

A Distant Tower

Tisiphone dove for the Wrathknight's feet. The blade of his sword plunged behind her, where she had just stood. His elbow crashed against her back, but she was already tumbling, rolling to his side. As he lumbered past her, she slashed her dagger at the back of his knee. He recovered, though, and pulled his leg back before her blade cut.

She skittered back, away from him. She kept low to the ground, dagger held ready. It was an absurdly mismatched fight. She gazed the surrounding area searching for a better weapon—her dropped sword, anybody's sword. But she dared not take her eyes from him for long. In the dark, in the confusion, she couldn't spot anything.

He turned, a wide grin across his mutilated face. His filed teeth promised that he might eat her alive once he'd subdued her. He grunted something in his language. She hadn't learned the language of the Sea People well enough to catch it when her concentration was elsewhere. From the tone, she doubted it was something conciliatory.

He growled and lunged, sword held high. Anticipating the downward cleave, she rolled to the side. He'd expected this, though, and twisted his own strike into a sideways blow. She only just managed to hit the ground, the heavy blade sailing just above. She struggled to her feet, but his fist caught her under the chin and she sailed through the air. Her back hit the ground hard a moment later, and she had to shake her head to recover her wits.

The Wrathknight bore down on her, walking purposefully but conserving his energy. Her hand played along the ground. She sucked in a sharp breath. Great. She'd lost her dagger now, too. Somehow, she'd have to get around him, back to the battle area, and find a discarded weapon. From the chuckling smile he wore, he clearly understood his advantage.

And then something whistled from the dark and struck the Wrathknight between the shoulder blades. He threw his head back and cried out, as much in rage as in pain. Another whistle, and this time she saw the arrow imbed itself into the back of his right knee. The leg gave out, and he crumbled onto his injured leg. His eyes locked on hers, and his grin turned to a menacing sneer. His eyes positively burned. He growled something in that alien tongue of his once again.

Now it was her time to smile. "That's right, friend. No one said anything about fighting fair."

A third arrow struck the Wrathknight, then a fourth, both of these in his back once again. He coughed once and blood flecked on his lips. He glared at her, amazingly managing to remain kneeling. Tough ugly bastard for certain. But his companions had failed him, whereas hers had not.

She stood, eyeing him warily. Chloe had rammed it into them never to underestimate an opponent, particularly when they looked beaten. She moved sideways so as never to allow him the opportunity for a last fatal surge of energy. Glancing back toward his dead Nightmare, she spotted her sword and took it in her hands. Then she returned to him.

He'd dropped his blade by then, on hands and knees, panting hard, trying to stay up. As she closed the distance to him, he watched her. Still, she was ready for him to make some move, have some last trick ready. Make the appearance of vulnerability work for him. That was the way Furies fought, though, not death knights. As she stood near him, the rage seemed to drain from his eyes, and his breathing became calmer. A thin line of blood trickled from the corner of his mouth. He refused to go down completely, using his strength to remain on all fours. And he lifted his head high, proudly, never closing his eyes or taking them from her.

The feeling of blade through bone and flesh was familiar enough to her. Never shifting her gaze, never fully believing he was done, she brought her sword down. Only when she felt it grind through his neck, did she allow herself to believe she…she and her comrades, had won. The crack of the blade through his vertebrae jarred her hands. His head spun away from his body, and a jet of blood sprayed across her arms. His torso collapsed instantly against the ground, twitching slightly. The head rolled away into the dark.

Tisiphone stumbled back a step and shook out her hand. Looking down at her sword, she realized the blade had cracked. She tossed it away and looked around. The night was dark and still. She couldn't even see her comrades who had shot the Wrathknight. For the moment, she seemed so alone. Then she staggered past the corpse, back over to the still mass of his mount. Somewhere about that spot, she'd lost track of Pandora. The younger girl had not reappeared.

The night had gone quiet, but there could still be some of the Wrathknight's group lurking in the gloom. She searched around among the rocks and bodies and finally found something useful as a weapon. She picked up an exotic-looking blade of fine bronze; curved along the single sharpened edge rather than the short double-edged blades they'd been given. The sword was of excellent quality, likely belonged to one of the Wrathknight's entourage, certainly beyond the means of any peasant. Although different from what she was used to, she liked the feeling of it. At any rate, she had little option.

Once rearmed, she resumed her hunt for Pandora. She gave the horrid Nightmare a few thrusts with her new blade to make sure it was dead. If Pandora had been wounded in the thing's charge, which seemed the most likely explanation for her disappearance, she couldn't be far.

Moving in ever-widening concentric circles, she found the younger girl within a few minutes. Pandora lay crumpled next to an outcropping of jagged stones. Tisiphone rushed to her side at once, cradling the young girl's head in her lap. The left side of her face seemed entirely purple in the dark, and Pandora didn't react at all to being moved. She held her hand up to the girl's mouth and nose. For a moment, she noticed nothing. Then, at last, she could feel the slight stirring of breath against her hand. At least she was alive!

Footsteps in the dark set her panicking. She reached for the curved blade, starting to stand. But it was only Galen, an arrow nocked in his bow. Meg trailed just behind him. Tisiphone's heart soared to see them both alive.

"Are you all right?" Galen asked, looking about.

"Yes, I'm fine. Pandora is hurt, though."

He kneeled and examined Pandora, running his hand along the purple side of her face and into her hair. "She took the hit above the hairline, I can feel the lump. I don't feel an obvious crack in the bone, but even a small one could be dangerous." He frowned and locked eyes with Tisiphone. "She'll either wake up within a day or two, or she won't."

Tisiphone swallowed and nodded, stroking the young girl's hair. "Did we kill all the Sea People?"

Meg remained standing, her bow at the ready. "Best we can tell for now. Dead or run off. Hagne took an arrow to the shoulder and a tumble from her horse. She's back resting on the other side of the path."

"What about Lysistrate? Have you seen her?"

Meg spat on the ground. "That bitch went chasing after those peasant boys that started all this. Took down a good number of the Wrathknight's companions first, I'll grant. Still, I'm going to stick my boot up her ass for running off on you and Pandora."

Galen laughed, but it made Tisiphone groan. Meg was right in her way. Lysistrate had an incomparable sword arm, but her lack of discipline could have hurt them.

"Here, I'll take your friend." Galen kneeled and took Pandora into his arms. As he lifted her, she seemed so small, so frail. Tisiphone felt a chill as she remembered they were all still little more than girls. "Best we get everyone back together. I count the

Wrathknight and his seven companions among the dead, but several of their militia allies got away. I doubt they'd come back, but we'll need to be on guard."

Tisiphone followed him, stopping to take a scabbard from one of the Wrathknight's companions to fit her new sword. Now that she was calming down, her whole body shook slightly, and her arm and shoulder began to ache from swinging a weapon. She couldn't imagine it would be possible to get to sleep at all tonight, especially with over a dozen bodies not a hundred orgyla's distance away.

Hagne waited for them, propped up against a boulder, the arrow still protruding from her shoulder. She gasped when she saw Pandora. "By the gods, is she…"

"She's alive, but got hit hard in the head. But let me look at you." She kneeled and examined the wound on her shoulder. The arrow had gone into her right shoulder high and emerged out the back. The tip was barbed, so it was just as well it had gone through all the way. They'd never have gotten it free otherwise without slicing her shoulder open. "I know this is easy for me to say, but I don't think it's bad, not as bad as it could have been."

Hagne frowned, knowing what was coming. "I wish we had brought wine."

Tisiphone glanced around, although the surrounding darkness prevented her from seeing much. "Damn, where is Lysistrate?"

Meg stood protectively over the others, bow at the ready. With Tisiphone and Galen each ministering to a wounded girl, Meg was now the only one of them armed. They could be vulnerable even if only a few fighters returned for them.

"Galen..." Tisiphone beckoned. He looked over at what she was doing and appeared to understand immediately what she had in mind. He shifted from Pandora over to Hagne and grasped the front part of the arrow protruding from her shoulder. Tisiphone kept a firm grasp on the back part of the shaft with the fletching.

"All right," Galen said with an even tone. "I'm going to break the tip off the arrow so we can remove it from your shoulder. Are you ready?"

Hagne nodded, two short jerks of her head, eyes tightly closed.

"Here we go. One..." He snapped the barbed head off the arrow with a forceful twist.

Hagne jerked and screamed loudy, "By the gods, be damned!" As she twisted, Tisiphone pulled the rest of the shaft from her shoulder.

"There, done," Tisiphone told the girl.

Galen motioned Hagne to remain still. "Let me look at it." He peered at the wound, front and back. After a moment, he seemed satisfied. "The bleeding is not bad. So long as the wound doesn't fester in the next day or two, you should be shooting arrows into Sea People warriors by a few days' time."

"Good, yeah, that's what I was worried about," Hagne grumbled, but remained still while Galen tended to her.

A moment of quiet passed. Tisiphone asked, "You can bandage her?"

Galen nodded, barely looking at her as he went about his ministrations. Tisiphone smiled, just a bit. He was keeping quiet on purpose, letting her lead. She decided then and there Galen was a good sort, whoever in Hades he was exactly. She stood, retrieved her bow from where she'd left it, and joined Meg on sentry.

"Hell of an evening," Meg murmured when Tisiphone joined her.

"Our first combat against real soldiers," Tisiphone observed.

"You think Chloe would praise us for this?"

"Nah. She'll be proud of us, but she won't say it. She'll probably beat us for letting a couple of villagers escape." They both smirked at that, but didn't allow themselves to laugh out loud. Tisiphone had the sense the danger had passed, but they couldn't be sure. It would have been best if they had gotten to their horses and ridden away fast, but with both Pandora and Hagne down, that wasn't going to happen.

Meg nodded in Galen's direction. "Good thing the Mycenaean trodded along. He's proven useful. What's in it for him, do you suppose?"

Tisiphone regarded Galen quietly for a moment. She hadn't given his motivation much thought, despite some initial suspicion of him. He'd proven himself valuable enough indeed. They owed their lives to his warning. "I suppose we'll have to ask him."

"Allow me," Meg suggested.

Something in her tone made Tisiphone look at her askance.

"What?" Meg shrugged. "Allow me my fantasies. I doubt he'll truly cast a look my way anyway with you or Lyz nearby."

The thought that flashed first to Tisiphone's mind was that Meg was not wrong. What other gifts the gods have given her in strength, courage, loyalty, they had taken from her in beauty. It was unfortunate. She might have made a good wife to a man who did not mind a strong wife without physical aesthetics. Still, Tisiphone opened her mouth to say something comforting.

"Spare your words," Meg said first. "You're a good friend for trying."

Footfalls in the darkness made both of them spin before they could exchange more words. Bow strings were drawn back, arrows aimed into the shadows. Through the haze a form emerged, small, long hair swaying, decidedly female.

"Lyz!" Tisiphone barked before the other girl even fully emerged into their view.

"Please, captain, let me shoot just in case," Meg grumbled.

The use of Chloe's title threw Tisiphone off just a bit as Lysistrate drew to a stop in front of them. Her armor was splattered with blood, her arms drenched in it to the elbows. She huffed and puffed, out of breath, though she grinned from ear to ear. At their feet, she tossed two round bundles before hunching over, hands on her knees.

From the ground, two faces stared up at her. Sethos and Nikon, their visages caught in the last moment of terror before Lysistrate had hacked their heads from their bodies.

Lysistrate smiled at them. "That will teach them to treat with the Sea People. Here, I got you a trophy." She tossed a small chain at Tisiphone, who nearly discharged her arrow to release her hand to catch it. It was Sethos' dolphin chain.

"Lyz, you shouldn't have run off," Tisiphone barked.

"And let these two get away? If it weren't for them, we wouldn't have had this trouble." Lysistrate didn't stop smiling, not taking the reprimand seriously.

Tisiphone's fury coursed through her. "Meg, would you give us a moment?"

"Are you sure you don't want me to put an arrow through her just in case she might be a Wrathknight in disguise?"

"Meg!"

"Fine." She spat at Lysistrate's feet and reluctantly moved off to keep guard out of earshot.

Lysistrate stood tall, her grin slipping a bit. "So, what now? Am I to be given a scolding?"

"You left the group. Left me and Pandora to fend for ourselves."

Lysistrate scoffed. "You had that lot well in hand, not to mention three archers shooting those fools down. I see they're all dead and you're alive."

"Pandora is hurt, and we don't know if she'll recover. I should have you flogged for breaking ranks."

Lysistrate's smile dropped entirely at that. "I'd enjoy seeing you try. I'm easily a match for you and your bitch sidekick together."

Tisiphone ground her teeth. "Look Lyz, you and I both know you think you should be in charge rather than me. That's something you're welcome to take up with Chloe when we get back. Until then, Chloe put me in charge, so if you disobey an order from me, it's akin to disobeying an order from her, and what do you suppose she'll do to you when we get back if I tell her about that?"

Lysistrate glanced down, then around, before glaring back up. Tisiphone could positively hear the other girl thinking. She guessed it had as much to do with Lysistrate's regard for Chloe, perhaps much more than any fear of the lash.

Tisiphone's heart quickened. She had the advantage and knew it. "So complain to Chloe all you like when we get back. Until then, you'll do as I say. And if you break the line again, I will have you flogged. Do you understand?"

Lysistrate's eyes narrowed. "Yes. *Captain.*" The latter word practically vomited forth.

"Good. Rejoin the group. I'll assign watches for the night. We ride out at dawn, whether Pandora wakes or not."

Lysistrate moved past her without a further word. Tisiphone watched her with a heavy sigh. Her eyebrows pinched together in a deep frown. Perhaps she hadn't made the right choice in Lysistrate, the skill of her sword or not. Only time would tell.

****

Pandora woke the next morning by the blessing of Artemis. She remained groggy, complained of splitting headaches, and clearly would be useless in combat. But the gods had not taken her. That was enough for now. Tisiphone helped the younger girl onto her horse and smiled proudly at her. Pandora had been bloodied, fighting side by side with her against the Wrathknight.

Lysistrate led their pack as they rode out. Meg kept close to the two injured girls, and Tisiphone took the rear, riding beside Galen. They needed to talk, and now was the time.

She let her horse drop back a bit, behind the others. No point in riding furiously now. They were almost inside Empire territory, and far away from the easy reach of the Sea People. With Pandora's and Hagne's injuries, a lighter pace would allow them to heal. As she had expected, Galen allowed his horse to slow pace with hers. Once they were out of earshot, she asked, "Who are you really?"

He laughed. "I told you my name. It is Galen."

"I don't mean your name. You are not from the villages of the wastelands. And if you were in league with the Sea People, you just missed your best chance to let us die. So why are you riding about in the wastelands?"

He looked away toward the rising sun, then back at her. "I serve Euboea and her Queen, Io. I was sent to convince the people of the wastelands to remain loyal to Io and the confederacy of city states along the eastern coast that unite, to defend themselves against the Sea People, and if need be, Empire of the North as well. From Euboea down to Athens in the south, we are united as the Ionian Confederacy, but we hold only the narrow strip of the eastern coast. We are few, and seeking recruits from the wastelands could have brought us precious reinforcements. But the Sea People have already gotten to them, convinced them through fear to shift their loyalties."

"Then they are fools. The Sea People have no allies. They take no prisoners."

"So it is true, but what help do those village people have? The men will not leave the villages to fight on the coast. We have too few soldiers to protect them in the wastelands. They are caught between the Sea People to the south and the Empire of the North. The Empire takes only slaves, the Sea People take only corpses. Only the Sea People tell them they will make an exception if they help hold back the Empire to the north while they finish us in the east." He turned to look at her, all but a silhouette against the sunrise. "The Sea People will not keep that promise, but what other choice do those poor people have but to place their hope in it?"

Tisiphone absorbed his words, and felt a flash of pity for those destitute people. She wouldn't have been able to point to the location of her former village on a map, but its circumstances before falling to the slavers wouldn't have been much different. "So why do you help us, then? We fight for the Empire to the North."

"The Ionian Confederacy and the Empire of the North are not yet at war. I have no doubt the Dorians would sweep down through Euboea and Attica if they could, but the Sea People are a more pressing problem." He shrugged. "And I really didn't like Sethos and Nikon. They were bullies, thugs, even to their fellow villagers. The worst sort to prey off of these troubled times."

No, not true, Tisiphone thought. The worst were slavers like Kriluss and Nyx. That made her think. "If you serve Io, do you know of her sister, Nyx?"

"Nyx?" He looked startled. "I know of her, although she has not been to Euboea in years."

A flash of disappointment pinched through her core. She'd hoped Galen might know something of the woman who might be her mother. "She has fallen out with your Queen?"

Galen sputtered for a moment. "I am not sure it is as entirely simple as that. It is still within Nyx's right to return as a princess of Euboea. She chooses not to. However, I am not sure it is my place to discuss such a matter."

Tisiphone frowned. Who, in their right mind, turned their back on a life of comfort to rut about with slave lords? "Tell me, at least…do you know if she had a child? She would have given it up."

He shook his head. "Nyx has lived for decades in the darkness. About her, anything is possible and nothing is certain. But why ask about Nyx? She has nothing to do with the Sea People, whatever mischief she might attend to."

Briefly, she considered confiding in him, but something held her back. "I am merely curious why one such as she would turn away from a life of riches."

"They say she is a great sorceress now. Perhaps it is as simple as that she preferred power to gold."

She watched him for a moment. "You have not asked us what we were doing in the wastelands."

"Would you tell me the truth if I asked you?"

"No."

"Then that is why I have not asked you." He smiled, not looking at her.

A moment passed. Then, impulsively, Tisiphone asked him, "Does a family await you in Euboea?"

"No, I have not been blessed as such. My life has been one of fighting and war."

"Then you have no love in your heart?"

He looked at her, curious. "It is amazing that a woman can become the fiercest of warriors and still be as any woman." He chuckled a bit. "I have love in my heart. A woman captured my heart long ago, but I lost her."

"She…died?"

"No, no. She was taken far outside my reach." He

looked down. "It matters little. She'd not remember me. Although I remember her." He looked at Tisiphone and smiled. "But it's nothing for you to worry over."

But worry over it, she did. She could not help but feel a stab of jealousy over this unnamed woman who had stolen Galen's heart. Curse the other girls, they were right! She'd allowed herself the foolish infatuation of a farm girl.

"I'm afraid our paths diverge just up ahead," Galen said, snapping her out of her thoughts. "I must return to Euboea, and you, my Dorian friend, to the Empire."

"Being a slave does not make me a Dorian, even if I have a Dorian name."

"What are you then?"

She considered that for a moment, the very question bringing with it a feeling of emptiness. "I don't know." Her eyes strayed to Meg, Pandora, Hagne, and Lysistrate, riding ahead of them, unawares. "I am a Fury. Nothing more."

Galen nodded, apparently satisfied. He took her hand in his and pressed it to his lips, then said, "Very well, Fury. I must part. Until we meet again."

He rode away toward the sunrise. As she watched him go, she felt certain of one thing. They would, indeed, meet again.

Chapter 13

Calm Before the Storm

Tisiphone held the wrathknight's head aloft in one gloved hand, fingers clutching the wispy strands of the human monster's hair. Strands of gore flapped down from the neck—although they were dry now, the blood had congealed, the fluids drained. Even in the cold, it had begun to stink a bit, but it was her trophy, and she was proud to show it off.

"Impressive," Chloe pronounced evenly, voice devoid of emotion after regarding it for a moment. Her one good eye glinted in reflected candlelight as she sat, back turned to her little desk. "The five of you took down a wrathknight and his entourage with no deaths among yourselves?"

Tisiphone couldn't stop a grin from spreading. She half thought she'd pay for that later with a beating, but she couldn't stop it. "We did. We had help from an Ionian named Galen, but we were still outnumbered, maybe three to one." All right, now she was overdoing it and she knew it. She stopped talking.

Chloe cocked her head and looked at the ceiling for a moment. "Be sure to stick that thing on a pole and display it outside your barracks. Under the circumstances, I suspect we can declare your cohort graduated from training, a bit earlier than expected, but affairs have changed."

Tisiphone lowered her hand, for her arm was getting tired anyway, and she guessed she'd gotten all the warm congratulations she could expect. That something was different from when they had left was already obvious. The other girls, the Furies who had remained behind, were all gone and their gear with them. Most of the male soldiers, too. The camp was all but deserted. Almost no one would be here to see their displayed prize.

"You've come a long way from the scrappy, foolish girl whose claim to join us consisted of beating a servant in a knife fight. But, impressive as your kill is, tell me of your primary mission. What of Adrasteia?"

"We found her. I met with her. She told me it is Bael, the Overlord of the Sea People who wishes me dead. She told me our fates are crossed so that one of us must kill the other."

That set Chloe chuckling. Tisiphone fought back the urge to strike her captain, which would be satisfying for only the briefest moments. "Well, you certainly have the most compelling of fate lines. Good fortune to you in killing the leader of the Sea People."

Tisiphone frowned and stifled the urge to say something snarky. "It would appear I have little choice in the matter. Your Adrasteia and the witch Koredyne seem to have conspired together to manage my fate, although Adrasteia refused to discuss my parentage."

"*My* Adrasteia?"

Tisiphone stammered. "She implied you and she had some kind of shared history. As, I think, did you when you sent me to her. She says she asked of you something difficult. And that you saved her life once, but that she'd forgiven you for it, whatever that meant."

Chloe laughed again. "Oh, Adrasteia, that old bitch. She deserves eternal life. I hope she rots in that cave of hers forever. This world would be better without the meddling of sorceresses and the folly of kings both."

"And yet she helped us as you knew she would."

"Helped us," she scoffed. "She helped herself. Learn not to mistake mutual interest for kindness."

Chloe fell silent and Tisiphone wasn't sure if she were dismissed or not. Nervous, she chose to speak instead. "I think Nyx may be my mother."

Chloe regarded her with a skeptical eye. "You haven't come to believe Artemis is your mother, at least."

"It makes sense. Why else would she help me? She's of the right age, no one can say for sure if she's had a child or not. It's possible."

"Anything is possible with the right amount of creativity and imagination. I've just been lecturing you about mutual interest, and here you see maternal instinct in the iciest of those witches."

Tisiphone felt her hackles raise, more out of having a perfectly reasonable theory dismissed so utterly than any particular attachment to Nyx. Her brain burst to say something in reply, but she could think of nothing that wouldn't earn her a lashing. So, her mind fluttered uselessly inside her skull like a bat caught in rafters.

Chloe raised her hand dismissively. "Besides, what does it matter? You had parents enough. I was given to understand your adoptive parents cared for you well. That's more than most of these girls ever had. Some of them, their parents sold into…"

"Yes, Chloe, I know, I know." Tisiphone interrupted, unable to bear another repetition of this particular lecture. She bit her tongue the moment the words left her mouth, though. That she had uttered the woman's name in her hearing would earn her a thrashing. That she had done it while interrupting gave her serious reason to doubt whether she would survive it.

Chloe's one eye bore through her like an awl. The woman regarded her coolly for a long, silent time, little doubt imagining all manner of horrid punishments.

"Forgive my impudence, captain. I accept the consequences for my rash words." Tisiphone began to unstrap her leather armor to ready herself for a beating.

Chloe held up her hand. "No, say what is on your mind. Entertain me."

Tisiphone breathed in deeply. "In no way am I trying to compare my own fate to the misfortune of the other Furies. And, yes, I have been fortunate to have the love of a mother and father who adopted me. But…" She struggled to find the correct words. "I don't feel entirely complete not knowing who they are, my birth parents. Maybe they are long dead. Maybe they are evil through and through like Nyx. I just want to know who they are. I want to know where I come from…who I come from. I don't even know if I am a Mycenaean Greek or Dorian. I don't understand why I am chosen to have my fate intersect with Bael. I feel as if I don't understand my own life."

Chloe watched her silently, the gaze of her good eye moving up and down as if inspecting Tisiphone for the first time. Finally, she observed, "You should take comfort in the memories of good parents who loved you, adoptive or not. The quest for the answers you seek may bring you no comfort at all."

"Before the Slave Lords came, before Kriluss and Nyx killed my adoptive parents, having them was enough. Even after their deaths, seeking vengeance might have been enough to sustain me. But Nyx's act of mercy…" She bit her lower lip and shook her head.

"She's infected your mind, nothing more. Learn to see nothing but selfishness in whatever she does, no matter how it may have benefitted you. Do not let her actions gain power over you."

Tisiphone looked evenly at Chloe. "What about you? Did you know your birth parents?"

Chloe scoffed at the question and looked away. "My father was a soldier for the emperor. He died in battle against the Sea People when I was twelve. He lived long enough to be sure my mother was left with eight children of all ages. My mother could not feed us all as a widow with no prospects and little money. My elder sister was indispensable in helping my mother with the younger children. And, though you'll not believe it now, but I was the most beautiful of us. So, she sold me into slavery to have money to feed my siblings. Because of my looks, I was too valuable to be any kitchen slave. I spent two years as a sex slave until the emperor, King Diadarian, assumed the throne and launched the idea for the Amazons. I was fortunate, despite what combat did to my appearance. I'd rather be cut to ribbons in battle, piece by piece, and turned into a hideous version of what I was than rut endlessly with filthy, strange men."

Tisiphone looked down. "I feel sorrow for what happened to you."

Chloe growled. "I shouldn't have told you. The pitiful look in your eyes as you've been moaning about your birth parents got the better of me."

Tisiphone held back a smirk. She'd gotten the woman to open up for once and wasn't about to press her luck.

Chloe brushed her hand in the air to dismiss her. "Go. We'll talk more in the morning. Get yourself some sleep. Events will move quickly enough henceforth. You'll need what rest you can get."

Tisiphone nodded and turned her back to her captain. Still holding the dismembered head, she left the shack and walked back into the cold night air.

****

When she awoke, the sun was already up, and her comrades already stirring. She couldn't remember the last time the sun greeted the morning before she did. It felt wonderful, like such an incredible indulgence, and her body felt wonderful. At the next bunk over, Meg sat on the edge, stretching herself.

"Chloe let us sleep in?" Tisiphone asked.

"That or the bitch died in her sleep. Either way, I'm thankful for the rest." She looked around. Pandora was the only other one in the barracks, holding her head with a wincing expression. It had only been the five of them during the night. As Chloe had said, the other girls were gone.

"Rather nice," Meg said, "to sleep the night without fifteen girls snoring or crying in their slumber."

"Speak for yourself. I was next to you," Tisiphone snorted. "Pandora, are you all right."

"My head still hurts all the time," the younger girl replied. "But less today than yesterday. At least we're

190

back here. I can make a tonic for the pain."

Lysistrate poked her head in the door. "Chloe had a tub and hot water sent up for us. Get yourselves going. I'm tired of riding next to you stinking girls."

As Lysistrate had said, Chloe had indeed sent up a huge tub, big enough for the five of them, and a bevy of women servants to keep it filled with a steady stream of hot water. It would have been an odd sight, the five of them bathing out in the open, cold air, steam rising from the tub, treated like princesses by quiescent slave women technically no lower in rank than themselves. But they luxuriated in it.

After they were bathed, Chloe summoned them to their old training hall. She stood over the large map of the Greek peninsula and, instinctively, they gathered round. They knew this map well enough, having been grilled on it repeatedly. Tisiphone traced the path they had just traveled from Iolcus to Astakos through the belt of unclaimed territory between the Empire of the North and the domains of the Sea People.

"What remains of the old Mycenaean civilization is clustered here along the east coast of the peninsula." She traced the area with her finger. "They hold little more now than the island of Euboea and the eastern shores of Attica down through to this village of Athens. They have united under the Euboean Queen and call themselves Ionians after her. The Sea People hold all of the Peloponnese, Boeotia, and Phokis."

They all nodded. This they already knew.

Chloe put her finger on the center of the great island of Euboea. "The Sea People have landed an army here at Kymi. They have moved to besiege Io's capital city of Eritrea. When the Sea People take this city,

Euboea will fall along with Queen Io. Only the Mycenaeans of Attica will remain, surrounded by Sea People armies. They won't last long."

Tisiphone saw Meg raise her eyebrows. That was certainly a shift in fortunes, although the Ionians were few and had been disorganized. Had they any hope of fighting off the Sea People, they would have done it long before they had only the eastern shores to cling to. They waited quietly for the rest, for surely more was to come.

"The Emperor, King Diadarian, has decided the Empire of the North will rescue these Ionians from the Sea People," Chloe declared.

That avowal generated only silence in the girls. Tisiphone looked from one face to the next, and realized it was for her to speak. They might have returned to camp, but they still looked to her as the leader. Even Lysistrate kept her mouth shut. So, Tisiphone cleared her throat. "How does the emperor see fit to do that? Euboea is an island, and the Sea People control the waters."

"The emperor plans to land an army here, at Mandoudi, to the North. Our heavy infantry will smash the Sea People raiders up against the defenses of Eritrea."

"They have to get across the sea first," Tisiphone persisted, "and the Empire's navy is..." She paused, searching for a careful word.

Chloe's functioning eye swiveled up and regarded her coldly. "Pitiful? Untrained? Incompetent?"

Tisiphone thought for a moment, then answered simply, "Yes."

Chloe smiled slightly as she looked down at the

map. "The plan is to avoid the ships of the Sea People altogether. The invasion fleet will sail from Iolcus at night and reach Mandoudi before dawn."

Hagne gasped with disbelief. "Those fools won't be able to see the coast. They'll crash against the rocks."

Chloe seemed to be enjoying this, leading them from one kernel to the next. "The harbor of Mandoudi has a lighthouse. The fleet will only be able to locate the harbor once the lighthouse is lit for them. It will be carefully watched, unless the Sea People are absolute fools. And I wonder if you can guess whose task it will be to light that lighthouse?"

Tisiphone furrowed her brow. "When does the Empire need it lit?"

"It will need to be lit after midnight, seven nights hence. That gives you a few days to rest and recover from your injuries. How you get to Mandoudi is of your concern. Most of the Sea People forces will be focused on Eritrea, but I would expect them to keep some levies on the other harbors in Euboea. With Io's forces defending Eritrea, I imagine the Sea People will have control over much of the rest of the island. So, you'll need to gain entry to the lighthouse and hold it through the night. If you fail, as Hagne pointed out, the effort to oust the Sea People from Euboea will fail, and the Sea People will be in a greater position of strength to strike at the Empire."

"What about the other Furies?" Pandora asked of their missing comrades.

"They've all been given other assignments to deal with this crisis. It is best you don't know their tasks…should one group be captured." Chloe turned to

Tisiphone. "Normally the unit captain would be fully informed of all her troop's movements to keep them coordinated. The timing did not allow it in this case. You'll have to content yourself with these four for now."

Tisiphone felt her face turn scarlet and nodded quickly. She glanced at Lysistrate, but the blonde girl held her gaze away, jaw set. Chloe's message had been clear enough, though. Tisiphone was to serve as captain of *all* the Furies once they were united. Whichever of them survived the separate missions they'd been sent on.

"Rest while you can these next few days. Whatever path you choose to Euboea will not be easy. I won't be coming with you. I must begin training the next batch of your replacements for when you die. While you rest, I suggest you begin planning." That last statement was directed, once again, to Tisiphone.

Tisiphone swallowed. "The Empire has done nothing before to help the Ionians. If anything, the Empire has eagerly taken Mycenaean land in the north. Why does the emperor extend a hand to Io's people? Why now?"

Chloe's mouth turned once again to a slight smile. Tisiphone began to understand that whatever brought mirth to Chloe would seldom be good news to her. "You can ask him yourself. He's already asked to see you."

****

Tisiphone made the trip down to the palace alone and on foot. She found the walk oddly refreshing. Strolling through the city of Iolcus openly, she felt freer somehow than she had since the night her parents had died and she'd been taken. Leather armor covered the brand on her shoulder, but that armor was enough to mark her for what she was: a slave soldier. But slave or not, the people of Iolcus did not molest a Fury. She began to understand a bit of what Chloe had intimated, that her worth as a human being was not determined by the status society gave her. As she looked from one side of the street to the next, she found nothing innate in free citizen or soldier that gave them worth over her. They were anonymous to her, shades of a city that was not her own. But she, to them, was a Fury, one of very few.

She found that she was expected at the palace. A courtier greeted her politely and escorted her in. She thought to ask after Spiro but decided that would be most appropriate to attend to after her meeting with the emperor. Moving through the corridors, she couldn't say she recognized them. Most of her time in the palace had been spent below in the kitchens, aside from the brief sojourn that had led to her fateful knife battle. Still, being here made her think of Iokaste, the kind woman who had given her life so that Tisiphone might live. She would forever be in her debt and hoped that the life Iokaste had given her would honor the older woman's sacrifice.

Up, the courtier led her. The palace corridors were wide but bare of adornments. The Dorians were not given to displays of opulence, a characteristic that apparently extended to their emperor. The courtier opened a set of wide doors out onto a limestone balcony. A chill breeze greeted Tisiphone, whipping her hair back. The courtier turned to his left and bowed deeply, "I bring you the Fury, Tisiphone." Maintaining his supplicant posture, the courtier turned back and slunk past her back into the palace.

Left to her own, Tisiphone stepped out onto the balcony. The view it afforded of the sea beyond was breathtaking. She'd become accustomed to the sea during her time training, although the camp had been perched high above the waves. And, of course, she had plunged into the cold waters to find Adrasteia. Here they were so much closer than the camp, crashing upon the rocks just below the balcony. Yet the waters here did not seem as cold and dark as on the west coast. She could see how people could come to think of the ocean as calm and comforting. It distracted her for the moment, a view so beautiful.

"It's striking, isn't it?" asked a woman's voice from her left.

Tisiphone turned, startled, although she naturally should have realized she wasn't alone. Ten feet away stood a woman in an elegant white dress. Her hair was straight and dark as night, her eyes piercing. Tisiphone guessed she might have crossed her fourth decade, although she maintained a strong and regal beauty. Beside her, in a plain white varnished wooden chair, sat a man in golden-hued robes. The robes were hooded to cover his hair, and a mask, like the sort actors wore in the theater, covered his face. It was not unlike the mask Koredyne had worn, only the expression was neutral, neither joyful nor sad. His hands were covered with cloth gloves, and he remained motionless for the moment.

Tisiphone found she didn't know much about how to act in front of royalty. She'd been trained as a soldier, remarkably little as a diplomat. She found she didn't have the will in her to play the subservient as had the courtier. She had her brand to remind her well enough. So, she decided just to be herself. "The view from your palace is unmatched."

The woman took a step closer, her expression unreadable. "I am your queen, Zinovia. This is my husband Diadarian, your king."

The seated man still did not move or speak. Tisiphone's eyes flicked from one to the other. "It is an unexpected honor to be invited to speak with you."

Zinovia's eyes assessed Tisiphone, gazing up and down over her. "You seem so young for a soldier. But then again, your mentor was younger still when she became an Amazon. Did you know that your mentor is a hero of the Empire?"

Tisiphone shook her head. Chloe had certainly never mentioned it in such a way, although being an Amazon or Fury was clearly no small thing.

Zinovia snorted. "So like her. Fame is wasted on the indifferent. I can remember Chloe at the same age as our young Tisiphone. Do you remember, Diadarian?" The man still did not move. "You will be like her soon enough."

Tisiphone wasn't entirely sure she considered that a desirable goal. "It was never my desire to be a…hero."

"Nor was it mine to be queen."

Tisiphone recoiled, startled. She wasn't sure entirely of the meaning of that revelation, but it couldn't help but sound unkind in front of her husband. "Destiny plays with us all, I suppose."

"And it is your destiny which intrigues us most of all," the man said suddenly, his voice silken and pure. His wife inclined her head toward him, and went silent, deferring. He chuckled a bit. "Yes, I can speak, Fury. Although even that tires me, so I leave as much of it as I can to the queen."

Zinovia turned back to Tisiphone. "The king is unwell, as I am sure you have heard."

Tisiphone nodded. "I had heard as much. Although I do not know the nature of his illness."

Zinovia frowned. "That is of no matter to you." Behind her, Diadarian shifted in his seat, his masked gaze turning toward them for the first time. Tisiphone had the sense that he disagreed with his wife's assessment. "We wished to see you for ourselves. We have heard how you killed the Wrathknight. And how your fate line crosses that of the Overlord Bael.

"As you might guess," Diadarian added in, "we are inclined to favor you in that particular contest."

"I'm not sure what it means," Tisiphone stammered, "why my destiny should cross his. I have no connection with this Bael. I'm still trying to understand it myself."

"The Sea People are a scourge on this land," Zinovia growled. "They destroyed the ancient civilization of the Mycenaeans, of which only fragments survive. We would roll back their conquests and revive the civilization of the Greeks, but the numbers of the Sea People are all but endless. There were old legends that have long told of one, a girl, who would appear to cut the head from the hydra. We believe this person to be you, Tisiphone."

"If it were not evident," added Diadarian, "we are rather in a position to help that along."

She nodded, understanding something for the first time. "That's why you've been training young women as soldiers. First the Amazons, now the Furies...in hopes that one of us would fulfill this legend. And you think it may be me."

"Since I first ascended the throne as a young man, when my body was whole, I initiated the training of the Amazons. Alas, in that cadre the legend was not fulfilled, although that initiative certainly resulted in the finest warriors this Empire had ever seen, Chloe being the finest of them all in her prime."

A moment passed while they watched for her reaction. Then Tisiphone asked, "How many of the Amazons still live?"

Diadarian's laughter was soft and sad before he answered, "One."

Tisiphone furrowed her brows. "This is the first I've heard of a legend. How do you know for sure it applies to me?"

Zinovia smiled. "Like all legends, the legend of the girl who would slay the hydra is vague."

"Then you don't believe it?"

Diadarian's silken voice answered, "What matters is that Bael believes it. And his people. If you succeed in killing him, they will believe themselves cursed and scatter like roaches in the light."

"And if I don't succeed?"

"Then we will be at the start once again," Zinovia observed. "But whether or not the legends are true, your fate lines certainly cross with Bael now."

Tisiphone ground her teeth. Had they brought her here simply to gloat about what a pawn she was in their games?

The Emperor sighed, audibly. "We have offended our guest." Zinovia opened her mouth to say something but the Emperor stopped her, his hand raised only slightly from the arm of his chair, the first time he'd moved at all. "Dear wife, give me a moment to speak with the Fury alone."

Zinovia looked at her husband aghast for a moment, then back to Tisiphone, her gaze icy. Finally, her expression softened, and she gave her husband a slight bow. "As you wish." Her eyes returned to Tisiphone just briefly before she stepped back inside from the terrace.

"She will get over her anger," the emperor pronounced with a tone that left Tisiphone unconvinced. "Nor had I intended to anger you."

"I am a slave. I can't imagine my feelings are of import to the Emperor of the North."

"On the contrary. Whether or not these legends are true, and as my wife says they are vague enough not to worry on them terribly, nor whether your path ever does cross Bael, I have no doubt you will be of considerable importance as has been your mentor before you. I understand that you chafe at a life you did not choose, but free or slave, the lives of the majority are ever at the mercy of war, pestilence, famine, luck. You have been risen above that, been given a sword and a destiny. Your name will be remembered forever more, long after they have forgotten the name of Diadarian."

She took several steps toward him, for alone in his chair, he did not seem so threatening. He could have her killed with a word, but somehow he seemed more of a pitiable creature.

The masked face turned toward her wearily, though the eyes were blackened and she could not see his irises within the mask. "Kings and emperors, too, are but playthings to the gods. Once I was a youth, every bit as beautiful as yourself. Though the signs of my illness had begun, when I ascended the throne as a youth twenty years ago, I was still handsome. Zinovia and I were able to share some years as normal husband and wife, just enough to truly bind her to me. Now she is as trapped as I." He shifted a bit in his chair, something that looked as if it took considerable effort. "Now, under these robes and behind this mask, I am a monstrosity. A curse, perhaps for some ill I committed long ago. I am certain to leave this earth before many more years have passed, and I will leave the Empire without an heir. But I will do all that I can, otherwise, to be sure I have left the Empire stronger, not weaker. And for that, I would have your help."

"By killing Bael?"

"Even if it is folly, Bael and the Sea People believe this legend refers to them. If you strike him down, they will believe the judgment of the gods has come against them." He chuckled a bit. "To be honest, we've been working on the inside for a bit to help that legend stick in their minds a bit. I'm glad it finally has. It gives us an unprecedented opportunity."

Tisiphone frowned. "But why me? When Bael's assassin came for me, I was entirely untested. There are other girls better with a sword than me."

"We didn't pick you. True, we provided a fertile ground for women warriors, who have proven more than useful to the Empire, legend or not. But our first batch, the Amazons, elicited no response in regard to the legend. I would have thought Chloe would have fit the story perfectly, but the Sea People's imaginations were not inflamed, not until now. Why they focused on you, of all the Furies, that I don't know. But it is why I wished to speak with you in person. Much rides on your shoulders. If you succeed in killing Bael, it will end the scourge of the Sea People against the Greek lands."

"I have no idea how to kill Bael, or even where he is."

"That, I suspect, will come in time." His body shifted again so that the mask faced the ocean rather than her. She doubted, somehow, he could see at all. "For now, we would make a hero of you, so that you could not be ignored. Thus, you must go to Euboea."

"I shall do as I am asked," she replied simply.

The Emperor remained silent for a moment. "I have been more than proud of the women soldiers of the Amazons and now, Furies. Our men in the cohorts and the phalanx form the thighs and the spine and the shoulders that thrust the spear through the enemies' shield. You and your sisters are the small bones of the wrist, slipping the dagger between his ribs. Each deadly in its own way." He went silent for another brief moment. "It is not enough that you go to Euboea because I ask it. You must go because it is the first step on your road, a road that will lead you to kill Bael, and keep Greece for the Greeks. If you are to be the hero I know you can be, then you must have your heart in it."

She thought on that for a moment, then nodded, though she wasn't sure he could see that. "I understand, Your Eminence. It will be my honor to fight for the Empire at Euboea."

Though she could not see it, she heard his smile.

"May I ask one question, before I go?" she asked.

"Of course you may."

"Why do you have the titles both of Emperor and

King? Is one not enough?"

He chuckled, his weak body bobbing in its chair. "Titles take on a life of their own, one building upon the next over generations, but a dynasty never lets go of the old ones. I am King of the Dorians and Emperor of the Empire of the North. One refers to the people, the other to the land. As I am to be the last of my dynasty, we shall see what comes of these titles with whoever assumes the throne on my passing."

She absorbed that for a moment and decided not to push it any further. "Thank you for answering my question."

"Of course. You will have to excuse me, though, for my energy has run its course. It was a pleasure meeting you, young Fury."

"For me as well, King Diadarian." She left the king there, alone on the terrace, and stepped back inside the palace. The constant roar of the ocean receded as she passed through the door and she found she missed its comforting sound.

She was not entirely sure what to make of her meeting with the King. She supposed it should be some form of honor for her, although as a slave she wasn't naturally inclined to feel pleasure at meeting the person who kept her in bondage. But Diadarian, in all his infirmities, had been a surprise. Although she couldn't say for sure that she looked forward to Euboea in the way he might have wished, her meeting him had given her some feeling of clarity and surety in her purpose in ultimately confronting Bael. That she was to be some form of hero, assuming she survived any length of time, was a new wrinkle and one she had difficulty believing, but it was something she could ask Chloe about.

Her thoughts were interrupted before she reached the stairs. Lost in them as she was, she hadn't heard the small frame slink up from behind her. Only when the woman's hand closed like a vice on her own elbow, did she startle. Instinctively, she reached for her blade only to remember, of course, she hadn't brought it to the palace. She spun around and found herself looking into the eyes of the queen.

Zinovia gave her a long, hard look, then smiled. "I am glad you have bonded with my husband. But I am not done with you yet."

Chapter 14

Kings and Queens

Tisiphone drew back, but found her elbow held fast in Queen Zinovia's grasp. She felt like a fly caught in a web. The Queen was no soldier, but Tisiphone could hardly lash out to free herself from the woman's grasp. That would earn her death. She couldn't help but tighten her hand in a fist, though, and stand strong before the queen. She wouldn't let the woman see fear in her.

"What would you have of me? I have already agreed to do as you've asked."

"My husband is a trusting sort," Zinovia said, her voice low, her face drawn in close to Tisiphone. "He's no fool and has led this Empire with a steady hand. But he believes in heroes and the power of his own voice to motivate the best in people."

"I assume you disagree."

"Consider me the pessimist of our relationship." She let go of Tisiphone's elbow but didn't step back out of her space. "I can see, hero or not, that you chafe with every fiber of your being at being a slave. In truth, I don't blame you. I never had much faith in the arguments that slavery is divinely sanctioned. But a young girl, potential savior of the Ionians, might find herself the recipient of new offers, better offers than the one you have here with the Furies."

Tisiphone frowned, confused for a moment, then understood. "You think Queen Io will try to steal me from you? By offering me freedom?"

"I wouldn't put it past the blonde bitch to do exactly that."

Tisiphone sized up the queen for a moment, taking her in more carefully than she had when she'd been distracted by the king's frail and diseased form. The queen was elegant and beautiful still, though age was beginning to mark her face and hands. Her persona oozed ambition and regret in equal doses. It wasn't lost on Tisiphone that Zinovia was of the proper age to have given birth to her. But Tisiphone knew she was looking at all women that way now, assessing their age, how much she resembled them physically. She'd eventually lose her mind trying to see her mother in every woman of stature she met. "You could give me my freedom first before she has the chance."

Zinovia pulled back a bit and grinned mischievously. "That would only free you to enter Io's service. No, I had some better ideas, a system of rewards and punishments for good or bad behavior."

"You really trust me so little?"

"I trust no one. Now listen so that we are in agreement as to the consequences. If you succeed with the lighthouse in Euboea and, most importantly, return to us after, I will grant you something that you want."

Tisiphone's interest was piqued, against her better judgment. "What?"

"I will grant you license to kill the man who enslaved you."

Tisiphone's eyes widened. "Kriluss."

"I have no doubt you planned to kill him anyway, but in this case, there would be no censure from the Empire. As you might imagine, we don't typically sanction slaves running off to execute the Slave Lords as it's not terribly good for business, but in this case, it could be overlooked. You would have freedom to do with him as you pleased, without fear of repercussion."

"And what of Nyx, the sorceress who aids him?"

"Fine, kill the bitch too."

"All right, I'm listening."

"If you fail to return, naturally you'll be hunted down and killed, although I imagine you've already factored that into your deliberations. But, in addition, I will take from you something you hold dear."

Tisiphone raised an eyebrow. "There are already too few of those things remaining."

"I've given it a bit of thought. We could kill one of your comrades in the Furies, but you are already so few, and it would likely be they who hunt you down. So, I thought, instead, we might kill your captain, Chloe."

"The woman who spent the last nine months torturing me? Killing her would be the punishment?"

"The death would be calculated to look like a Sea People assassination, of course. Give her a martyr's death. And I'm calculating that your attachment to her is not quite as flippant as you make it sound. If I am wrong, well there are still the positive incentives and avoiding your own death."

Tisiphone pursed her lips, considering it. She had to admit, however much a hell fiend whore Chloe was, the idea of leaving her to die didn't sit right. Zinovia had guessed improbably well. "Very well, I understand."

Zinovia stepped back, a satisfied smile on her face. "Good. I apologize for being so unpleasant, but a good king must have a good queen to cover the pragmatics of his plans. How old are you anyway, child?"

"Fifteen."

Zinovia shook her head. "We send children into battle. If only they didn't fight so well, we might stop."

"It is just as well. War was the best of the futures that lay open for me once my parents were killed."

"How sad." Zinovia cocked her head to one side, regarding Tisiphone as if she were a strange bug. "You must harbor resentment toward us for creating the market for slaves that gave rise to Kriluss' raids."

Tisiphone shook her head. "I can't be mad at the whole world. Once Kriluss is dead and Nyx…" She trailed off, still not sure what she wanted to do with the woman who might be her mother. "It will be enough. I will consider their deaths avenged."

Zinovia regarded her silently for a moment, eyes narrowed. "Very well. I am satisfied for now. When you come back from Euboea and hear the roar of the crowds, you will know you have made the right choice. Diadarian and I are not jealous to allow our women warriors to enjoy the adulation of the masses. So long as you remain loyal to the Empire."

"Of course, my queen."

Zinovia waved her hand in the air, "You may go, Fury." She turned away and stepped through the door to the veranda to rejoin her husband.

Tisiphone watched her go before heading back down the stairs. Diadarian, she decided, she rather liked. Zinovia, not quite so much.

****

When she returned to the camp, Tisiphone found her comrades in the most unexpected of circumstances. They lay about in a small field of dry grass upon bits of cloth and ate in the open. The sun was at its zenith, making the temperature tolerable. They relaxed in civilian clothes, lolling about in laziness they had not been allowed in months. And with them was Chloe herself, not in armor for once. If she were more reserved and less inclined to smile than the girls, she did not stop their revelry and that, in and of itself, was amazing. She lay across a strip of cloth, her long, curled hair spilling about her shoulders and taken up by the breeze. She wore only a simple woolen shift, and her feet were bare. Somehow it struck Tisiphone that this was the first time she'd seen Chloe in daylight without greaves on her shins. Until one got close to her, the viewer could be excused for believing her to be beautiful. Tisiphone could not help but stand before them, mouth agape.

Chloe looked up at her, expression unreadable. "So, did you enjoy meeting our king and queen?"

"I didn't know you were some kind of a national hero of the Empire," Tisiphone responded.

Chloe scoffed. "You can see for yourself the fortune it has built up for me." She waved her hand toward her primitive hut.

"Hero?" Meg gawked. "I thought Amazons, like Furies, were creatures of stealth and surprise."

"And intimidation," Chloe added. "Our mere existence advertises to our enemies that they might die unexpectedly at any time. Thus, the Emperor, King Diadarian, enjoys showing us off. You lot wouldn't know, living as you have mainly in the sewers or in scattered villages no sane people would even bother to invade."

"Hero," Meg scoffed. "If only the masses had to live with her for a week."

Chloe looked over at Meg, but her expression didn't change, and she did nothing.

"What's going on?" Tisiphone demanded. "This is just not possible." She stared at Chloe. "You should be beating her for saying that."

"I am no longer your captain," Chloe observed calmly. "You are their captain. Although technically, you have the right to beat her if you like."

"Then we can call you…"

"Chloe, yes, it is my name."

"I need to sit down."

Pandora sat up onto one arm. A broad swatch of purple still stretched across her forehead. "Chloe is keeping us company until we head for Euboea. I think she is allowing us to enjoy these days because she believes we are likely to die."

Chloe pursed her lips but said nothing.

Pandora's observation brought the chatter among the girls to a halt.

"It's remarkable none of us were killed fighting the Wrathknight," Hagne said. "As it was, two of us were hurt badly. We'll be fighting far more Sea People at the lighthouse, I'm sure. We might all be dead in a week."

"Not me," boasted Lysistrate. "I'm going to outlive all of you."

That set the others laughing.

"Will you miss us?" Tisiphone asked Chloe.

The older woman shook her head with a smile. "No. I'll have a new cohort of young brats to turn into girl soldiers by the end of the week. Come now, though, what did our fine king and queen have to say to you?"

"King Diadarian said that we are his special soldiers. Like the small bones of the wrist, he said of us. Zinovia told me that if I don't return after the lighthouse, she'll have you killed."

If her words had any impact on Chloe, they did not show.

"Well, that would seal the deal for me," Lysistrate said. "I'd be in Assyria by the end of the month." The other girls laughed.

"Wait, did she say all of us or just you?" Pandora's brows furrowed.

Tisiphone shrugged. "She spoke to me personally, but I imagine it must apply to all of you."

Pandora's brows remained furrowed. She did not appear satisfied.

Tisiphone rounded on Chloe, hands on hips. "Does it not bother you in the least that the queen is threatening to kill you in order to blackmail me into returning should Io offer me my freedom?"

"On the contrary, I'm rather flattered it seems to bother you."

"It makes sense the queen would target Tisiphone," Pandora observed. "Lysistrate has too much sense of honor to abandon the Furies under any enticement. Meg and Hagne don't really care one way or another about freedom. Living on the streets, they've never seen its benefit, anyway. I might be tempted, but I'd be ashamed to give in to enticements if you did not, Tisiphone. Other than Lysistrate, we would look to you to see what you chose, and likely follow you, if for different reasons. She is very smart, is our queen."

"So would you take an offer of freedom from Queen Io, if she offered it?"

Tisiphone felt the blood rising in her face. She didn't know what inflamed her more, that they were discussing her possible betrayal of Chloe in front of the woman, or that Chloe watched with complete emotional detachment.

"I would have taken an offer from Io if Zinovia hadn't threatened the Cap...Chloe. I won't be responsible for the death of one of our own. Although from the look on your face, I seem to be more worried about it than you are." She turned and paced off a few steps, then realized more thoughts were bubbling furiously in her mind and turned back, facing the older woman as if none of the other girls were even there. "I can't believe that you have given your entire adult life to this Empire and the moment it suits them, they threaten to kill you. It's what we all face, isn't it? But what's worse for me is that you seem not to care. Like you don't even value your own life any more than they do. Or maybe you think this is all some kind of game. But I'm getting sick of everyone treating me, you, the girls, like some kind of pawns. Between the Empire, the Sea People, and a bevy of sorceresses, it's just exhausting me."

She stalked off again.

"Tisiphone..." a young voice called weakly from behind her, Pandora maybe, she wasn't sure.

Somehow, she wasn't even sure why, but that set her off again. She spun around once again on Chloe, although it hadn't been she who spoke. "You know, we may technically be equals now, whatever that counts for among a bunch of slave girls, but we still look up to you, depend on you for guidance. What does it say to us if you lay about treating your own life like it has no value? This Empire might treat us like livestock, but does that mean we have to think of ourselves the same way?"

Chloe cocked her head slightly to one side and blinked, but said nothing.

Tisiphone fumed. "Fine. I give up. I'm going to bed." She stormed off. "And yes," she called back without turning around, "I know it's midday!"

She slammed the barracks door behind her. Away from the others, she only became angry with herself for getting angry. Why on earth did she let Chloe's reaction, or lack of reaction, get to her? She had no idea. Maybe she should take an offer of freedom from Io after all. That would teach the bitch to be so…smug, or carefree, or whatever it was that she was. Of course, she'd never do it, because then she couldn't live with the guilt. She growled loudly in frustration and furiously worked the straps of her armor to undress.

Behind her, the barrack's door squeaked open and gently rapped closed.

"Couldn't I *possibly* have one moment alone?" Tisiphone breathed. She turned around and found not Meg or Pandora, who she expected, but Chloe. Dressed in the shift, rather than armor, the woman looked so…normal, and somehow that only infuriated Tisiphone anew. "Perfect. By all the gods, you haunt me like a ghost." She kept stripping her armor. "And let me tell you, if you've come to beat me, for once, I'm not taking it passively. You might still be able to best me, but I swear I'll fight you with every ounce of strength that I have."

"Calm yourself, Tisiphone. I've not come to beat you." Chloe took a few steps into the barracks, glancing about as if seeing it for the first time. "I rather had the impression you are angry with me."

Tisiphone stopped fiddling with her armor and fixed Chloe with a glare to turn her to stone.

"Because the words of Queen Zinovia do not fill me with dread?"

"Because you're not..." —her mind struggled to find the right word— "...upset! You don't seem at all betrayed. And I'm not sure...maybe because you seem to take my loyalty to you for granted."

"I do take your loyalty to me for granted." Tisiphone sagged at Chloe's words, but Chloe kept speaking. "As you may take my loyalty to you for granted. I would never betray your trust, not to a queen or king, not for freedom or any amount of gold. That is what it means to be an Amazon or Fury. We may be slaves to the Empire, but we are loyal to each other above all else. Zinovia knows that and used it to her own advantage against you. But it is a quality that makes us strong, that makes us fight together as one machine. So, if I am not upset, it is because I never had any doubt about what decision you would make."

Tisiphone sighed, anger flowing out of her as if a dam had been released but feeling only an emptiness in its wake. "Doesn't it...depress you at all, that the queen treats you like you're nothing, after all you have done for this Empire?"

"My mother sold me to become a whore before I was even your age, and my salvation was learning to murder the Empire's enemies, not all of them from outside the Empire. You'll pardon me if I've grown cynical about the motives of my betters over the years." She leaned against one wall. "I'm sure you understand that repeating that first part to any of your comrades *will* get you beaten."

Tisiphone nodded. "I won't tell anyone."

"I wouldn't have told you if I thought you would. And I wouldn't have named you captain of the Furies if I didn't think you were the best of them." She tapped the side of her head. "That was my decision, although I could tell the king was thinking the same, probably given your connection with Bael. He is keen to highlight you as a hero."

"So he said, more or less. Do you speak often with the Emperor, King Diadarian?"

Chloe shrugged. "Often enough. You will too. The orders of the Furies, like the Amazons, come directly from the king and queen. We are answerable to no one else."

Tisiphone's eyes widened at the implications of that, but she said nothing. She fell silent.

"Are you still angry with me, then?" Chloe asked.

Tisiphone looked up and shook her head.

"Good. Since my life is apparently in your hands, I would hate for us to part on bad terms." She moved gracefully, almost dancing, rather than walking back to the barracks door. She opened it and moved through, turning back only just before the door closed. "Do enjoy your afternoon nap."

Tisiphone collapsed on her bed, more emotionally drained than physically tired. She might not be angry at Chloe anymore, but the woman was still a pain in the ass.

Chapter 15

The Edge of the Storm

Tisiphone reined in her horse at the edge of the cliffs overlooking the sea. Far below, the ocean ebbed and flowed, the now familiar crashing of waves a comforting sound. Having grown up in an inland village, she'd never have imagined she'd see so much of the water. Then again, there were a lot of things she'd never imagined she'd see. If someone had told her what her life would be like now, a year prior, she'd have found it entirely fanciful. But here she was.

Meg skidded her horse to a stop beside her. "So, now what?"

They were a hard day's ride south of Iolcus, back in the uncontrolled borderlands where the last pitiful remnants of the Mycenaean Greeks scratched a living from the rocky soil, caught between two conquering peoples. Across this water was the northern coast of Euboea. They needed to cross to get to the lighthouse at Mandoudi.

The crossing was wide enough that the opposite shore remained hidden over the horizon. They might have ridden further south into Boeotia where the crossing was much narrower, but that would have taken them firmly into Sea People's land. They'd be dodging marauding armies enough once they got to Euboea. As it was, the crossing would be treacherous. In the distance, Tisiphone could see a ship bobbing in the waves, a sail set against the wind. A Sea People's raider, no doubt. Those scoundrels from a distant land were not foolish enough to leave the waters open. There, on the waves, even the Empire of the North could not dare to contest them in open battle.

"We'll need to steal a boat. At nightfall, we'll cross. We'll find a sheltered area nearby here to rest until nightfall."

Meg nodded and spun her horse around to help the others set up camp until they had cover of darkness.

Tisiphone watched the waves with apprehension. Sailing had not been part of their training. To say that the Dorians were clumsy sailors would have been putting it kindly. Powerful though the Empire was on land, its navy could barely keep Sea People's raiders from pirating far up the coast in Empire territory. Once they stole a boat, Tisiphone didn't much know what to do with it other than to point it at the horizon and row in the hope of good fortune.

She nudged her horse away from the cliff edge, feeling a sudden desire to be apart from the group, to think. Not too far, of course. It wouldn't do to be out of earshot of the group. They might not be in conquered Sea People's territory, but that didn't mean the Sea People didn't send patrols through the wasted lands. Slowly, she walked her horse across a small field toward a small copse of trees.

There, among them, waited a dark form, small and bent, shrouded in a thick robe, the downtrodden mask hiding the face. Tisiphone felt fury grind within her as she neared the figure until, from atop her horse, she towered over the old hag. "And have you used your sorceries to trick my mind into coming here for your convenience?" She turned back to make sure she could still see her comrades. Her friends were still at work in the makeshift camp and had taken no notice of her.

"I have wandered on foot from the Peloponnese and back to follow the lines of your fate, girl," Koredyne growled, shuffling a bit further back into the woods. "Do not think it a convenience."

"And what augury do you bring me now? Will you tell me just enough to be afraid, and little enough to be able to do anything of use about it?"

Koredyne stopped and looked up at Tisiphone but said nothing. Below them, waves crashed against the shore. The only sound for a long moment.

Tisiphone had not yet mastered the art of using silence as a weapon, and though she might be armed and towering astride a stallion, was not yet a match in a battle of wills against one as old as Koredyne. So, she filled the silence herself with indignation. "I see you and our Emperor have the same taste in face wear." She had to marvel at the completeness of the masks. For neither Diadarian nor Koredyne could she even discern eyes beyond the blackened holes. She'd half suspected Diadarian might not have them at all; so little did he seem to see. But with Koredyne, it was different. She clearly had no loss of sight. It was more as if there were only night behind the mask.

"I suspect neither the Emperor nor I have faces fit for the eyes of mere mortals." She shifted again, back toward the tree line. "And Diadarian is no emperor of mine."

Tisiphone did not stir her horse onward. "Once I

followed you into the woods to hear your valueless soothsaying. Not again. Speak your peace out here in the open, woman, where the sun can cast light upon your words."

Koredyne turned back. "Such anger in you. Have I merited it thus?"

"You didn't merely take me from my parents. You let them die. You could have told me—"

"And if I had told you your parents were to be slain by slavers—"

"Not just slavers," she spat through ground teeth, "Nyx…"

Koredyne paused for a moment before continuing, "Slain by slavers and the woman you think may be your birth mother, what would you have done differently? Fled with them into the night, fought and died beside them?" She waved a gnarled hand through the air as if shooing away flies. "No course would have led you to be astride that steed today but the course that was taken. Besides, I did not know what you think I knew. Even to one such as me, time yet to be is a murky thing. I knew only that your time with Alexis and Myrrine had come to its end, but the circumstances of that end were hidden from me."

"But you suspected."

"I suspected that they must die, yes," Koredyne confirmed quietly. "It was not of my choosing. But everything in this life comes with a price. And look at you now."

Tisiphone squeezed her eyes shut instead and looked away from the crone. Tears burned her corneas as she could not help but think of those last minutes, her father cast down by Nyx and Kriluss, her mother still inside their home, alive for only moments more. She wiped at her eyes after a moment with her arm, but the leather of her armor was not suitable for daubing away moisture. "And what price have you come to ask me to pay today?" She looked back toward her comrades. "Is it one of them?"

"Yes," Koredyne replied simply, her directness disarming. "Or you. At least one will die. I know neither who nor how many. But if you do survive this, your power and influence will be unmatched among women since Chloe herself was in her prime as an Amazon. I told you before I would come to you at times of transition in your life to try to guide you in the small ways that I can. You are at one of those points. Either you succeed or your path ends. There is no middle ground."

Tisiphone managed a scoffing laugh at that. "I managed to guess that much already. You've wasted a trip, if that was all you meant to tell me."

"I am here to give you one of the small nudges I am allowed. I know you plan to wait for nightfall, then take a boat across the waters to Euboea. A reasonable enough plan under the circumstances, but all mortal plans are at the mercy of fortune. Unfortunately, your plan is one of those. If you leave tonight, it is certain you will be caught and killed, all of you. That much I can see clearly."

Tisiphone frowned, surprised by that, but remained silent.

"Instead, you must stay hidden for the night. As the sun casts its first rays, go down to the beach and walk to your right, to the west. Not a hippikon along you will find a small boat. As the sun rises, keep the prow just to the right of the orb. This will lead you to Euboea without fail."

"During the morning? The Sea People's raiders will see us for sure!"

"I know you think you have no reason to trust me, young Fury, but nothing I have ever done has been against you. You may never find with me the love you think you need, but I live with no purpose but to see you safe."

Tisiphone pursed her lips and considered that. The other girls would think her mad when she told them. Even as she considered their reaction, she knew she had made up her mind to heed the witch's words. "I am becoming quite weary of sorceresses interfering with my life like I were some plaything."

Koredyne chuckled wearily. "If only it were as simple as that. Although, by the gods, I do not blame you. We are a weary, meddling lot. Adrasteia and I at least understand that. Nyx will as well, in time."

Tisiphone's horse shifted slightly under her. "I suppose, like Adrasteia, you will not tell me whether Nyx is my mother?"

"It is not for us to say. Part of the grand bargain struck at the time of your birth, forbids us from speaking openly about your bloodline."

"But you know who my mother is?"

"Oh yes. I was there at your birth."

Tisiphone clenched her jaw, frustrated to be so tantalizingly close to the truth, and yet further from it than ever. "And why is it forbidden for you to tell me this?"

Koredyne remained silent for a moment and then said, "Because it would send you astray from your path.

The knowledge you seek will not bring you the peace you long for. You enjoyed the love of Alexis and Myrrine for fourteen years, more than many are granted. But if you are unable to see the wisdom in finding satisfaction with your adoptive parents and the time you shared, then you must find the answers of your own volition. Only in this manner will the information you crave not destroy you."

Tisiphone shook her head. "I don't understand."

Koredyne laughed, more genuinely this time. "Neither entirely do I. But it is what we have seen, Adrasteia and I. Knowledge of your heritage must come from your own efforts if you are to learn it at all. It mustn't come from our lips."

"And if I were to ask Nyx if she is my mother?"

"Nyx is not bound by the same ties as us. What answers she gives you will be upon her own conscience."

"And you would counsel me to forget the matter altogether, to be unconcerned with whom is my mother or my father, despite that they may be but arm's reach away."

"Or worlds away. But it does not matter what I counsel. I know very well that I have no authority to tell you what to do. Other than I hope you will heed my advice and sail for Euboea at dawn rather than dusk."

Tisiphone frowned. As ever, speaking to any of these witches confounded more than clarified. She'd be just as happy to be done with the lot of them, although if Koredyne truly had some form of cosmic awareness of her immediate path, she'd be foolish to ignore it. "Very well. We will travel at dawn. But why is it that you should even care so much? Why are you and

Adrasteia so concerned about what happens to me?"

Koredyne remained silent once more before speaking. "Adrasteia has no particular affection for you. But she has guided and protected your bloodline for many generations, past the time when even her abilities could keep her soul in a mortal body. For you to fulfill your path will bring rest for her. For that reason, she is your ally. As for myself, as I said, I attended your birth and cared for you in your first months before Alexis and Myrrine. I still have a fondness for that infant even if she has grown into a typical, ungrateful youth with a sharp tongue for her elders." Tisiphone frowned but held her tongue. Koredyne continued. "But I, too, am aged beyond mortal years and would see my end come before, like Adrasteia, I become little more than a voice."

Tisiphone considered her words. So, they were allies, as much as anything because their goals suited one another. At least the crone had been honest. But so, too, had she emphasized how little connection Tisiphone had left in this world, now that Alexis and Myrrine were gone. Only her friends among the Furies and with the life they led either she or they would soon be dead. Without bothering to reply to the old woman, she pulled her horse around and began to ride away.

"We will see each other again," the hag called after her. "That is, if you do not die tomorrow."

Tisiphone glanced back only briefly but said nothing. Riding back to her mates, she was lost in thought, all the more for the fact she had difficulty sorting out exactly what her thoughts were. One of them would die. At least one of them. Well, she'd already known that was a possibility. Now it was a certainty. And Koredyne's words had only served to remind her of her aloneness in this world.

She had the girls, though. And for tomorrow, that would be enough. They looked up when she returned; toward their captain. "A slight change in plans," she announced, still astride her horse. "Be prepared to settle in for the night. We sail tomorrow at dawn."

****

Tisiphone would never know what might have happened to them had they sailed under the cover of darkness as she had originally intended, and as common wisdom would have dictated. Her comrades initially protested the change in plans, but Dorians and Mycenaeans alike are superstitious folk. Once she told them of Koredyne's visit, the concerns died away. Greeks were not inclined to go against the advice of a seer.

And so, with the dawn sun sparkling over the water and their hearts in their throats, they found the little boat where Koredyne said it would be, and set to rowing across the expanse of water. The sun they kept just to the left of the prow, although it rose higher and higher and still no land came into view. Now, out on the open ocean with no land in any direction, their anxiety increased, and conversation among the girls ceased, their concentration locked on the task at hand, rowing and scanning the horizons for Sea People's raiders. There were four oars and so they took turns resting, the fifth taking primary responsibility as a lookout. Once they did see a ship on the horizon, back toward where they'd come from, and it quickened their pace. But, if it were a raider, the ship didn't see them and continued skirting the horizon until it passed from sight.

The sun began to sink back down behind the boat, and they kept it behind them and to the left to be sure they weren't rowing in circles. At last, nearly toward dusk, land appeared and set off such jubilation in the boat that they nearly capsized. They collapsed on the sand, arms, shoulders, and backs aching worse than from any beating Chloe had given them.

Once recovered from exhaustion, they pulled the boat into the trees and navigated by map through the Euboean forests toward the lighthouse at Mandoudi. Despite being an island, Euboea's size was not insignificant, and they'd landed on the island's northernmost coast. Traveling to Mandoudi took two hard days of shifting through the dark forests, avoiding trails and roads, and eating off the land as best they could to preserve their supplies of food.

The island itself was in chaos, with villagers hunkering down or fleeing before the Sea People's invaders. The Sea People seemed to roam freely across the island, although their numbers and patrols were relatively few. Despite the panic and aggressive displays of the few uncontested Sea People's patrols, both armies were likely concentrated near Io's capital at Eritrea. Fortunately, this made it relatively easy to make their way stealthily to Mandoudi.

At last, dirty and tired, but on schedule, they reached the harbor and spotted the lighthouse. Mondoudi was but a small city, a third the size of Iolcus, perhaps. However, its harbor was generous and deep, the waters dark and smooth. The harbor receded from the sea into the land in a massive semicircle like a bite taken from a pear. Rocky cliffs guarded the entrance, although the harbor itself boasted both sandy beaches and some small piers intended for fishing boats. Two raiders were currently berthed at the piers, their numerous crews overrunning the town like a pack of wolves. The lighthouse was perched on the southeastern cliff, a beacon for finding the harbor in the darkness.

Balanced along this outcropping of rock, the lighthouse itself did not need to be terribly tall. From the distance, Tisiphone judged it to be perhaps a plethron in height. Not an insignificant height, certainly enough for a deadly fall from the platform up top. Nonetheless, it would be possible for soldiers on the ground to throw up ropes or use ladders to ascend. The lighthouse wouldn't be secure even if they could bar the lower door.

Hidden among clusters of grass overlooking the town and lighthouse, Tisiphone frowned, her mind working. Meg crawled through the grass to lie beside her. They were silent, observing together for awhile.

"Lighthouse is lightly guarded," Meg observed after a bit. "Six or seven of those oafs inside it."

"Mmm hmm," Tisiphone grunted in acknowledgement. Taking the lighthouse wouldn't be problematic. The Sea People didn't seem to have prepared for the possibility the Empire would use it to make an amphibious landing. To the best Tisiphone could tell from the damage, they'd done nothing to disturb the operations of the lighthouse, although it was not lit at the moment. "How many do you figure in the town?"

"Two raiders with full crew. Hard to see them all coming and going from the buildings. Enough to keep that whole town cowering, though. I'd guess maybe two hundred sailors and soldiers together."

"The distance from the town to the lighthouse is perhaps fifteen stadia, a little over a dilichos. Once we get the lighthouse lit and they figure out it's not supposed to be lit, I'd guess we'll have perhaps twenty minutes for them to cross the distance."

"And how long do we need to keep it lit?"

"Lit after midnight," Tisiphone replied with a shrug. "Until the boats show up. Assuming they do. Until dawn for all I know. Even if the boats are offshore, waiting for the signal, I'd imagine it would still take at least two hours, maybe three, to get into the harbor and begin to offload the phalanxes."

"So, the five of us will have to fend off two hundred rabid goons for three hours, maybe more." She grinned. "I don't see why that's a problem."

"We'll need to strike before midnight at the lighthouse, clear it, and get the furnace working so that it is lit."

"We have the right night, don't we? I've lost track. It would be embarrassing if we had the wrong night."

Tisiphone gave her a stern, level look without speaking.

"Just a joke, of course." Meg smirked. "If we bar the door in, they'll have to climb for it. They'll be in a far more precarious spot than us. Only a few of them are on the platform at a time. I don't mind the odds."

Tisiphone studied the lighthouse carefully. Windows ran up on either side of the lighthouse, left and right, although there were none to the back, the side of the door. She couldn't be sure if there were any in front, facing the water. The windows were a problem, easy points of entry, even if they barred the door. Tisiphone had an idea for that, although she needed to know if any windows faced the water. She hoped not. The windows appeared oriented due east and west, presumably to let in light for the stairwell. Given the position of the harbor, the lighthouse faced almost due north. Hopefully, the designers had thought there to be no need for north-facing windows anymore than south-facing windows.

"We've got a bit of time," Tisiphone observed. No sense in overtaking the lighthouse so many hours before midnight and potentially having to fend off attacks for hours on end.

"Great. I can't wait for the opportunity to whittle away the day talking with Lysistrate."

Tisiphone smiled. But as they edged back toward their makeshift camp among the trees, the smile faded. One of them, at least one of them, would die tonight. But which one? Which one.

Chapter 16

The Tower

In the late spring months, the sun still set rather early, which meant they had only a few hours to wait while darkness fell and a chill set into the air. They kept quiet and hid in the forests with their quarry just in view. Away from the lights of the town, it was barely visible. Whatever occupants dwelt within the lighthouse, produced little illumination. Certainly, they didn't fire up the lighthouse furnaces. Had they done that, the Furies could simply have waited out the night in the forests without risk, but no such blind luck was forthcoming.

Judging when it approached midnight was more difficult, but Tisiphone just waited until the strange mixture of boredom and apprehension nearly overwhelmed her before motioning to the others that the time had come. "Keep any Greeks alive," she commanded. Running the furnace would be easier if the lighthouse operator were still alive to assist.

With Tisiphone in the lead, they sprinted across the distance between the tree line and the lighthouse. This consisted mainly of open field, although in the dark and away from the town, they had little concern for being spotted. Their leather armor was black, and they covered their face, forearms, and the backs of their calves—the only parts of their bodies not armored—with dirt and mud.

Blood pounded through her veins as Tisiphone sprinted toward the stone tower. Pure exhilaration coursed through her as they charged their target. By the gods, how a part of her had begun to love war! She hoped it would not grow too strong, nor her heart so weak that she might begin to seem like Chloe. But the animalistic thrill in her chest could not be denied. Even the thought that, at any moment they might be seen, that they were fooling the Sea People's warriors, charged through her with a sense of elation.

No call or warning interrupted their charge. Tisiphone hadn't really expected one, as much as the sense of danger had thrilled her. It would take some imagination or paranoia for the Sea People to conceive of a Dorian seaborne invasion. And defending territory was not the strength of the Sea People, so she had learned during their training. They were marauders, powerful and unpredictable on the offense, and devastating against unprepared foes. Not to mention the most capable sailors in the Mediterranean. But they could be knocked off guard when put on the defense. They burned territory; they did not hold it effectively.

Tisiphone pressed herself up against the lighthouse wall, feeling the cold brick against her face and hand. The others slapped up against the stone beside her. All around them the sounds of waves smashing against rock roared, ebbing and flowing. Nothing else disturbed the cold night.

Tisiphone remained silent, although, with the crushing sound of the waves, they probably could have openly spoken without being heard. She motioned toward the door, and Pandora moved for it first. Her fingers were the nimblest and if the door proved to be locked, she would be able to make short work of it.

Locks, though, were the purview of the wealthy, and no one would typically think to lock a lighthouse. This was no exception. The door nudged open easily and Pandora looked to the others expectantly. Tisiphone pushed forward and sidled her way through the narrow opening into the room beyond.

Solid walls instantly cut the cacophony of the ocean down to a murmur. Her eyes took a moment to adjust to the dark. She'd hoped the Sea People might have left some light burning, but there was no such fortune. This was a dangerous moment, silhouetted against an open doorframe. Had the Sea People prepared a proper sentry, she would have been vulnerable.

As it was, this entry chamber was empty. Once her eyes adjusted, she could see that, to her immediate right, a staircase spiraled up along the outer wall of the building. The base of the structure was large enough to incorporate multiple rooms, however, and this entrance chamber was just the first. Before her, a corridor receded into darkness. She took up a ready, defensive position, while the rest of the Furies filed inside.

The building remained quiet, and they entered unopposed. The Sea People were complacent, unprepared, so much the better. Foolish brutes for all their numbers and brutality.

Tisiphone crept down the hall, the curved sword at the ready. The walls were bare stone, the building simple for all the majesty it conveyed from the distance outside. The rock walls were cold and dank and smelled of mildew. It gave her a memory of Adrasteia's cave and the crippling cold of that witch's horrid prison. Her body shuddered.

To the left, an open archway beckoned although the corridor continued still. She peered into the darkness. A single narrow slit in the stone wall let dim light into the chamber. Within a small room, filled with shelving and these shelves with clay pots. Oil, she guessed from the smell of the place. Priming fuel to quickly light the furnace.

On the floor lay a human form curled into a ball, shivering. He had no blanket or means to warm himself aside from the simple woolen tunic he wore. An old man from the look of him. He wore his white hair long, and his beard looked to have gone untrimmed for some time.

"Greek," she whispered to the others. She kneeled next to the old man's face and drew her dagger. She nudged the old man several times with the hilt until finally, he stirred.

He looked up at her, eyes wide, mouth open revealing his broken and uneven teeth.

"Not more than a whisper, old man, or I slit your throat," she warned, letting the blade swim before his eyes. "Who are you?"

He swallowed, looking from one girl to the other. In their armor with blades drawn, they must have truly looked like Furies to him. "I am Nachor, mistress. The lighthouse master."

"And the Sea People, how many are there and where?"

He looked down at his hands for a moment as if to count on his fingers, though they didn't move. "Six, I think. Most rest in the large room at the end of the hall. I keep most of the wood for the furnace there. Some may be up top, although I haven't kept an eye on their moving. So long as they don't disturb me…"

Tisiphone looked meaningfully at the others. They began to move back to the hall, their blades thirsty.

"Stay here, and keep quiet until we return for you," she told Nachor firmly.

"You mean to kill them, don't you?" he asked.

She nodded.

He raised himself higher, his hand clutching her shoulder. "Good for you. Nasty brutes they are."

She stood up, over him, slipping her dagger back into its sheath. She moved off to follow the others, aiming the blade of her sword back his way. "Remember, not a rustle, or we kill you first, Greek or not."

He nodded with a swallow.

A bit harsh with the old man, she thought once back in the stone hall. But they were here to kill Sea People not make friends with the locals. He'd serve his purpose well enough when the time came for it.

Down the hall they crept. Now the outline of a door became visible. A rectangle of faint, flickering orange outlined their goal. The vermin beyond had left a lamp burning. Careless. It was the nature of the human condition to assume safety, to take comforts where one could. But Chloe had brutalized them, pushed them past the limits of humanity, so that misery, cold, and pain became comfortable companions. Rest and comfort were sources of anxiety. They'd dallianced with ease only briefly on their last return to Iolcus, and only because Chloe had led them. At her side, they could imagine no danger. If she took ease, then no danger existed in the world.

But that was a fleeting illusion. These bastards from across the water thought they had this land secure. They assumed no Dorians would cross the sea for them. They didn't place proper guards, no doubt slept easy, and took to drinking. Best they take what comfort they could, for it would come to its end soon enough.

Tisiphone nodded toward Meg and Pandora. Slowly and quietly, they sheathed their blades and pulled their bows from their backs. The five of them took up positions. Lysistrate, at the front, to take the door, Meg and Pandora to follow with bows, then Hagne and Tisiphone herself to rush past them and go behind Lysistrate into the melee. The assault would be fast and catastrophic.

Lysistrate put her ear against the plank door. She nodded back to the others. Talking from the other side. The blonde gently tried the door latch, working it carefully, until she'd edged the door just a little, to confirm nothing barred entry.

Then, without a sound, she pushed the door full open. She crouched and moved down and to the right, out of view. At that moment, those within might have thought a stiff breeze had blown through the building, knocking their door open. Meg and Pandora moved through next, shades against the flickering light within. From the back of the group, Tisiphone could see several hunched figures around a table, dressed in the unfamiliar clothes of the Sea People.

Before she even got through the door, she heard the flip of bowstrings, the slashing of blades through the air, the screams of dying, and the slosh of blood through the air. With a singleness of purpose, she charged through the door. Her eyes immediately scanned the movement of the tall, broad men in the room. Her brain recognized the writhing of the fallen, the dying, the incapacitated. She moved past these. Past the table, to the rough cots on which several more slept. These began to rouse like pigs.

Tisiphone picked her first target—a dark hairy thing, just pushing himself up onto his arms. She slashed across his elbow, sending him crashing back down. Before the breath in his lungs formed into a cry, she brought her blade down through his chest, snuffing that sound before it was ever given a voice.

She turned to her right and found herself looking into the face of another of their warriors. A young man, barely older than herself. Eyes of light blue, fierce and beautiful. His nose thin and well-shaped. His skin was light, like the finest beach sand. A slight stubble played along his chiseled cheeks. Strong as they were, they seemed just slightly feminine. She thought him a beautiful young man, almost like one of the statues the Mycenaeans left behind in their crumbled cities.

All of this her brain processed on some parallel track that in no way slowed down the commands it gave her muscles, and she swung her sword for that very same face. The blade dug into his head with a hard crack, tracing a similar path from eye to nose to cheek as marred Chloe. This strike bore in deeper, though, cleaving the front of the skull so hard it made her arms quiver. The youth collapsed at once, without a sound. Blood spurted hot and sticky over her arms. Her blade became stuck in his skull. Stupid, overdone blow, leaving her weaponless. She glanced about, judging no immediate threats present. She would have drawn her dagger and made the best of it had there been any. But instead, she planted her boot against the side of the man's head and wrenched her sword free.

By then, the fight was over. Nine bodies lay strewn about, hacked to bits, or shot through with arrows. It had taken seconds. Tisiphone's lungs heaved and her heart pounded. Her head swiveled left and right, her brain unready to acknowledge the danger had passed. "Up the stairs," she ordered. "There may be more up top."

They filed back into the stone hall, tracking blood with their boots. As they passed the room with the oil, the old man Nachor emerged, tottering on his wobbly legs. "Are they dead, girl?" he asked.

Tisiphone stopped for just a moment. "They are. We'll need you to fire up the furnace. Can you do that?"

"Of course, I'll see to it. But by the gods, what do you need the light for?"

"Just get the furnace alight and be quick to it." She turned without waiting for a reply and followed the other girls up the stairs. The steps were fairly broad, given that they took up most of the tower. Their bodies were tuned to endurance, and the climb did little to wind them. Still, the ascent seemed endless, running round and around until dizziness began to set in. Here, they had little light to guide them, only that from the moon and stars let in through narrow windows. Tisiphone was gratified to find that, as she hoped, windows opened up to the east and west, but not to the north.

Only toward the top did the staircase suddenly

narrow, with a door to one side. This proved to be the entrance to the furnace room, currently unoccupied. Up further they climbed the now narrow staircase.

Finally, they came to a sturdy set of double wooden doors. These they pushed out with ease. Cold night air flowed back toward them as they emerged atop the lighthouse. Above them, a stone overhang arced, partially shielding the platform from rain. Just beyond the doors, a plain stone wall shielded them. Out of view on the other side of the stone wall, a pair of male voices chattered in the barbarian tongue of the Sea People. Tisiphone knew enough of their harsh speech to know they spoke of trivial matters, as men do.

Tisiphone and her companions made their way slowly around the edges of the wall. Just beyond it, the overhang ended, shielding only enough to protect the flame of the furnace below. On this side of the stone wall, a long, battered bronze mirror had been hung to amplify the light of the furnace out toward the sea. The platform beyond was generous enough, with decent room to move about if necessary, Tisiphone observed. At the edge of the lip, a small stone wall, coming to about waist height, prevented one from slipping easily over the edge. It was a beautiful space in its way, the front part of the platform naturally open to the night sky.

The two Sea People warriors sat perched on the stone wall, legs dangling over the side. Their weapons, axes, rested near them. They appeared to be sharing a moment of true camaraderie, talking low and laughing, their backs toward their approaching deaths. They shared one last joyful laugh before arrows pierced their hearts through their backs and together they toppled silently over the edge.

"There," Tisiphone said, once it was done. "This lighthouse is ours. But we must prepare it if we are to keep it. Pandora, see to Nachor. Help him however he needs. Hagne, I'll need you to keep watch here. Meg and Lizzy, we're going to need to make it difficult for them to get in through the bottom of the tower."

Pandora ended up with the worst deal, it turned out, needing to help Nachor heave wood and oil up to the furnace room to make sure the light had enough fuel to burn through until morning. Her looks to Tisiphone as they crossed paths on the lower level said enough. Tisiphone, for her part, vacillated between guilt and stifling giggles. She resolved they'd all lend a hand once they'd gotten the lower levels prepared for unwanted guests.

The lighthouse had not been designed as a fortress, naturally. Theoretically, it had numerous entrance points, given the windows running up along the staircase. But it had been fortuitously designed in its way. Only one actual door leading in. The windows began high enough such as they wouldn't likely be initially appealing as an entrance point. And, most crucially, the tower had no north-facing windows. As such, Tisiphone figured, if they could make the stairway impassable, the Sea People would have no option but to climb to the platform, where the Furies would have the advantage of position.

Thus, Lysistrate, Meg, and herself set to work piling the entrance chamber full of fuel wood and dousing this with the oil. They kept only a narrow walkway for Pandora and Nachor to finish their business. But once this was done, they'd both effectively barricaded the door and turned the entrance chamber into a fiery death trap. And once the fuel wood got burning, it would fill the entire staircase with smoke, making it effectively impassable, and thus removing the need to defend the platform from that direction. The smoke would pour out the windows to the east and west. Coupled with the offshore breeze, the smoke would be kept away from the platform, so that the light wouldn't be obscured. It seemed a viable plan, at least in theory. At the very least, it had been the best Tisiphone could devise and none of the others complained of it or suggested much by way of improvement.

They needed to hold the lighthouse only long enough for the Dorian sea invasion to arrive. And if it didn't for some reason, well, this would all be quite an impressive but futile show. Even if they held off the Sea People in the town for that long, the column of smoke would certainly summon reinforcements come morning. By then, the five girls, if still alive, would be exhausted.

Once they were done with the entrance, they all set to help Pandora and Nachor, aside from Hagne, still on watch up top. With them all working together, the work went quickly as it needed to. Nachor got the furnace fired up with evident glee. And the lighthouse was back in function. Up top, the flame roared to life, with the extra benefit of bathing the platform in welcoming warmth. The Dorian fleet, assuming it was out there in the dark, would now have their beacon.

Tisiphone sent Pandora down to keep watch over the main door. Nachor remained in the furnace room. The rest went up top to wait for the inevitable.

Lysistrate and Hagne prepared bundles of arrows for easy access. Tisiphone examined the platform for its defensibility. She was glad for the little wall at the edge that came to waist height. She would have liked it to be even higher, but of course, that would have blocked the light from the furnace. But it would serve well to protect them from furious arrow fire from below.

"What do you think?" Meg asked, her voice neutral.

Tisiphone drew her hands in around her and shivered a bit, thankful for the heat from the furnace. The platform would have been unbearable without it. As it was, her body was buffeted between waves of heat from the fire, and cold winds blowing off the ocean. "I think we can hold it until morning. For what it is, I think we've made it as defensible as possible. They'll have to use ropes to get up to the platform. We can cut them down easily enough. If they try to come over the top..." She motioned at the partial roof. The Sea People would never be able to climb up the front face of the lighthouse where the Furies could cut their ropes. They'd ultimately have to come over. "...we'll have the more advantageous position. We kill them as they touch down on the platform."

It wasn't lost on her that their position was not entirely ideal, however. The trail that looped from the village ended on the south side of the lighthouse. From the platform, they would have poor visibility of enemies mustering just to the south. Their ability to engage the Sea People with bows would be reduced.

From their perch, they could spot three of the Sea People's warriors ride out from the village on horseback. They galloped out at a quickened though not

240

panicked pace, making the loop around the port toward the lighthouse. As they passed to the south, they could only watch their progress by hanging along the wall of the tower and looking around the outside.

"I guess they noticed the light," Meg observed without emotion.

"Bound to happen," Tisiphone agreed. "They'll think their drunk comrades have lit the thing up. That won't last long though. What do you think the odds are of hitting them from here?"

"All three?"

"Two of the three, say."

"At this angle, at night, from this distance…it would be a tough shot. As I'll assume they won't be sitting still on their horses, the whole time, I'd bet I could get one but not the other before they ride away."

"Do the best you can, then, once you see them bolt and ride for the village." Tisiphone grabbed her own bow and made for the stairway down.

"Where are you going?"

"I'm going to answer the door." She bounded down the stairs, round and round, until she got to the bottom. By then, one of the Sea People warriors was pounding on the door. He shouted something in his barbaric tongue, but through the wood, she was unable to translate his words in her head. She gathered enough by his tone, however, angry, but not yet in war mode. As she expected, he must have thought his fellows were having some drunken fun. That the lighthouse door was barricaded rather than barred, he could not know.

Pandora was already at the door, perched on several pieces of the fuel wood, trying to avoid the trails of oil. She looked at Tisiphone uncertainly.

Tisiphone drew an arrow and notched it. She drew aim at the edge of the door. She nodded to Pandora to open it.

Barricaded as it was, the door would only open a small amount, but it was all she needed. Cold air rushed in through the narrow gap between door and wall. Beyond, she caught a sliver of the man's appearance—a tall, middle-aged fellow with a patchy beard and weathered, wrinkled face. He turned to peer through the gap with his gray eyes and opened his mouth to speak.

She fired the arrow between his lips.

As he fell, she tried to see the other riders, but couldn't. From the whinnying of their horses, she knew they'd bolted in alarm. She thought she heard one of them cry out, possibly in pain. She motioned to Pandora to close the door again and barricade it even more securely. "Stay here and be ready," she ordered, and immediately ascended the stairs once again. She ran as if her life depended upon it, emerging on the platform as before.

"I don't suppose you got the other riders?" she asked with a thin line of hope.

Meg shook her head. "I did the best I could, might have wounded one of them, but they've ridden off."

Lysistrate picked up her sword and took a few practice swings in the air. She didn't look concerned in the least. "I, for one, am more than pleased to get the excitement going."

Hagne merely picked up her bow and notched an arrow, her expression unreadable.

"When they come," Tisiphone told the others, "I'll go down below with Pandora. We'll delay them at the main door as long as we can, then set the wood alight.

We'll make our final stand atop the platform, side by side."

They had a bit of time, though, to watch the horde summon itself against them. The dull sleepiness of the village began to stir with lights and murmurs and shouts carried over the water across the harbor. They could see men milling about, horses moving, and torches being lit. Then, like a horde of locusts, the mass of Sea People's warriors moved as one back down the dirt path toward the lighthouse.

Tisiphone picked up an unlit torch and headed back for the stairs. "Good luck, girls," she called back. "I'll see you back up here in a bit, or on the other side of hell."

Chapter 17

Fire and Panic

Tisiphone rejoined Pandora at the bottom of the winding staircase. Here, she lit the torch using the little clay lamp Pandora had set up. Then she set it down on one of the lower stairs. Lighting it was a risk. It would be better to remain hidden in the dark as the Sea People barbarians battered their way through the door. But they'd need to light the waiting conflagration at the right moment, and she didn't want to risk the possibility someone might knock the little lamp over in the initial fighting.

The entrance chamber now smelled horrid. The acrid stench of copious fuel oil rendered breathing difficult. Surely even the brutish Sea People would notice the smell and not be fool enough to come in stumbling over the combustible wood. She hoped to time the lighting to catch a few in the conflagration but achieving or not achieving that was a minor issue. Getting the wood lit was essential to her plan.

Pandora gave her a quick, almost curious glance, but said nothing. She kept her recurve bow pulled back halfway, prepared for fire. Like Tisiphone, she kept just up the stairs a bit, ready to retreat once the fire was lit. Tisiphone felt a swelling of pride in the younger girl. She might only be a year younger, but the girl looked much younger, almost comical with the powerful bow drawn. Her gifts to the group were more intellectual than physical, but she was as brave as any of them.

Down here they couldn't see anything, but from the buzz that accumulated outside the sturdy door, they knew the Sea People's host had gathered around them. No escape now. Either they fought the horde off before the Dorian fleet arrived, or they died trying. Hopefully, they'd make a good show of it, at least.

Outside, the general cacophony coalesced into discernible voices, male voices raised in anger, threatening violence. They shouted among themselves in that babbly tongue of theirs. Tisiphone's pulse quickened. She drew the first of what she assumed would be many arrows and notched it.

Presently, something smashed against the outside of the door. It rattled, but held. Then again, another and another. More and more incessant banging as the throng sought to burst through into the lighthouse. The door held admirably, and Tisiphone began to worry the door almost might be too strong. She'd hoped to take down a few of their number here, but if the door proved to be uncooperative, she'd just have to light the fire and be done with it.

Soon, however, the banging changed to a new sound, crisper, more violent. This set the door shaking on its foundation. They'd taken axes to it. Hopefully, it would still take them time as the hard wood resisted. Every moment it bought them, with the barbarians trying to get through, would be more time for the fleet to arrive.

Then the first edge of an axe blade burst through the material. It was wrenched back and then plunged back, hacking free a considerable triangle of wood. The blade pulled free again, revealing a sliver of darkness beyond. Tisiphone and Pandora both fired through this sliver at once. Their timing was so close they almost knocked each other's arrows off course. They could see no targets, but at their angle, slightly up the staircase, their shots should plunge into what they assumed was an assembled barbarian mass. Beyond, there were shouts, although whether these were of pain or anger was difficult to tell. It didn't much matter. They needed to take every opportunity to hurt as many as they could.

The axe shattered more of the door now; a good chunk of the upper portion hacked away. A long, dark hairy arm reached through this opening, reaching for the bar. Pandora shot an arrow into the arm at once and pinned it to the door. The dirty bastard howled and wrenched his arm free, doing the flesh horrid damage in the process. Tisiphone fired another shot into the darkness. This time, their fire was returned, several arrows soaring into the entrance chamber and bouncing off the walls. Tisiphone resolved to keep firing into the dark so that an archer could not place a shot directly in their path without being hit first.

More axes joined the first, so that quickly most of the upper part of the door was gone. Still, the portal resisted, for the lower half was not merely barred but fully barricaded by the wood they had pressed against it. This forced the barbarians to crawl in through the upper part. When they did so, they were helpless to Tisiphone's and Pandora's arrows. The men, dirty, snarling, horrid, would push their bodies in, moving quickly like leopards, only to be felled by bronze arrowheads.

The barbarians would look up as they crawled over oil-soaked wood, growling for blood, eyes rolling like furious stallions. At this range, the recurve bows put arrows straight through them, penetrating their bronze armor, and straight through their skulls. Their fellows had to pull their bodies back through the door or push them out of the way to make room so they could crawl to their own deaths. Still, they came, a relentless wave of male rage. They seemed to take no notice of all the flammable oil in which they quickly became soaked. Tisiphone had to admire their courage, if nothing else. They kept pushing through to certain death despite the fate of their colleagues and showed not a moment's hesitation.

Soon they began to come through like rodents, three or four at a time. Tisiphone knew the sheer force of numbers would overwhelm them. She took up the torch and hurled it into the wood. For a moment, it teetered atop a stout log before falling into the mass. Nothing happened. Tisiphone despaired it might have landed in an oil-free spot in the wood. But then, with a whoosh, the trap caught, and flames roared to life.

Tisiphone and Pandora both put their arms up to protect their faces from the sudden wave of heat. The oil caught quickly, and the fire spread across the wooden mass right to the door. Several of the Sea People horde were caught stumbling through the barricades and their screams as the fire took them were demonic, a mixture of panic, fury, and hideous suffering. They whirled and flailed about, their armored bodies disappearing into the mass of fire and smoke.

Tisiphone didn't wait to watch their awful deaths. "Let go!" she ordered Pandora, and the two girls turned, sprinting back up the long, circular stairs. Now the danger was that they'd be caught in their own trap. They were outracing not Sea People, but the growing cloud of thick black smoke pouring from their own fire. If they were caught in it, they'd suffocate, victims of their own cleverness. Fortunately, their feet were light. Tisiphone only stopped at the furnace room to implore Nachor to join them atop where he'd be safe from the smoke.

"I'll tend to the light!" he insisted, his round body glistening with the sweat of his exertions. "I'll give my life to this furnace if it will give Greece even the slightest chance against these foul bastards!"

Tisiphone gave the old man a smile and closed the furnace room door, hoping that would offer him some protection. Then she turned, coughing, and made the rest of the way to the platform. She emerged just as the smoke in the stairwell became intolerable. She slammed the door behind her and, although smoke certainly wafted through at the edges, she was assured too little smoke made it so high as to obscure the light or make defending the platform unbearable.

The other four girls were aligned along the stone wall along the lip of the platform, firing arrows down toward the ground below. Return fire was light, arrows plinking against the roof or walls. Tisiphone set her bow and quiver aside. Hunched over, she joined the others, surveying the ground below.

Only a handful of the Sea People had made their way to the front of the lighthouse. These hid behind whatever cover they could find; rocks or the few trees. Already two bodies lay stretched along the ground. As she watched, Hagne put a shot into another, the body toppling over an embankment of rock and into the sea. In this type of archery exchange, they had a clear advantage in height and line of fire. This was merely the opening, however. A few archers to keep them busy and pinned down until the real assault began. Looking up, she could see that the stone overhang ended behind them. If, as Tisiphone presumed, the Sea People warriors climbed up the lighthouse from behind, they would drop down behind them, which wouldn't work at all. And this seemed the only possible route for the Sea People warriors to come. She was certain the stairwell was no longer viable. But even with the smoke billowing from the windows, coming up from the south, the smoke outside the lighthouse would not be enough to deter resolute climbers.

Meg fired an arrow that sunk into a tree behind where one of the warriors hid. She looked back at Tisiphone. "Is the wood all lit up then?"

Tisiphone nodded. "That should keep them from coming up behind us."

Meg furrowed her brow. "And you're certain the fire won't distort the stone at all? Send the whole lighthouse crashing down with us atop it?"

Tisiphone instinctively ducked as an arrow whistled overhead. "Well, I really hadn't thought of that, had I? Do you really think setting a fire could damage the foundation?"

"I don't know. You're the blacksmith's daughter."

"Well, we didn't cover lighthouse toppling, did we? A little late to worry much about it now. We'll just have to hope these Ionians didn't use rudimentary mortar." She looked up again, considering. "We can't stay like this. They can fire arrows at us all night, but they'll have to eventually come up and remove us if they want to put out the light. We'll need to be prepared for that. With the space we have, we'll keep two archers back, and three with swords in front. Keep all our arrows together so the archers have access to them all. Meg and Pandora, I'd like to keep you behind with bows. The rest of us up front to kick attackers back off the platform. If one of us three falls, Meg, you'll join the rest in the line. There will be a lot of them coming, but only a few can drop onto the platform at a time. We'll need to dispatch them quickly. If they're able to build up sufficient numbers, they'll overwhelm us."

The others nodded. Lysistrate and Hagne drew their blades and arranged themselves so that Lysistrate and Tisiphone covered the flanks with Hagne in the middle. They all kept their bodies low, for the pattering of arrows did not abate. The things flew in an arc, mainly over their heads, although some were quite close. They hit the ceiling, or went completely above the overhang, or glanced along the walls. Some skittered into the furnace, ironically adding to the light.

Overhead, something clunked and scraped along the roof. A climbing hook, little doubt. This was followed by several others of the same.

Tisiphone looked around at her colleagues. "It seems we will have company soon enough. Whatever may come, I want you to know it is an honor to stand beside each of you. And if we fall, then I will see you at the Ferryman."

They were granted a moment's reprieve as the arrow fire died down. Then they could hear shifting up above, atop the stone room. Tisiphone gripped the hilt of her curved foreign sword tight in both hands. Her heart quickened. She steeled her mind to end the lives of whatever men came before her tonight.

Above her, at that moment, came the first signs of movement. A pair of legs began to dangle over the edge as a man lowered himself down. Either Pandora or Meg, Tisiphone didn't know which, for she had her back to them, fired an arrow through one calf. The man yelped, then fell, landing awkwardly in front of Tisiphone. She raised her sword but hadn't even time to swing, as he lost his balance on his bad leg and toppled over the stone wall out into the dark night, screaming.

His fellows learned quickly from this, though, and dropped straight down to the platform without lowering themselves carefully. A first landed before Tisiphone, a tall man with a flowing red beard. He came down with a heavy thud and raised a war axe, eyes gleaming in the flaring light. An arrow went through his throat immediately and he dropped the axe, clutching noiselessly at the gaping wound the arrow left behind. Tisiphone needed only to kick him to send him toppling after his comrade.

For a minute or two, the battle went like this. The Sea People would come in ones and twos and, before a sword could be raised on either side, an arrow would finish the barbarians. Tisiphone, Hagne, and Lysistrate seemed to have little to do other than to make sure they went over the edge rather than cluttering up the platform. Tisiphone began to wonder if it would have been wiser to keep them all with bows and simply slaughter the bastards as they came down on the platform.

The Sea People began to come down quicker, more coordinated, and then the melee was joined. Fists, blades, hammers, blood, they all began to fly free. It became difficult to keep track of the other girls, as Tisiphone's focus narrowed on what was just before her. She used her size to her advantage in the narrow fighting space. Get in, deliver a lethal wound, get back out, and prepare for the next target, which would come soon enough.

She barely had time to register their faces. One jumped down in front of her. Big, that was all she registered of him. A good, big target. She stuck her blade into his stomach before he could get his bearings. She felt hot blood spurt onto her hands and gave him a kick over the ledge before he could even scream.

To her left, she saw movement, and turned and swung her blade against the back of another one fighting Hagne. The blade stuck in his armor, digging in enough to wound but not to kill. With a roar, he turned toward her. Hagne's blade swung up in an arc, slitting his throat while he was distracted. He slumped to the floor and Tisiphone pulled her sword free. No time to push him over the edge. Gradually, bodies were accumulating. They'd made maneuvering difficult. And the blood they leaked made the flooring slick.

Her foot slipped in the ichors just as she thought that, bringing her down to one knee. Yet another of the beasts landed near her and, without rising, she swung for his knees. Her hands jarred as the bronze connected with bone. The hulking warrior dropped his axe and reached for his knees, crouching. Tisiphone brought her blade up as she stood, connecting with his chin and sending him staggering back over the ledge into the dark night beyond.

She couldn't resist a look back at Pandora and Meg

with a grin. They looked to be doing fine, firing furiously, but their supply of arrows held. To her left, Hagne and Lysistrate were whirlwinds. Tisiphone was proud of her girls. They were like goddesses of death up here atop their tower. And these fools kept coming.

Another dropped before her to meet her blade. Then another. Then another. They fell, their lives but gossamer strands before her blade. Her arms began to tire. Her hands began to ache with the force of each thrust. But still, she swung. And she would continue to kill until her body gave out or one of them managed a lucky strike against her.

A smaller fellow slipped down from the roof, barely taller than herself. She thought him to be quick work and swung for his head, but he ducked this, faster than most of his comrades. Immediately, her mind registered alarm. Here was one, faster, quicker, smarter, closer to one of their own than the rest of that horde. She stepped back instinctively, knowing he'd follow her clumsy attack with a strike of his own.

His blade glided across her armor, the leather fortuitously holding and protecting her. An arrow whizzed past, fired from behind, but the small fellow dodged this, a long ponytail swaying as he weaved. He came at Tisiphone again and their blades crossed, clanging roughly and launching a few sparks. She tried to push him back, but he was faster, and his foot swept behind her own and pulled her off balance.

She fell heavily to the stone floor. For the moment, she felt more frustrated than anything else. But she needed to dispatch him fast. Every moment he delayed her, more of his fellows could follow him, and they'd quickly overwhelm the five girls if given a chance.

Tisiphone saw his blade arcing down toward her, and she rolled to the side. The sword smashed against the stone where she had lain only moments before. She rolled over onto her back, ready to confront his next attack.

To her surprise, though, he had turned to his right, where Hagne's exposed back lay open to him. She was engaged in battle with another of his comrades, unaware of the danger.

"Hagne!" Tisiphone shouted, her chest feeling as if it might split.

Hagne didn't hear her. The other girl had no idea at all how much danger she was in. Not until the small man's sword drove into her back. Hagne arced her back and looked over her shoulder in sudden alarm.

Rage coursing through her, Tisiphone scrambled to her feet, her vision narrowing on the man who'd knocked her down and injured her friend. His sword buried in Hagne, his throat lay open to her now. He turned toward her, a grin fading just as her sword cut through the sinews of his neck. His head lolled back in a great gush of blood, and he toppled backward.

His sword remained in Hagne, though, and as he fell, she began to tumble with him. Hagne dropped her sword, her hands flaying wildly as she lost her balance. Tisiphone reached out to help her, their fingertips just brushing against each other. Tisiphone called out to her friend again. Hagne's face was a visage of panic and pain. And then the body of the dead barbarian pulled her over.

"No!" Tisiphone screamed. She turned and jabbed her sword into the stomach of the big warrior Hagne had fought before being felled. As he dropped, she rushed to the ledge. Some foolish part of her hoped Hagne had somehow grown wings and taken to flight, or perhaps the gods had sent Pegasus to save her. But her swirling vision could discern nothing, only the great darkness below.

Instead, for her troubles, she heard the sound of something singing through the air. Stunned, she only pulled her head away at the last moment. Her left ear erupted in agony as an arrowhead sliced through it. She screamed and put her hand up to her ear, feeling hot blood flow through her fingers. There, with her hand pushed up against the side of her head, for a moment, all she could hear was the thud of her own pulse as her heart drove blood between her fingers.

Then a hand grabbed her shoulder and pulled her back. Meg, her bow dropped, and sword now drawn, stepped into Hagne's spot as she'd been ordered before the battle. "She's gone," Meg said.

Tisiphone nodded. She wiped an arm across her face instinctively, to try to clear her eyes from swelling tears, but she managed only to smear blood along her face.

Wounded, despondent and tired, she fought on with Meg now at her side instead of Hagne. They kept coming, the barbarians, one after another. Furious, unrelenting, seeming unconcerned for their own lives. And still, she killed them. This orgy of death continued endlessly it seemed, until her bones shook to their core and her muscles seemed to tear loose from their moorings. She no longer thought, no longer counted the dead, no longer worried for her own safety. She would kill until she could kill no more, and then she would be ready to die.

Only, eventually, the tide of the Sea People finally ebbed. The pace with which they assaulted her slackened suddenly. In a moment, the Furies were left alone atop the tower. They looked around at each other. No longer recognizable as women, they were monsters coated in blood. Only Pandora, furthest from the melee with her bow, had been spared the shower of gore.

Tisiphone wondered at first if this might be some kind of trick, if the Sea People had discovered some other means to attack them. Down below, there was much commotion, the shouting of men, the sound of bronze on bronze.

Reflexively, she put her hand to her ear, which throbbed unrelentingly. She stepped closer to the ledge. Below, among the heaps of the dead, men fought. Among some of them, she recognized the armor of hoplites. Dorian warriors.

Her eyes shifted to the harbor, and there she saw boats slipping out of the piers, whilst others took their place. Men were vomited forth from these ships. Men in the bronze armor and spears of the phalanx.

"They've come," Tisiphone said, barely able to hear her own voice. "The Dorian fleet."

"We've done it," Meg said, then gave a little laugh. Lysistrate looked over at them and grinned.

But their grins did not last long. Hagne was gone. Aside from Pandora, each of them had taken injuries. And their bodies had been pushed beyond the limits of endurance.

Tisiphone collapsed, tossing her Egyptian sword to one side. She sat in a pool of fluids with her legs crossed. Her chest heaved as her lungs struggled to find enough air. Tears suddenly threatened to spill forth, and it took what remained of her resolve to force them back down. Not in front of her soldiers, not now.

The others sat down too, not caring in what puddles of gore. Lysistrate could hold herself up a little better than Tisiphone and lay back, using the ledge for support. Meg seemed in better condition and Pandora the best of them, for they had fought less hand to hand.

Pandora looked up and behind them. "How are we going to get off this tower?"

Tisiphone looked up as well. Even in the darkness, they could see the column of smoke rising up and behind the lighthouse, small glowing embers carried with it. Smoke from the fire they had set, still filling up the staircase and their only way down. Tisiphone couldn't help it but began to giggle. Soon, they all were laughing at the ridiculousness of their predicament.

Still, it was over. The fighting and the killing were over. Whatever may come, they were now in the hands of the gods. Later, Tisiphone couldn't remember that the girls said anything more to each other that night. She remembered only their maniacal laughter before they, one by one, lay down across the cold bloody stone and slept as if death itself had embraced them.

Chapter 18

Blood in Her Hair

Tisiphone awoke with the sky alit within the morning sun, the receding image of her adoptive mother Myrrine decaying with the memory of some dream. She sat up suddenly, startled to find herself in this bloody, cruel reality, surprised to be wrenched from a dream she'd already forgotten. Her hand slid in slippery fluid and her hair pulled free from the floor with a thick slurp.

From head to toe blood covered her. Mainly that of others, mostly men whose names she never knew, although perhaps part of her rested in the fluid that had once kept Hagne alive. The exception was the left side of her face and neck, which she could feel coated with her own blood, still oozing slowly from her burning left ear.

Her arms ached furiously, and her body rebelled with a series of nausea-inducing shakes as she moved to ease up into a sitting position. She'd pushed her body past its limit. They all had. Meg, Lyzzi, and Pandora all still remained stretched out in puddles of gore, exhausted. Meg even rested her head on the corpse of a man she'd killed, his leg more comfortable than the stone below.

By the gods, what a wretched scene, and how

wretched they were. Tisiphone crawled over to the ledge and managed to haul herself over it to look below. Scattered just under the tower were dozens of the dead. Men they'd killed, now watched over by crows and carrion feeders. So much life they had taken in such a short time. It was unfathomable. Tisiphone forced that line of thought from her mind. It would lead her nowhere useful.

Beyond, the sea lapped up against the shore, somehow more peaceful seeming in the day than during the darkness of night. The Dorian ships, those blessed shapes that had slid into the bay to rescue them, were gone. The bay was now empty, even the Sea People's raiders gone. Nor was there a Dorian army in sight. The fortuitous arrival of the Dorian fleet might have been itself a dream if she did not spot just a few of the hoplites mingling about the town, a rearguard left behind while the main army moved on to lift the Sea People's siege, at least so she hoped.

"Tisiphone?" whispered a voice from behind her.

Tisiphone turned to find Pandora struggling to stand. "Are you all right? Are you injured?"

Pandora shook her head as she managed to stand. Her drawing hand looked raw and inflamed, but otherwise, there was not a mark on her. The gods could be praised for that. "I feared you and the others might never wake. That exhaustion might kill you where the Sea People had not."

Tisiphone smiled. "Never. Why, we merely needed a nap."

Together, they woke up the others who, like Tisiphone, were quivering from the overexertion of the night before. They replenished their stock of arrows from the unbroken ones that had been fired up at them. Then, limping and holding onto each other, they began the long climb down the tower that seemed far more daunting than it had the night before. Fortunately, the fire they'd set had burned itself out. The stairwell was coated in ash and smelled horrid, and tendrils of smoke still wafted through it, but it was no longer impossible to breathe.

Tisiphone checked in on the old Greek who'd bravely managed the furnace for them, keeping the light lit. Sadly, the smoke had gotten the better of him, and he'd suffocated, feeding the furnace until his last moment. With a prayer for his safe passage to the Underworld, they left him where he lay. Eventually, they stumbled through the remnants of the fire they'd set and into the fresh ocean air.

Here, on this side of the tower, were the remains of the Sea People contingent they'd battled, along with a few Dorian dead as well. If any of the Sea People had gotten away from the Dorian invasion, they'd been few. Silently, moving as one, they went to the north face of the tower and, there, searched for Hagne's body. To their distress, they could not find their comrade and ultimately had to admit her body must have fallen into the ocean or, less likely, been carried off by what Sea People had survived.

They limped to the bay next, past a few hoplites who regarded them curiously. In full armor, they waded into the cold ocean to bathe themselves. Blood, brains, gore and flesh spread out across the water in a discernible layer of filth. Tisiphone worked hard to scrub away the viscera from her hair, from her armor, from her skin. As she did, she could feel small fish in the water swimming around her legs, grateful for the unexpected bounty of organic matter she brought them. Whatever it took. She couldn't bear the thought of carrying such offal on her person for much longer. Her ear stung as she immersed her head underwater. She shivered, but she endured the cold. It was a small sacrifice to pay to clean herself.

Eventually, when they had washed themselves the best they could, they set a fire and warmed themselves, and ate. They took turns ministering to each other's wounds. It was Meg who stitched Tisiphone's ear back together. Tisiphone couldn't help but flinch and squeal as the bone needle pierced through the hard cartilage of her earlobe.

"Shush, girl," Meg ordered. "To think with what you've been through, you can't handle a few stitches. Would you prefer to go through life looking as if a dog had chewed on your ear?"

Tisiphone glowered, though Meg, sitting behind her, couldn't see it. "What does it matter how I look, anyway? Soon we'll all look like Chloe, if we're not killed first." She sat silently for a moment, trying to take mental stock of herself and discovering mainly that she didn't really know how she felt. Drained and exhausted, for certain. Aside from that, she didn't seem to feel what she might have expected. They'd participated in a slaughter of Sea People warriors of such an epic quality they'd be talked about for generations, certainly. But Tisiphone couldn't help but wonder if she'd been party to a great tragedy. And then there was the death of Hagne. She'd know Hagne least well of their group, but she'd still been a valued colleague. She'd be missed. And Koredyne had been right: they'd had to pay a sacrifice in flesh.

Truth was that her mind shuddered to think much about what they'd experienced the night before. Better something to leave behind, to forget. There'd be enough death awaiting them in the future to bother reflecting too much on the past.

"You led us well last night," Meg observed as she jabbed the bone needle once more through Tisiphone's ear.

"Gods!" Tisiphone growled, then quieted. "What do you mean? We lost Hagne."

"One lost against dozens of enemy dead and the success of our mission. Hagne died with honor. We will mourn her, just as we will celebrate the heroism of her death."

Tisiphone moved her head back a bit, a dangerous move given Meg's pluckings with the needle. "Do you think so? Is it as simple as that?"

"I know that no one, not even Chloe, could have led us with more success than you. None of us had any reason to expect to survive, and yet we did."

Tisiphone processed that silently. Where she saw failure, Meg saw success. Somehow, this revelation only served to confuse her, to make her less certain of what to think.

****

Once they had sewn their wounds, and eaten and warmed themselves, they set out across the island to follow the Dorian army. They did this at a leisurely pace, still weakened and not feeling obliged to join a full battle. Serving as soldiers of the phalanx was not where the Furies shone. And they'd done their fair share already.

Following the army was not difficult, as three thousand men naturally trampled everything in their path. Halfway across the island, they stopped and made camp and slept well for the night. They woke up again mid-morning and resumed their journey.

The first hint that they approached Io's capital at Eritrea were plumes of smoke. Five or six of these rose lazily into leaden skies. They were spaced about, not from a single source. Warily, the Furies ventured closer until they could see what had befallen Eritrea.

The city walls, in fact, still stood secure. Like Iolcus, Eritrea nestled the seacoast, facing the west and the coast of Attica across the narrow waters. From the land, tall stone walls protected the city, and these had held against the Sea People's siege until the Dorian army had arrived. Arrayed around the outskirts of Eritrea was the Dorian army the Furies had themselves helped to land. The hoplites now gathered about in small clusters, setting up camp and looking bored even from a distance. The battle with the Sea People was over. Those plumes of ash rose from the bodies of the dead raiders, heaped into piles, and burned.

Tisiphone led her girls down into the valley toward Eritrea. They walked openly among the men, who regarded them curiously in turn. Tisiphone remarked to herself of the men of pure muscle, armored in bronze. So different from themselves, yet killing machines in their own way. Technically, the men were free, unlike the Furies, but what difference did it make, really?

The hoplites stopped what they were doing as the Furies passed. The men regarded them without hostility, yet the Furies received no words of thanks either. In return, the women said nothing to the men. It seemed as if they weren't part of the same army at all, merely distant and even mutually suspicious allies of circumstance.

So, too, it clearly was between the Ionians and the Dorians. The walls of Eritrea remained closed even though the Sea People had been slaughtered. No fighting emerged between the two Greek peoples, but it seemed a wary situation as any.

Tisiphone had no intention of sleeping out here with the men, though. Straight to the gates, she led her soldiers. There, she looked up and called, "I am Tisiphone of the Furies and I ask for entrance."

After a moment, a lone face peered down at them from above. "Furies? Dorian slave warriors? What business have you in Eritrea?"

We just saved it, Tisiphone grumbled inside her mind, but decided not to give voice to those thoughts. "Tell the Queen…tell her I have news of her sister."

The face disappeared from the wall. Tisiphone looked around at her comrades and shrugged. It wasn't entirely a lie, exactly.

A moment later, the gates began to grind open, just enough for them to pass through. One by one, they slipped through the stone slabs and into Eritrea. The city that waited beyond was small, but impressive. Tisiphone immediately thought it rich, with buildings of better construction than Iolcus and a palace by the sea that was plainly visible even from this distance. People bustled about their daily business, apparently unaware a Dorian army camped outside their palisades, and unconcerned about the battle fought there just recently.

Just on the other side of the gate stood a man. Galen. Tisiphone rushed into his arms, and she couldn't stop a foolish grin as they embraced. He greeted each of the Furies in turn. Then his look turned more serious. "What of your friend, Hagne?"

Tisiphone felt her eyes well up at her name. By the gods, when would she stop reacting this way? It made her feel like a girl, not a soldier. "She…she…"

Galen put his hand on her shoulder. "I'm sorry. She was a fine warrior." He looked around at them all. "You've been expected. I've told Io about you and your exploits, which I'm told now includes fighting a thousand Sea People warriors on your own." He grinned.

"Barely two hundred," Meg corrected with false modesty.

"Io will be interested to meet you," Galen said as he led them toward the palace. "She has a banquet planned for this evening. You'll be the guests of honor. And don't worry about anything. She has rooms set aside for you in the palace, and clothes, and anything else you need."

Lysistrate whistled at that. "Nice to see we're getting some appropriate thanks for our hard work for once."

"You wouldn't know it by the tense stand-off between Io's people and the Dorians, but we're all quite thankful for what you've done. The city couldn't have held out indefinitely under siege."

Galen brought them to the palace. The soldiers and courtiers deferred to him, and he went about the building as if it were his own. This impressed Tisiphone, who was used to seeing him as a rough-hewn archer.

Like the palace at Iolcus, Io's palace was designed

for comfort, not war. It was an open building, meant to capture the sea breezes, cooling during summer months and warming during winter, although the openings could be shuttered against the worst gales. This palace was old, much older than the Emperor's palace. Airy though they might have been, the corridors seemed ever haunted with ghosts.

Galen brought them to a chamber high up, where four slave women waited. He turned to the Furies. "Here I will leave you. You will be taken to your separate rooms, where you will be bathed and attended to. You may rest if you like until you are called for this evening. I will see you again then."

Tisiphone found herself in the care of a young woman by the name of Agapita. As the slave girl led her away, she felt a moment of disorientation. Aside from brief moments, she had barely been out of contact with the other Furies for nine months. Now they would be separated in an unfamiliar place. They were putting considerable trust in Galen and his liege.

Agapita led Tisiphone to a spacious room overlooking the sea. Comfortable bedding and luxurious clothes awaited, as did a bronze tub of steaming water. Tisiphone frowned on seeing it. "This is for me?"

"While you are here, yes," Agapita responded with a smile. She reached for Tisiphone's belt, and Tisiphone instinctively reached for her sword. Agapita frowned. "You must be bathed, and you cannot be bathed in armor."

Which, of course, made considerable sense. Tisiphone sighed and willed herself to relax while the slave girl went to work undressing her. Tisiphone stood, arms outstretched. She did not care about undressing in front of other women. The absence of privacy was a fact of life for a slave soldier. But to suddenly be waited upon in this manner was jarring. She could not resist chattering to fill the awkward space. "Have you been here, at the palace, all your life?"

"As a slave, you mean? Yes. I was born into slavery. I am not worked unduly hard here. Io is kind, and our health is looked out for."

"You don't wish to be free, then?" Tisiphone couldn't fathom why she'd asked that as soon as the words had come out of her mouth. Hardly a polite conversation to start with.

Agapita chuckled. "I suppose we all think of it sometimes. But what would I do with freedom? Seek out employment at the palace where I might help bathe Dorians who talk when they are nervous?"

Tisiphone frowned. "You have considerable nerve for a slave."

"You are a slave as well," Agapita reminded her. "I see the brand on your shoulder. So, I say we talk freely as sisters. Do you wish for your freedom, sister?"

Tisiphone felt a weight lifted from her as Agapita pulled the leather armor away. She thought about the question for a moment. "I wasn't born to slavery."

"What did you plan to do when you were free?" Agapita helped her out of her undergarments and into the tub. The water was still quite warm.

Tisiphone eased into it, feeling the soothing warmth seep into her muscles. "My father was a blacksmith. I suppose I would have helped him with his forge."

Agapita raised her eyebrows. "A woman

blacksmith?"

"And why not? You are ruled by a queen without a king."

"So that is true, although these are troubled times." Agapita moved behind her and began rubbing some small white berries into the water. These began to form a light foam as she worked them. Then she plunged her hands into Tisiphone's long hair, mashing in the frothing berries. She was not gentle.

"Take care! I haven't fought my way here just to have all the hair plucked from my head."

"She may be a strong queen, but Io does not like to greet guests who have bone in their hair. Now settle down and try to relax. Did you wish anything else of your life but to be a blacksmith?"

Tisiphone did try to settle down, particularly once Agapita found a rhythm for washing her hair. "To marry and have children, I suppose. Do they allow you to marry as a slave here?"

"It depends on the master. We may form marriages, but they are not recognized by the state, and our families can be sold apart at any time." She said this without emotion.

Tisiphone thought on this, comparing this uncertain lot to her own, forbidden to marry or bear children at all. Perhaps that was better than to see her husband and child torn from her arms.

Agapita seemed to sense Tisiphone's mood. "I didn't mean to darken your spirits with this talk. You will be celebrated tonight like few are. You should enjoy this moment. Besides, whatever worries I may have, they are fewer than most. Io treats us with kindness, and I need not worry after my next meal, or a warm bed. There are few others, free or slave, who enjoy the security I do."

"You are quite right, and a wise woman." Tisiphone nodded, although she remained deep in thought. Security and slavery or freedom and the risks that came with it? She wondered which she would pick if that were the choice offered to her. Then again, she knew firsthand that, even if Agapita lived in some comfort, the life of the typical slave was brutish.

After bathing, Tisiphone was allowed a few hours to rest. Then Agapita returned and helped her dress in a peplos of emerald green, with silver shoulder clasps. Never before had she worn such luxurious or comfortable clothes. By now, so used to being adorned continuously in armor whilst not sleeping, wearing only the peplos made her feel all but nude. Agapita then spent hours applying cosmetics and working wonders with her hair. Tisiphone watched the entire process in a brass mirror, amazed by the transformation Agapita wrought in her. She might have passed for a princess. Any hint of the slave warrior was gone for now.

With her work done, Agapita then led Tisiphone to the banquet hall. A chill breeze blew in now from the sea, but the corridors were lit with fiery braziers, casting off waves of heat, so that Tisiphone's skin was intermittently cooled and warmed as they walked. Night had fallen, and as they walked at one point along the landward side of the castle, Tisiphone thought even the campfires of the Dorian host looked beautiful arrayed in the dark.

Agapita stopped at the foyer of the banquet hall and motioned for Tisiphone to enter in such a way that Tisiphone knew Agapita would not be following.

Within, a modest hall was packed with men and women clustered around a series of wooden tables. The din was considerable—laughter, shouting, each person trying to be heard over all the others. Like the halls, the room was lit by several immense braziers that cast such heat winter clothes were not necessary within. Wine flowed freely, and women and men intermingled in such a way the people of her village would have considered it licentious.

Tisiphone stepped into the room, not recognizing anyone at first. She turned back, but Agapita was already gone. Stepping in further, a tall man jostled her and moved past. Then she spotted Lysistrate across the room, surrounded by no fewer than three Ionian youths and laughing as if she had not a care in the world. Meg, she spotted a moment later. Unlike Lysistrate, Meg raised a cup toward Tisiphone when their eyes met. But she too had Ionian admirers, perhaps a rare moment when she enjoyed a surfeit of male attention, and Tisiphone had no desire to take her from that. She looked about for Pandora but couldn't find the younger girl at all. She looked about for Galen as well, but he too was missing.

Then she felt a touch at her elbow. She turned to find a handsome youth beside her. He was of moderate height and fair looks, with curled brown hair and brown eyes. He was slender and athletic and smooth of skin, such that she initially doubted he could have ever held a shield and spear. "You are one of our saviors, our guests of honor?"

Tisiphone laughed nervously. "I suppose that is true. I am Tisiphone, captain of the Furies."

"I am Praxis. You must be hungry. Won't you sit

with me…we can dine and talk for a bit."

She pointed toward her comrades, "I really ought to…"

He smiled, his tone more thoughtful than pushy. "They appear to be indisposed at the moment."

"Then Galen…"

"Is with the Queen."

"Will she not be attending?"

"That is hard to say. Although she called this banquet, she is not often seen in crowds. If she arrives, I would be sure to introduce you."

"You know her so well, do you?"

"Just enough to make a polite introduction." He motioned toward a rare open spot at one of the tables. "If you find my company objectionable, I won't press my suit further. However, if you might find me a reasonable momentary distraction from your fellows and from Galen, it would be a considerable pleasure to speak with you."

She blushed but nodded her assent. It felt good to receive male attention that didn't involve a swinging sword or thrusting spear. As she had not yet eaten, the table certainly called to her as well. It was piled high with fruits, all manner of beasts, and confections of every sort. An opulent display of the wealth of Euboea. The Ionians might not have much by way of military might, but they had riches still. It would make them a tempting target for either the Sea People or the Empire of the North.

Like the others, Tisiphone ate with her hands, using only a knife provided when necessary. Praxis proved himself a worthwhile companion. He was both charming and dexterous in his manner with her, never pushing his luck further than she might welcome. In a moment of laughter, he might touch her shoulder or her thigh, and his touch electrified her. It occurred to her she might lay with him if she so chose. She'd never lain with a man before. But he was handsome and kind. If she had no connection of love with him, perhaps that did not matter so. She might die in battle tomorrow without ever knowing a man's embrace. She knew Chloe would approve, so long as she took the precautions against pregnancy Chloe had taught them all.

Whatever came of it, whether something or nothing at all, she enjoyed his company. He made her feel like her company was worth enjoying as a woman, not as a slave soldier or the supposed focus of some vague prophecy. It was thrilling, made her feel human, and it was over too quickly.

Galen appeared suddenly, his hand gently on her shoulder. "The Queen has sent for you."

"Galen," Praxis scolded good-naturedly, "the Queen has three other Furies to choose from. Can she not leave Tisiphone in my able hands?"

Galen smiled, though without warmth. "She has sent for Tisiphone specifically."

Tisiphone actually felt disappointed, and she gave Praxis an apologetic smile. "Thank you. You made me feel very welcome."

"Welcome, you are. Perhaps we will meet again, my Dorian friend."

Galen led her by the elbow through the crowded dining hall, out a different door from the one she entered through. This hallway was dark and quiet, the sound of the crowd quickly receding. Several soldiers stood at watch here.

"Why does Queen Io not attend her own banquet?" Tisiphone asked, still feeling a bit piqued to have been taken from Praxis in such a manner.

"The Queen is not fond of such events, frankly. She called the banquet in your honor because she felt you deserved to be celebrated. She is not one for crowds herself. But she was insistent on meeting you."

"Why not Lysistrate, or Meg, or Pandora?"

"You are their captain," he answered simply. But she knew that was not all. She was also at the center of this talk that her fate lines crossed with Bael. This would interest the Ionians as much as the Dorians.

At the end of the hall, Galen motioned her through an open doorway. Within, a dark chamber waited. Nearly as large as the banquet hall, this one was lit only by a few candles. A small table sat just next to the open door, laden with food and drink just like the banquet hall. Beyond that, she could barely see. The room filled with shadows and flickering bits of light from the candle. "Io awaits you."

"Aren't you coming?" she asked.

"Io wished to speak with you alone." He winked at her. "You will be fine. Be yourself."

"I've never figured out who else to be." But she swallowed and stepped through the doorway. Galen was gone almost immediately. She felt a bit like she'd been led to some monster's den. Perhaps that was true. Io was sister to Nyx. Perhaps another witch, for all she knew. She stepped near the table, squinting into the darkness. "Queen Io?"

"Tisiphone, captain of the Furies, I presume?" a voice echoed from the darkness. A moment later, she

273

emerged from the void like a ghost. Wearing a peplos of white, her face framed with long, golden hair, Io, the queen of Euboea, who led the shattered remnants of Mycenaean Greece. She approached the table with such grace it seemed she levitated. Like Nyx, she was beautiful, but light where Nyx was dark, warm where Nyx was cold. They were sisters such as the face and inverse are both sides of the same coin. Io was older than Nyx, she knew from somewhere, but it was hard to tell.

"I am Tisiphone." She didn't bow or prostrate herself. Be yourself, Galen had said, and bowing before a master wasn't her. She hadn't bowed to Diadarian or Zinovia, and she didn't feel like starting now.

Io came fully into view of the shimmering candles on the near table. Her blue eyes appraised Tisiphone. Then she motioned toward the food. "I've taken you from your banquet. Eat, please. If you wish for something that is not here, I will send for it. I've taken you from the company of the youth, Praxis, as well. I can only beg your forgiveness for that, for I've only my own company with which to replace it."

Tisiphone sat on a bench at the table and plucked at a few grapes. Io sat across from her and, likewise, picked lazily at the food.

"You, no doubt, wish to ask me questions," Tisiphone observed.

"And you, no doubt, wish the same of me," Io replied. She popped a berry into her mouth and smiled. "Which of us shall go first?"

"It is your right, Queen."

"Very well. First, let me say how grateful I am to you and your comrades for what you have done. I am told that five of you held off a thousand Sea People's warriors?"

"It was only two hundred." Tisiphone pursed her lips to keep from grinning.

"Only two hundred?" Io repeated. "I was saddened to learn that one of your number died in the fighting?"

"Hagne. We did not find her body."

"No matter. A shrine will be erected to her honor on the site of the battle." She smiled broadly, and in the silence that followed, let her smile slowly fade. "Of course, you must imagine, effectively I have replaced outside my walls one hostile army for another. Granted, the Dorian host is not trying to scale my walls as of yet, and I am grateful they have rid me of the Sea People's horde. But the Empire to the North has hardly been remiss in plucking up the lands of the Mycenaeans any more than have the Sea People. And since the Dorian navy fled soon after unleashing the phalanxes, it appears we will play host to them for some time."

Tisiphone looked into a goblet and found it full of wine. She tasted it and found it sweet to her liking. "You worry the Dorians will attack your city?"

"Yes. We cannot hope to expel the Empire's phalanxes any more than we could the Sea People's hordes. Have you met with the Emperor, King Diadarian?"

Tisiphone nodded. "I have."

"And did you have a sense of his mind on this matter?"

"If he wished to rule your lands, he'd have asked me to kill you once you brought me here. And if I had any such orders, I would already have done it."

Io leaned back. "You've no weapon. There are

guards just in the hall."

Tisiphone grinned. "Unless you've some skill at arms you've masterfully hidden, I could be across this table and snap your neck before you had time to flinch. I'm confident I could kill your guards too and be away in the night." She laughed a bit, then realized what she'd said. She cleared her throat. "Which I tell you to put you at ease. If King Diadarian wished you dead, you would be dead. Of that I am confident." She tore a piece of bread away from a loaf and spoke while she ate. "It's true he's left you with the responsibility to feed three thousand men. The Dorian navy won't have a chance to recover them until the Sea People's navy is broken. And that may be never. But Dorian phalanxes in addition to your own men. Euboea will not be targeted by the Sea People again soon."

Io did not seem unduly threatened by Tisiphone's words. "The Empire of the North has so many troops, that to leave three thousand here is not a strategic mistake?"

Tisiphone considered it. "I don't know how many soldiers the Empire has. Fewer than the Sea People to be sure, but far more again than you, I think. I can say King Diadarian struck me as no fool. If he sent these phalanxes here, he knew he could not recover them easily and gauged that worth the risk."

"To keep us fighting?"

Tisiphone shrugged and took a drink from her goblet.

"And, let us say, the Sea People are defeated. Will King Diadarian allow us to live in peace in Euboea and in Attica? Is that your impression?"

"I can't say he said as much. I think he'd want the

lands the Sea People now occupy, Boeotia, the West, the Peloponnese. But I think if you honored him as the savior to the Ionians he would find more value in that than land."

"But I am given to understand King Diadarian is unwell. What if there were no Emperor, only an Empress, the Queen Zinovia. What then?"

Tisiphone paused, remembering her own brief and unpleasant encounter with the Queen. She searched for careful words and found none, continuing the search. Eventually, she realized, too late, that her own silence had answered the question.

Io shifted on the bench, and regarded Tisiphone for a moment. "You said at the gate that you had news of my sister."

Tisiphone looked up and nodded. "It was she who made me what I am. With a man named Kriluss, she destroyed my village, murdered my parents, and enslaved me. Kriluss meant to sell me as a sex slave, but Nyx sent me instead to the kitchens of the palace at Iolcus. From there, I was made a Fury. I think she knew, somehow."

Io looked down at her hands. "I am sorry for what she did to you and your family. My sister has chosen a dark path. We have not spoken in years."

"Why?"

Io narrowed her gaze. "Why have we not spoken?"

"Why did she choose a dark path?"

Io recoiled from the question as if struck and watched Tisiphone as if stunned for a long moment. "That is a difficult question with a complex answer."

Tisiphone met Io's gaze evenly and, once again, let silence speak for her.

Io leaned in across the table. "Why do you want to know this?"

"She set me on this path for a reason. I'm trying to understand what that reason might be. My parents, who she killed, were my adoptive parents. I don't know my birth mother. One explanation for why Nyx took an interest in me, saved me from becoming a sex slave…"

"You think she may be your mother," Io reasoned. "How old are you?"

"Fifteen." Her birthday had passed unnoticed, during her training.

Io considered that for a moment. "She left Euboea before then. I know nothing about whether she became pregnant. It is possible then. But be wary; Nyx may have an altogether different ulterior motive for sparing you. Don't become misguided by a fantasy."

"I'm not sure having Nyx as a mother would be called a fantasy, but I have to know."

Io sighed. "I'm not sure I can make any sense of it for you. Nyx and I were never close. She was four years younger than I. Our parents…our father was a good king, my mother a good queen. But they had little time for us. Nyx especially, for she was withdrawn, shy…strange even as a child. She wore black, always, when she could. She never worshipped the gods, but seemed to murmur only to older spirits, things long forgotten by man. She had few friends, and though she had an unearthly beauty, a beauty I frankly at times envied and despised, she had no suitors. Well, that is not true, but I am ahead of myself.

"As I said, Nyx and I were not close. When it became evident my parents would have no sons, my father began to prepare me to rule. Not alone, of course.

A suitable husband would be found. In these days the Sea People were already assaulting the Peloponnese and the Western shores, although they were just making their appearance, their raids temporary, and hope remained they would be repelled. But I would marry and bring a king to the land. As would Nyx because, if I died, then all hope would rest with her. So she, too, was destined to marry an appropriate husband of our father's choosing. Only one day, against everyone's expectations, Nyx fell in love."

Tisiphone ate quietly while she listened, fascinated by this glimpse into the early years of the woman who might be her mother.

"The youth who captured her heart was a commoner, a charming fellow full of life. He had found employment at the castle, and they began spending time together. My parents, involved in the affairs of state, did not notice for a long time…too long perhaps. I can't say that Nyx ever changed into a spritely girl, but she seemed alive for the first and only time I ever knew.

"When our father finally learned of the affair, he forbade it most angrily. We were most desirable as virgins, you see, and the shame of such an affair would tarnish our family's honor, he felt. But by then the matter was well past the stage where young women listen to their fathers, and he was all but a stranger to her, besides."

Io sighed and looked down at her hands. "In truth, I took only a cursory interest in all this. I suppose I thought that by keeping out of it, keeping Nyx's secret until my father found out on his own, I was doing my little sister a favor. I will always wonder if I had done more…spoken to her more about what she was doing…if things might have been different for all of us."

Tisiphone sat frozen, no longer even able to eat, so rapt was she in Io's tale.

"One day, our father found them together, wrapped in the embrace of the most intimate lovers. He flew into a rage. To him, I think he saw it as the ruin of the family's honor, crushing his hopes for a good marriage for Nyx. Perhaps he thought even I would be less desirable given a stain on the family's honor. He locked Nyx up for a time. Our father had Nyx's lover…he was executed publically and in a most cruel manner."

Io stopped for a moment, remained still, then looked up and met Tisiphone's gaze. "I think he regretted it almost at once, that murder. He set Nyx free, and isolated himself from public view in his own shame. I went to Nyx then, did what I could to be a comfort to her. But that life I'd seen in her was gone, and the darkness that had always brooded within her was given full voice. She spoke to almost no one, she never cried, never raged at my parents. Anyone could see that a storm spun within her, but she remained as cold as ice and as distant as the Titans."

Io went silent again, this time minutes ticked by without further words. The Queen appeared to be lost deep in her memories.

Finally, Tisiphone timidly asked, "So what did Nyx do?"

Io looked up and blinked as if she'd almost forgotten Tisiphone was there. Her glance darted around as if searching for a ghost visible only out of the corner of her eye. At last, she answered, "She murdered our parents, of course."

Chapter 19

The Dark of Night

Io wiped a tear from her eye as she uttered those horrible words. The darkness seemed to stretch further over the walls and ceiling, driving back the pitiful efforts of the waning candles. Cold permeated Tisiphone's bones. But she didn't dare to press the Queen further.

At last, Io spoke anyway, determined perhaps to see the story through. "She did not stab them or anything so clear as that. But murder them, she did, I'm sure of it. Her love had been turned to hate, and she enacted her vengeance. She'd had no love for them prior, and that was of their own making. And my father had slaughtered the only thing she'd ever cared for. Even then, our mother did nothing to comfort her or to stop our father, so she too must have seemed complicit in Nyx's eyes.

"One evening, after supper, our parents took ill and retired to their beds. By the still of night, the illness became a violent, raging fever, coughing blood, and painful contractions of the limbs. Morning brought them both death. The physicians said it was a bloody flux, a natural illness, but I knew better than that."

"Nyx poisoned them?" Tisiphone ventured.

Io shook her head. "The physicians looked for that,

looked for signs of poisoning. It was the bloody flux, sure enough. Only no one else in the palace had contracted it." ,Io met Tisiphone's gaze once again. "She cursed them, not poisoned them."

Tisiphone looked down at the table, letting that declaration sink in. She'd experienced Nyx's malevolent force directly herself, so it wasn't difficult to believe Nyx had the power. But to kill her own parents? It was unimaginable.

"I know," Io whispered. "I had no proof. With my parents dead, I was made queen. And when Nyx left Eritrea a few weeks later, I did nothing to stop her. I unleashed her on the world, a bitter, enraged monster. Truth be told, I was afraid. I was glad to see her go." She laughed a cold, brittle laugh. "So if she cast you forth from her wretched body, it would have had to have been about four years later, when the Sea People truly washed up on our shores. And if she is your mother, then may the gods help you."

Tisiphone looked up toward the roof and inhaled deeply.

Io reached across the table and grasped her wrist. "But from what you've done, even from seeing you this short time, you are nothing like her. If her blood runs through you, she must have given you that one moment of life and love she felt and held back the rest. I would be proud to call you my niece."

Tisiphone wiped her free hand across her face. "I'm just a slave, Queen. Not fit to be of your blood."

"We are all slaves in our own way. I won't compare my lot to yours, of course. I can only imagine the physical horrors you went through to become a Fury. All my horrors are up here," —she put a finger to her temple.— "Any week my city might be burned by Sea People or Dorians, or perhaps simply strangled in my bed when one of my own courtiers decides he might have just enough support to become king." She regarded Tisiphone for a moment. "I'd make you free if I could, but if I know Zinovia at all, I'd guess she's already ensured it would be impossible for you to accept any offer I might give you."

Tisiphone's eyes widened in surprise. Io was clearly wise to have guessed Zinovia's manipulations so clearly.

Io nodded. "I could offer you almost anything she could. So, she must have threatened you with something. Something or someone dear to you, perhaps?"

Tisiphone could only nod, although it was a strain to hear Chloe described in such terms.

"Should your future circumstances change, know you will always find an offer waiting for you here."

"Thank you, Queen, you are most generous." She hesitated for a moment. "Queen Io, I would like to ask you a personal question."

Io laughed gently. "You may ask, but I reserve the right to refuse to answer."

Tisiphone nodded and smiled. "Why did you never marry? Never have children?"

Io raised an eyebrow at the question and sat silent for a moment. "For one, the great irony is that Nyx was the only one of us to actually find her heart stirred by a man. Once I became Queen, to marry would have meant to subvert my own authority under that of a man, perhaps a foreigner. Perhaps I should have married Diadarian and united the Dorians and native Greeks against the Sea People before they became an unstoppable wave. But Diadarian was already in love with Zinovia even in those days of our youth. All choices, even the right ones, come with regret."

"You have regrets then?"

"I regret never having a daughter as strong and beautiful as you," Io replied with a smile.

Tisiphone was wise enough to know that the complement signaled a change in mood and an end to the interview. "Thank you, Queen. I will take my leave of you." She stood.

Io nodded. "May the gods be with you."

****

Unlike the Dorian army, the Furies could have snuck back across the sea with minimal risk of being caught by Sea People's raiders. But Tisiphone did not feel tremendous pressure to return to Iolcus. They could not dally indefinitely, but Chloe's life would be at risk if Zinovia thought they changed allegiance to Io. But surely Zinovia would not kill Chloe so quickly. A week to heal, indeed to relax as Io's guests, did not seem unreasonable.

Io arranged a tribute for Hagne and a stone was placed by the lighthouse at the site of her death. It was a beautiful memoriael, and Tisiphone felt somewhat better to think her friend's sacrifice had been honored. She wondered if her own death would be so honored or if she would be quickly forgotten.

Aside from that, she actually spent little time with the other Furies. Most of her time was spent with Praxis. She enjoyed his company, his vitality, his humor. His affection for her was obvious enough, and she enjoyed that. It made her feel like a woman rather than a slave or a soldier. Her feelings for him were complex. Certainly, she liked him, found him beautiful, and was pleased by his company. But her heart resisted anything deeper developing. She couldn't stay long, and the likelihood of returning soon seemed slim. And there was still the matter of Galen, to whom her mind remained drawn. That Galen was a lost cause seemed obvious enough. Galen treated her only with affectionate paternalism rather than Praxis' clear adoration. Yet her heart wouldn't entirely see reason.

"To hell with Queens," Praxis proclaimed one day while they sat together by the ocean, their arms entwined. "You should stay in Eritrea, Zinovia be damned."

She smiled and tossed back her hair. "You know I can't. Much as I'd like to."

"Why don't we mount a rescue operation for this Chloe of yours, much though she doesn't sound worth it? We could ride into the Empire, snatch her from Zinovia, and bring her here before the bitch is any wiser."

"Which bitch?" Tisiphone giggled. "Zinovia or Chloe?"

He laughed. "Either one. We'll kidnap one and leave the other to steam in Iolcus."

She joined in the laughter. It felt good, the idea of turning the tables on those who held power over her. It made her marvel for a moment to think to what degree it was that women held power in her world. Io, Zinovia, Chloe, Nyx, Koredyne…for good or for evil, these women held real authority in a man's world. Compared to them, Diadarian was but a well-intentioned wisp, Kriluss a simple brute, and Bael a distant rumor. That latter might change some day, would have to change if prophecy was to be believed. She leaned into him a bit, enjoying his warmth as protection against the cold sea air.

"Eritrea is beautiful, is it not?" Praxis asked with evident pride.

She nodded without turning to him. It was true. Eritrea was a beautiful city. Despite the recent siege, despite the Dorian army still camped outside their walls, the Ionians evidenced an optimism and contentment she'd not experienced before.

"You'll come back to Eritrea one day, you'll see," Praxis said, half teasing, half serious from his tone. "Once you have experienced her, she gets into your heart and there she will stay."

She turned to look over her shoulder, to read what was written in his eyes. "You Ionians speak very freely of emotion."

He chuckled, unselfconscious. "I suppose it is in our culture to be honest about what is in our hearts. Unlike Dorians, who place walls around their own." It was a gentle jab, made with a smile, but observant in its own way.

"I'm not a Dorian," she said, and turned back to the sea, relaxing with her back against his chest. "I don't know what I am, really. The village I was raised in was Mycenaean, but I was adopted. If Nyx truly is my mother, I would be Ionian like you."

"Eritrean, in fact," he said with a tone as if this would be of the highest compliment. "I tell you, the city is in your heart."

"Perhaps," she whispered. Moments later, she said, "I don't have the freedom though to decide when I can come back. I am a slave. A slave who can neither marry nor bear children. Surely of little interest to a man of respectable bearing."

He laughed and repeated, "Respectable. After all you have done here, you think your name is not respectable in Eritrea? Why, even your former captain Chloe's name is well known. Were she to consent to it, she'd find a thousand suitors in Eritrea alone. The gods will judge you for your deeds, Tizzy, and I think you will find I would do the same. Besides, a year ago, could you ever have imagined you would be here, a hero of Eritrea and a soldier of the Empire of the North?"

She shook her head.

"Then who is to say what time will bring us with another year?"

"But for a twist of fate, or Nyx's intervention, I might have been lost forever into the horrors of an altogether different slavery. If we are to think I am a lucky slave," —she had difficulty even speaking these words,— "by what grace should I enjoy that when so many other girls are lost forever?"

Praxis let out a long breath. "I am sorry. I did not intend to add to your burden."

"I know that, I do. And it's I who am sorry. I am ruining a wonderful day. You've done nothing wrong. I think on things too much." She reached up and stroked his cheek. He deserved as much as that.

"And I am given to flights of fancy. And I cannot say what is right or fair to the suffering of so many others. Only I hope that fortune would bring you back to Eritrea and to me soon. Our time together is too short. But I think if we had more time to share, we might become quite fond of each other. Don't you think the same?"

She looked at him again and fashioned him with a smile. In the back of her mind, she thought of Galen. There was still Galen there, but no sense in saying anything of that. It was likely as not she'd be dead before she ever had a chance to return to Eritrea. So why not allow Praxis his moment of hope? Besides, he wasn't wrong. "Yes, I think so, very fond of each other."

"Then I will be off to Iolcus at once, to ask Queen Zinovia to set you free!"

She giggled at his proclamation. "You fool, you can't even get across the water! And if you did, Zinovia would likely have you poisoned for even suggesting such a thing."

"You Dorians have the most difficult masters."

"I'm not a Dorian," she insisted with a grin. She stubbornly refused to let the grin slip even as footsteps announced their moment was coming to an end.

Someone stood waiting behind them. Only with reluctance did she let the moment go and turn. Galen.

"I am sorry to interrupt you," he said, his expression neutral. The lack of emotion he displayed irritated her. A selfish part of her hoped to see jealousy in his eyes, but there was nothing. "I have news Queen Io thought would interest you."

She turned around fully to face him. "Go on, Galen."

"Despite the Dorian army camped on our gates, we've been sending out patrols to reestablish control over all of Euboea and remove any Sea People's stragglers. One of our patrols in the north set upon a band of slavers. They…"

"Kriluss!" She knew at once and stood, feeling suddenly naked without her armor and sword.

"…they fought the slavers, took some prisoners but a number escaped. From our interrogations, we have learned that they were, indeed, traveling with Kriluss."

"And Nyx?"

Galen hesitated for a moment. "And Nyx, yes."

Tisiphone set off at once for the palace. Galen kept pace with her on one side, Praxis on the other. "It was bold of him to come here," she observed. "Fate has brought him to me."

"No doubt he saw profit to be had in the chaos of war," Galen replied. "Only to find himself as surprised by the Empire's intervention and the reversal of fortunes on the island. I have no doubt our patrols will run the rest of the slavers to the ground. When that happens, I could show you Kriluss' head myself."

She shook her head. "No, I'm meant to avenge my parents. I'll get the others at once." Not for a moment did she question that the other Furies would join her, that, in fact, they would be greatly dishonored if she did not assume as much.

"I'll come as well," Praxis volunteered. "I may not be a Fury, but my arm is strong."

She reached out and touched his arm. "Dear Praxis, you cannot. Your place is here with the queen and I fear in the dark days ahead, she will still have need of you, just as with Galen. If what we have shared is meant to grow, the Fates will bring us together again. I have no doubt of that."

There were many reasons she wanted him safely in Eritrea. Though he might be a reasonably good soldier, he was no Fury, and she feared for his safety. But she also didn't want him to see her that way: vicious, deadly, bloody…she felt the need now to keep some part of her life, whether it ultimately be small or large, separate from death.

Praxis looked disappointed but did not argue with her. He'd already learned the tone she used when her mind was settled.

"If it is vengeance you seek, there is the matter of Nyx," Galen said. "She is still a princess of Euboea."

"Queen Io wants her kept alive, even though she has returned to enslave her own people?"

"I don't think either of us believe Nyx is here to help Kriluss collect slaves, even if that is what Kriluss believes."

Tisiphone stopped and stared at Galen. No, of course not. Coming across the seas to Euboea in the midst of war was a terrific gamble. Nyx must have planted the notion in Kriluss' mind. Which meant Nyx was here for another reason. But what? To overthrow Io? And if so, why now after so many years of indifference toward her sister and her kingdom? She set back off toward the palace. "I will do as best I can, although much of her fate depends on Nyx herself."

Chapter 20

Nyx and Day

When the Furies caught up with Kriluss and his
men, they found the slave lords on the northern shores
of Euboea, laying low, and no doubt trying to find a
passage back to the mainland. Ionian patrols had
decimated the slaver ranks and taken from them their
captives, leaving only a core band remaining. A
massive fall for the man who had so drastically altered
Tisiphone's life course. And the remaining band of
slavers, cowering in the woods, were no match for
Furies who had fought off hundreds of Sea People
warriors.

The Furies cut through them mercilessly, falling
upon them like dogs on rabbits, tearing them apart,
showing them no mercy. For Meg and Pandora and
Lysistrate, it was not personal, save perhaps that each
of them had been cast into slavery by similar men, if
under different circumstances. But it was enough that it
was personal for Tisiphone. And there was a profound
sense that by causing these deaths, they removed a stain
from the world, a disease that inflicted misery wherever
its infection spread.

Only Kriluss himself put forth any respectable
resistance. Tisiphone marked him for her own. She
recognized him only by the helmet with the ram's

horns. Once she struck this from his head, she realized she had never learned to recognize his face. His was a commonly ugly and brutish face, and though he had peered on her and judged her a sex slave, her brain had refused to register him as anything uniquely worthy of memory. He might have passed her on the streets in Iolcus and she would not have remarked upon him, just one more loutish man among many.

He was strong, though, and even as his men fell, determined to survive. His cunning kept him alive longer than the others. He did not ask why the Furies attacked him. He showed Tisiphone no recognition, knew her certainly even less than she remembered him. But he must have guessed. They wore Dorian uniforms and were renowned already as slave soldiers, so he must have known.

She let him chase her, swing his heavy sword until he tired and could no longer match her speed. Then she struck his hand from his arm and opened up his stomach. Even as he fell to the grass, his back up against the ruins of a forgotten stone wall, holding in his entrails with his good hand, he asked for no mercy.

Tisiphone stood over him, watching him as he panted, blood oozing between his fingers and into the grass. Behind her the others waited, their own quarry dead.

Kriluss looked up at her and laughed. "It was bound to come one day. I didn't expect it to be a girl. Damned Empire and their women soldiers. I don't remember you at all. Just one slave among thousands."

"I didn't expect you to," she said calmly. Now that the moment was here, she felt no particular elation. There was just peace and a sense of balance restored to the world. It was less about vengeance in the end and more about returning this sense of balance. It saddened her just a little to think that death, even of such a horrid man, would be something to bring her peace. But such was the world she found herself in. It was not of her making. "Where is Nyx?"

"Nyx? In the end, not where I needed her." He looked down at his torn belly, then back up again. "You're one of her pet projects, aren't you? Should have guessed that woman would be the end of me. Been batty lately, for sure." He sucked in a deep breath and his body shuddered for a moment. "Temple of Artemis. Just to the north, by the shore. Hasn't left it since we made camp yesterday. I have a feeling she'll be expecting you." He coughed hard and grimaced.

Tisiphone watched him die. It didn't take long. As she did, she wondered what path had brought him to his end. Not the choices he had made as a slaver, to suck like a parasite from the blood of the world, but his path before that. She had been cast on her own path, but if she had chosen to live the life of a Fury fully, that path had nonetheless been initially thrust upon her. What life course had thrust the life of a slaver upon Kriluss? What had he endured at her age or younger? What choice did he have but to embrace the life of the slave lord, and what other paths, if any, might have been open to him? It didn't matter, though, she supposed. Whatever he had endured, he had chosen to inflict suffering on others. He could have chosen the life of a beggar, if nothing else, to avoid harming others. Everyone, ultimately, had choices, and Kriluss had made his. When, finally, he drew his last breath, she felt at peace.

When it was done, she turned to her comrades, who watched her as one might an overboiling kettle. "I'm fine," she assured them.

Meg put her hand on Tisiphone's shoulder. "The sun will burn brighter that the world is without him. Artemis will praise what we have done here today."

Artemis. Nyx had chosen her location purposefully.

Pandora stepped closer. "Do you want us to come with you?" It was hardly a question of where Tisiphone would next go.

Tisiphone shook her head. "I must face her alone. I won't be long."

Meg nodded. "We will wait here for you. However long it takes."

And so Tisiphone rode north. She thought she understood this meeting as well as could be expected. Kriluss may have found himself unexpectedly trapped in north Euboea, but Tisiphone guessed it was a trap set by Nyx, not Io or the Sea People raiders that kept him from crossing the seas to safety. Nyx had orchestrated all of this, no doubt lured Kriluss with the promise of easy slaves. And she had abandoned her colleague in the moment of his greatest need.

This, Nyx had done for Tisiphone herself. Not out of some streak of repentance or goodness, certainly. Nyx would be following her own designs as ever. But Kriluss had been offered up as a sacrifice, of this Tisiphone had no doubt. Which meant Nyx wanted to talk, not battle. Tisiphone wanted the same, at least for now.

As she drove hard for the coast, the temple of Artemis rose into view. It was old, now unused, its grounds reclaimed by the forest. Mighty columns held up a heavy marble roof, and walls still kept the temple inside in darkness. Once, this temple had enjoyed considerable local prestige, although its congregations had moved off elsewhere generations ago. The sun was on the horizon by now, the temple bathed in the orange and purple of dusk.

Tisiphone dismounted and tied her horse to a tree. She approached the temple cautiously, although she drew neither her bow nor sword. She couldn't rule out that Nyx would ambush her somehow at this moment, although she didn't think it likely.

She took the marble steps up to the temple gingerly. Within, the temple was dark, unlit. Only the faintest light from the setting sun carried within. The floor was dirty, cracked, caked with dead leaves and dirt. To the north, a tall statue of Artemis the Huntress stood, forgotten by her worshippers, now covered with a long vine that wove around her like a snake.

Before the statue of Artemis stood Nyx, adorned in a purple chiton and her hair flowing freely about her shoulders. Nyx had her back to Tisiphone, for all appearances admiring the statue. Tisiphone had a moment's temptation to fire an arrow into her back and be done with it. No doubt the world would be a better place for it. But it wasn't what Io wanted and, truth be told, it wasn't what she wanted either. And she had enough sense to figure Nyx would not be so easy to kill as that.

"I have answered your call," Tisiphone said to announce her arrival.

Nyx lowered her head, but did not, as yet, turn. "Then you have executed Kriluss?"

Christopher J. Ferguson

"I have."

"And how did it make you feel, to kill him?"

She considered it for a moment. "I felt at peace. I felt my parents avenged. But I do not feel it has changed me. I do not feel that my purpose has run its course."

"Nor should you." Nyx turned now, her dark eyes appraising Tisiphone. She took a few steps closer. "Have you come to kill me as well then, young Fury?"

Tisiphone shook her head. "No. Maybe. I don't know. I've come to try to understand you."

"Understand me?" Nyx laughed at that, although her laughter seemed more self-deprecating than cruel. "May the gods help you with that! If you have any success, I hope you will share it with me. Tell me, you consider Artemis your patron Goddess, don't you?"

Tisiphone nodded.

"You are similar in so many ways, it makes sense. Tell me, does the Goddess ever speak to you?"

Now Tisiphone shook her head.

Nyx shrugged a bit, seemingly disappointed. "No, not to me either. There are some, as you well know, oracles who believe the gods speak to them. Always in riddles. What use is it to ask a question of the gods and get a riddle in return? Not knowing the answer was already riddle enough."

"The gods don't speak to you, then? Are you not a witch?"

"You may call me that if you like, but what force I have does not come to me as a gift from the gods. It is something far older and more primitive than even they. But we are not here to speak of magic. Tell me, did Kriluss die well?" She moved closer to Tisiphone, showing not a hint of fear.

"As well as any."

"Good. I had no fondness for him, but I am pleased to know he did not dishonor his sacrifice." Nyx circumnavigated Tisiphone, moving around behind her. Tisiphone maintained her ground, showing no fear in return. "It is amazing to think of how young you are, basically still just a girl, and yet you have done such amazing things, particularly in the past few weeks. Already your name is being spoken of in tones of admiration."

"And that is something I owe to you. Is that what you hope for me to say?"

Nyx stopped. "You wish to know why I did it. Why I set you on the path that would make you a Fury."

"Yes, I wish to know."

"Why do you think?"

Tisiphone swallowed and looked away now, unable to face the very truth she had come for. "I don't know. I hoped you might tell me."

"Oh, nonsense, girl." Nyx waved her hand dismissively. "You were doing so well, standing bravely, showing no fear despite that I could stop your heart any moment I chose. You have given this much thought. You are not here out of some idle curiosity, that you wish to know the mind of Nyx. You killed Kriluss but you've made no move to kill me, though you could have shot me in the back had you chosen. I killed your adoptive parents just as sure as he did, but you've excluded me from your plans for vengeance, for which I am quite thankful, I will add." She stopped and stared at Tisiphone.

Tisiphone didn't respond, but she forced herself to meet Nyx's gaze.

Nyx broke the silence. "For what little it might be worth, if I could undo the death of your adoptive parents I would, but that is beyond even my power to do. So we are clear, I do not apologize for it, nor does it fill me with sorrow, but I like you well enough that I would undo what I have done if I could. Perhaps that would be unwise though? We are all the product of our pasts, and your pain is as much a source of your greatness as anything else."

Nyx looked away, and a moment of silence passed. Once again it was the princess of Euboea who broke it, her voice softer now. "You met with my sister."

"I spoke to Queen Io, yes. Do you remain fond of her?"

Nyx laughed softly. "I am as fond of Io as I am fond of anyone. She has given me no reason to hate her. That is no small compliment, I suppose, for my heart is full of hate."

Tisiphone thought to say something about Nyx's parents and what they had done but thought better of it. Tisiphone felt her boldness to be more fragile around Nyx. She was not frightened of Nyx, not like she should be perhaps. But there was something else that held her back.

"This is the first time I have set foot in Euboea in nearly twenty years," Nyx observed, looking around the dilapidated temple. "If Io were to die, I would be Queen," she said with a sneer. Her eyes met Tisiphone's. "There is nothing I would loathe more, so you needn't fear for the safety of your new patron."

"I am still the instrument of the Empire of the

North," Tisiphone corrected her.

"Perhaps less so than you were a week ago. I remember my sister well, and unless she has changed much in these last years, she must still be the light to my dark, forgiveness to my rage, and hope to my dismay. Whether she wishes to or not, she will one day force upon you a difficult choice."

"I am sorry for what happened to you, Nyx. But why don't you come back? Why don't you return home to Eritrea? Io could use the power you would bring to fight the Sea People." And the Empire as well perhaps, she thought but did not say.

Nyx recoiled as if she'd been stung by a wasp. "Return to Eritrea? And what would I do? And what would they do with me? Should I settle into the life of a princess, to marry and bear some bore of a man child after dirty child? And would I pretend not to hear them whisper as they serve the princess they all believe to have killed her parents, their king and queen?"

"Did you kill them?"

Nyx regarded her evenly for a moment and it seemed she might answer and answer truthfully. But then she drew back. "What does it matter? If I am innocent, they will never believe it, and if I am guilty, like with the slaughter of your parents, it is not something that can be undone. If even I would wish to."

"Doesn't it matter to you?"

Nyx snorted. "That is of my concern only. But come now; let us not draw the moment out. You've come here to ask of me a question, and I've come to answer it."

Tisiphone drew herself up, nervous now that the moment had arisen and could be put off no longer. "I want to know why you changed my path. Why did you help me even after you killed my parents?"

"You still ask things in a roundabout way, but very well, I will give you a roundabout answer. In the heat of battle, you were no more than one potential slave in a village full of them, but once all was settled, and we had you safely in a cage, I could smell the stink of Koredyne all over you. She'd been nudging you well enough along already, it was not difficult to see that. And I knew enough about what she and Adrasteia had burned their lives on…prophecies and tinkering with bloodlines…to have some guess about what that meant. And though we have no love for each other, sister sorceresses though we may all be, we share a common enough goal in our desire to see the Overlord of the Sea People dead. Since you were an integral part of that, I diverted you along onto the proper path."

"You wish to see Bael dead? Why?"

Nyx wagged her finger in the air. "No, no, no, no, you go too far. Like the circumstances of my parents' death, there are some matters I wish to keep for myself. Suffice to say we find ourselves two passengers on the same boat, and we must decide whether to row together or row in opposing directions. It is enough for you to know that I hope you will succeed rather than fail."

"You say you wish to answer my questions, yet you give me no answers at all."

"I said that I had come here to answer a question, the one you've truly come to ask, but you have not yet asked it."

Tisiphone ground her teeth. "I want to know…I want to know if you are my mother."

Nyx looked up and to one side, as though

considering a difficult problem of arithmetic, although a mischievous smile played along her lips. "I will answer your question and I will answer it truthfully, but before I do I wish to know some things."

"What things? Once again, you are not answering my question."

Nyx held up one hand. "In one moment only. Such a momentous question should not be answered lightly. I have told you that I have come here to answer that question, and I will. I presume that Adrasteia and Koredyne have refused to answer that same question?"

Tisiphone took in a deep breath. "They have. It was due to some rule, or they thought it was for my own good."

"I, of course, worry little about the rules that bind those two, although whether this knowledge will do you good or ill, I do not know. If I had reason to think it would impede you in killing Bael, I would reconsider, but perhaps the danger to you comes after that." She paused to consider once again. "Which answer would you prefer? That I am, or am not your mother?"

"Truly I don't know." Tisiphone looked at the ground.

"It would be nice to have a mother, to know from whence you came, but if you had your choice, I would not be she."

Tisiphone looked up but did not answer.

Nyx laughed. "Do not worry. I am not insulted. I don't blame you at all. I make no claims to being well suited to motherhood. Truth be told, you've already been well blessed with loving parents, even if adoptive. You should be satisfied with that."

"You're not the first to say so."

Nyx pulled a face. "Tell me I'm not thinking alike with that old crone Koredyne, now. Tell me, if I were your mother, could you find it in your heart to love me as such, despite what I had done to your adoptive parents?"

Tisiphone felt tears burn her eyes as she thought of Myrrine and Alexis, Nyx with Kriluss over Alexis at the moment he fell. "Truly, I do not know. Now, will you tell me if you are my mother?"

"I will tell you," Nyx said, and glided across the floor as if she were a shadow until she nearly touched Tisiphone. "Let me savor that sweet sense, that tenuous chance for forgiveness. Unfortunately, it is not for me, the answer is 'no.'"

Tisiphone let out a breath so fierce it was nearly a bark. She hadn't been aware she'd been holding it in. Tears rolled down her cheeks, and she wiped them away furiously, feeling as if Nyx had merely played games with her. "Do you enjoy this?"

"I wonder if you are more frustrated that your guess was incorrect, or relieved about the same? Perhaps a little of both. But our conversation is not over. What is less interesting is that I am not your mother. What is more interesting is that I know who is."

Tisiphone's gaze narrowed on Nyx. More tricks? "Do you?"

"I do."

"And my father?"

"I know of only your mother for the moment. Consider, though, you may like or not like the name I have to give you. This will be your last chance to reconsider, to decide whether ignorance is superior to knowledge."

Tisiphone didn't need any time at all. "I want to know."

"A woman of my own heart if not of my womb." Then she leaned over and put her lips next to Tisiphone's ear and into it whispered a name.

Chapter 21

The Name of the Rose

Io offered the Furies the option to stay in Eritrea for as long as they liked, but of course, they could not. Little doubt she would have liked them to stay to act as emissaries with the Dorian army stuck on Euboea. At least these troops began to disperse usefully to guard all of Euboea's coasts rather than remaining clustered like a quietly besieging army. But the Furies were eager to return to Iolcus.

Io provided them with a swift boat, and near Eritrea, the distance to the mainland was narrower. Fortune once again smiled upon them, and they were not accosted by Sea People's raiders on their journey. Over land, they had to travel some, through the overrun territories of Boeotia and once again through the contested wastelands, but by now they had learned to put their skills at stealth and infiltration to good use. They lived off the food Io had given them, and then off the land when this ran out. It was a difficult existence, but the Furies had become hardened to a difficult life.

Through this time, Tisiphone remained aloof from her colleagues, if anything a more stern and determined leader, although she shielded her thoughts from them. She did not tell even Meg about the name Nyx had given to her. Not yet. She needed to be sure it was true.

She wouldn't let that bitter witch make a fool of her.

There was a part of her that still thought she'd have done the world a favor to murder Nyx there in cold blood. There was no doubt the woman's intentions remained sinister. Perhaps the thought was moot; Nyx's power likely remained considerable, and she hadn't shown the slightest fear of the young Fury. But it was an unchosen option her mind kept returning to.

At last, they reached Iolcus. The city was a welcome sight. Spring, by now, was just beginning to poke through the cold of winter, and the Dorian city seemed alive and vibrant after their long journey through war-torn lands. Small flowers of pink and lavender bravely pushed their way through the frosted tundra outside the walls, and the trees were budded with new leaves. Over the sea, the sun rose and cast the palace towers in gold. Farmers moved and prepared seed for the spring planting. It was easy to believe that Persephone herself had returned from Hades to welcome the new cycle of life and harvest. They might have enjoyed a heroes' welcome had they come in announced but, instead, they chose to come in quietly. Let Diadarian make a fuss of them if he wished.

Tisiphone parted company with her colleagues at their old barracks, although these were now occupied by new recruits. These girls seemed impossibly young, like babies. It was hard to fathom that the Furies themselves were only a year older on average. Tisiphone felt a flash of compassion for these girls, just now enduring the year of horrors that would train them to become the next wave of the Empire's slave-girl soldiers. Perhaps one of them would step, likely briefly, into Tisiphone's own shoes once she inevitably fell in battle.

But she did not have time to dither at the training camp. With a few inquiries, she knew where she must go. She made her way quickly to the palace of Diadarian and Zinovia, where, by now, she was recognized and admitted on request. She didn't even have to hand over her sword, so great was the Empire's trust in the Furies now. It occurred to her they would make the perfect assassins for some other group...the Sea People, Io...if only they could be turned. Diadarian's trust in them was immense and knowing that made her feel a flicker of guilt for even considering desertion from the Empire for Io.

She bounded the stairs up to the higher floors, remembering the way easily. She passed unobstructed. Diadarian was in the recess just inside the balcony where she had first met the Emperor King. He sat draped in robes with the mask covering his face, barely moving. In front of him, a table and on it a map of Greece, she suspected he couldn't see. But it was there for the woman who helped him to plan the Empire's strategy against the Sea People.

He shifted in his seat a little as Tisiphone approached, and she had the impression he wasn't capable of much movement beyond that. "Ah, from the sound of the boots, military but light-footed." His voice was strong and clear. "I suspect I hear the return of one of our exalted Furies! Tisiphone, is it? I cannot tell you how remarkable your success in Euboea has been. Your name and that of your companions will be praised throughout the Empire!"

She could sense him smiling behind the mask with whatever remained of his face. She met his proclamation with silence at first. It had simply not occurred to her that he would wish to shower her with praise. That was not why she was here at all. She wasn't here for him, in fact, but for the woman next to him. "My King," she said. "I am gratified to have pleased you…" —she managed that much at least,— "…but…" Her eyes shifted to the woman, and she took a moment to steady herself, and drew in a deep breath. "You are my mother."

From where she'd sat next to the Emperor, explaining to him what the map told, Chloe now stood, her long curls flowing around her shoulders like a fire. Her one good eye glimmered as it narrowed its gaze on Tisiphone.

For what seemed an eternity, the three of them remained like that in silence. It was the Emperor who broke it. "Well, it would seem that I am an unfortunate interloper in a most unexpected family discussion. I would excuse myself, but that would require one of you to carry me. Perhaps you would prefer to use the veranda?"

Without a word, Chloe strode past Tisiphone, her cold eye on her the whole time. She opened the door to the veranda and stood aside, letting Tisiphone go first.

Now that she had blurted out what Nyx had told her, she felt like a fool. She couldn't know that Nyx had told her the truth. Certainly, she shouldn't have blurted it out in front of the Emperor. It hadn't been the way she had meant for the conversation to go, but on seeing Chloe, the words had just spilled out. Chloe would be seething with rage, without a doubt.

Already humiliated, Tisiphone slunk out onto the veranda. Her heart felt like it had been turned to clay.

She waited a moment for a verbal lashing, or perhaps a physical one, but it did not come. Nor was Tisiphone embraced in the warm arms of a long-desired reunion with a woman who, until now, had no face.

When the silence persisted, Tisiphone forced herself to look up. Chloe's face was unreadable, and Tisiphone found herself staring at the horrid scar that ran across it. In the days of the journey that had taken her from Eritrea to Iolcus, she had somehow never bothered to ask herself how she felt about the notion of Chloe as her biological mother. She had sought only to know the truth. Now that she looked on the woman who had trained her, who had sometimes beaten her mercilessly, who had treated both her and the other Furies with an incomprehensible mixture of respect and coldness, she felt she still didn't know. Was it better than having Nyx as a mother? Almost certainly given Nyx's wickedness and murderousness, although Nyx was at the very least capable of great emotion. Chloe was a cypher, perhaps further beyond reach than Nyx might have been.

Tisiphone tried to compare herself to Chloe physically. Neither of them was tall, their physiques were similar enough, but that was hardly surprising given the exact training they both endured. Chloe's face was beyond making a reasonable comparison, and they shared neither eye color nor the texture of their hair, although their hair color was similar.

Chloe certainly gave no indication of her thoughts to Tisiphone now, but rather regarded the girl silently with her withering, one-eyed stare.

Gradually, Tisiphone's humiliation and fear twisted to anger, and she straightened her back. "Say something!" she demanded, rage burning heavily in her heart.

"What would you like me to say?"

"Is it true?"

Chloe's jaw tightened a bit, her only response for several seconds. At last, she said, "When I was a sex slave, but fourteen, I became pregnant. Pregnancy is about as useful to a sex slave as it is to a Fury, but here my path crossed Adrasteia. I still don't understand why to tell the truth. Back then, she was still an old crone like Koredyne is now, rather than a shapeless voice in a cave, and she came from nowhere to the hovel where I was kept with countless other girls. She told me I was pregnant, which I already knew, and offered me an exchange—if I gave her the baby I was carrying, she would deliver me from the cruel life of a sex slave. I agreed in a heartbeat. There was no sense not to; it might be no more than a fantasy, but I had nothing to lose. They would never have let me keep the baby, I thought, and the life of a sex slave is short and brutal.

"She must have weaved some magic, for they did not beat the fetus out of me like they did with most girls. Nor did they stop me from working, however. Almost until I went into labor, they found men who would still pay for my services. It turns out there is a market for all manner of unexpected preferences."

Tisiphone blanched at that, and suddenly realized she would have preferred an abridged version of this story.

"When the child came, it was Koredyne who came to take her, a girl. I was barely conscious, never knew the girl's name, never held her. Koredyne did nothing for me, nor did Adrasteia return. I remained a sex slave for another year until I was fifteen, cursing their names and their betrayal the entire time. Only after a year had passed did Diadarian begin his concept of the Amazons, and I was made a slave soldier instead of a sex slave. I suppose that was my reward for turning over my child to them. As they agreed, they took me from one brutal life by moving me to one just a notch less brutal. But at least I no longer needed to humiliate myself before a stream of endless men. I owe them that at least." She drew in a long breath. "I could not say for certain you are my daughter, but I've had my suspicions. If Nyx says that it is true, then I've no reason to doubt it."

The words washed over Tisiphone like a cold wave. "Suspicions? When did you begin to suspect?"

"When you returned from Adrasteia with your stories of her refusal to explain your parentage and your wild theories about Nyx. I knew that much, at least, that Adrasteia was bound not to reveal I was the mother of the child she took away. Why, by the gods, that mattered, I have never known. I imagined that whatever pedigree they had in mind for the child, knowing it had come from a sex slave did not fit well with its future life."

"And my father?"

Chloe shrugged. "One of hundreds of men whose names I do not know and whose faces I no longer recall."

Tisiphone's stomach turned, but her mind was exhilarated at the same time. She imagined the brilliance of that. Chloe certainly brought her own pedigree: physically and mentally she was the most impressive of women, destined to be an Amazon, although they could not have known at the time. But whoever her father had been, if his union with Chloe had been critical to these schemes of the witches, to this prophecy, what better way to mask his identity from even the mother by making him but a drop in an ocean of suffering? It was brilliant, if hideous. She wondered if such a scheme belonged to Adrasteia or some other force.

"If you suspected, when were you going to tell me of all this?"

"Never."

The word was like a slap. "Did you not think I deserved to know?"

Chloe's jaw set with a glimmer of anger for once. "It is not a matter of what we do or do not deserve, for we are all slaves. It is a matter of what was best. Adrasteia and Koredyne had their reasons for hiding the truth from you, and who was I to doubt that? But more to the point, I was your captain and even now we are comrades in arms. Was knowing that we might share blood going to make us more efficient in battle?"

Tisiphone stared at Chloe, aware for the first time that tears ran down her cheeks. She wiped them away with both hands, suddenly embarrassed to show emotion, to show weakness in front of this woman of stone.

"Do you not see?" Chloe seemed to relent just a little, her tone softening. "The day may come when I must send you to die in battle, or you must do to me the same? How could that be possible if we were to think we could form bonds of family?"

"Then it means nothing to you to have borne me in your womb for nine months?"

"That was fifteen years ago!" She held her arms

out as if helpless, explaining perfect sense to an imbecile, although her voice betrayed emotion for once, even if it were frustration. Tisiphone seized upon it.

"What can time possibly matter to the bonds between mother and daughter? Even if those bonds are only of blood?"

"Tisiphone, I am pleased with the woman you have become. I am proud to stand beside you as a comrade in arms. And I am glad that you had the good fortune to be loved by adoptive parents who gave you the home I never could. What more could you possibly expect? That you would rush into the palace with your big revelation, and that I would swoop you into my loving embrace and we would span the broken time that had stretched between us? If I had wanted that, I would have embraced you when I first had my suspicions!"

From the look on her ruined face, Tisiphone could tell Chloe regretted, truly regretted her words as soon as she spoke them. But this regret was weakness and Tisiphone ached to her very core. She was wounded not by a careless statement but by the truth that underlay that statement. She again could not help but to compare Chloe to Nyx and in this moment of pain, Nyx came out ahead. Whatever Nyx might have been, she would have taken an interest in Tisiphone as her daughter. Perhaps that interest would have proven self-serving in the end, but at least it would have been there. Tisiphone, in this moment, though, she would have preferred that to the indifference of Chloe.

Chloe stepped toward her daughter, but Tisiphone stepped back, knowing it would deepen the older women's regret, however shallow Chloe's emotions would be. She wanted Chloe to suffer as she suffered, if even just a fraction.

"Tisiphone, knowing I am your mother is a weakness others will exploit. Even not knowing it, Zinovia used me as a hostage to keep you loyal. Imagine what it will mean now that you know I am more than just the woman who trained you."

Chloe was right, of course, in her pragmatic way. But Tisiphone couldn't see that any of it mattered. What mattered was, whether sensible or not, Chloe had had no interest in reestablishing any bond between them. Tisiphone now understood that the fantasy of her biological mother had been more pleasant than the truth. Sometimes the truth was not what we really wanted. It could rob us of hope.

"Tisiphone, is it not enough that you had Myrrine, a woman who loved you as a mother for fourteen years? That is, of itself, much more than many girls have?"

The thought of Myrrine made Tisiphone's heart sink and ache even further. Somehow, she felt repulsive, as if seeking her birth mother made her faithless to her adoptive mother. The rejection by her birth mother made this feeling worse in turn. All of this had ended in ruins and if it wasn't the outright danger Kerodyne had made it sound like—it was an emotional disaster to be sure. And she'd shouted her declaration in front of the Emperor, no doubt for all the palace to hear. Her shame could not be deeper.

"Then tell me you have not an ember of feeling for that daughter you lost. You have no interest in knowing her?"

"I do know her as a warrior I am proud to call a comrade." Chloe did manage to look apologetic, a rare enough look from her, but this only deepened

Tisiphone's disappointment as if some real connection was tantalizingly close, but yet out of reach. "Whatever maternal abilities I might have had were long ago ground out of me. You deserve what you seek, but I am sorry. I am not able to provide it to you."

"Fine," Tisiphone said, by now as much as anything eager to be free of her, free of the palace, the place of her humiliation. "I was foolish to even say anything. I know that now." She stepped around Chloe, keeping out of arm's reach. She wiped her arm along her face, for all the good that did. Leather armor was not effective at drying tears. Gods, what a wreck she must look like, and still needed to walk past Diadarian.

But Diadarian was no longer in the alcove—some servant having tactfully removed him so that Tisiphone need be shamed no further, perhaps. She picked up a determined pace, wanting to be free of the palace as quickly as possible. She made eye contact with no one. She hoped no one would choose this moment to congratulate her for the victories at Eritrea.

A part of her hoped she might hear Chloe call to her to stop. It was unlikely, but still, she fantasized about it. She imagined what she'd do if Chloe called to her. Perhaps she'd keep going and ignore the older woman. Perhaps there'd be just a hope that Chloe would change her mind if Tisiphone turned around, though. Perhaps. Perhaps. But this, too, remained just a feeble fantasy, for no call came.

Tisiphone walked and walked, with no destination in mind. She didn't want to see anyone, tell anyone what had happened. She wasn't yet ready for the consolation that Meg or Pandora might offer her. For now, she wanted to wallow in her misery, to experience it raw.

Eventually, she found herself on the cliffs above Iolcus, beyond the training camp where she could be alone. She sat on the rocks and let the cool ocean breeze soothe her raging mind, if just a bit. She thought about the past year and all she'd lost and the things she'd gained. Aside from a small number of emotionally battered girls, she had no one in the world. And yet, by tomorrow, she and her comrades would be proclaimed heroes. Perhaps someone would think to make a statue of her. That was what she wished to be, a statue. A block of stone that did not feel and could not be injured. Like Chloe.

But she did feel, and she could be injured, and perhaps that in the end, would make her unsuitable to be a Fury. For Chloe was right, whether she reciprocated the feeling or not, Tisiphone now knew the woman to be her mother, and that couldn't be undone. It would indeed be a weakness to be exploited and that, too, could not be helped. She sighed, hoping the great exhale of breath might take some of the pain with it, but that was not how things worked.

As night fell, she curled into a ball there at the edge of the cliff and shivering, fell into a fitful sleep. Before she did, she prayed the gods might deliver her from this path somehow. Turn her into some new exotic flower that, weeping, grew only on the cliffs by the sea. Or perhaps weave their magic and take her memory from her. Or perhaps Artemis would make her stronger, braver, less caring, and make her into a true warrior. She could see many avenues the gods might take to show mercy on her.

But in the end, in the morning, she woke up cold,

but the same.

****

Far away, in the Peloponnese at nearly that moment, the man named Bael, Overlord of the Sea People in Greece and nemesis to the girl Tisiphone, brooded on the destruction of his war band in Euboea. To say this was an unexpected turn of events would be an understatement. The five thousand warriors lost had been recent arrivals from the homelands, eager for blood and booty. His reputation as a fierce warrior and conqueror had drawn them to him. Euboea was to be theirs. His fleets mastered the seas. How had that damned Empire of the North managed to land soldiers to reinforce the crumbling empire of the Mycenaeans (as he thought of the Ionians)?

Five thousand troops were, relatively speaking, a trifle. But this was his first significant loss and a blow to his reputation. An Overlord was not to lose. The tide of the Sea People could not be held back. An Overlord who could be defeated by weaker people would not attract new warriors. There were plenty of other rich lands to plunder, many other Overlords. Even his own current followers in Greece might trickle away or, sensing weakness, topple him and replace him with someone stronger.

It enraged him still further to learn that the girl, Tisiphone, had been responsible for the loss. The one the soothsayers said he must kill if he was still to rule. He hadn't known how seriously to take such prophecies. What was some strange Greek girl to him? What harm could she possibly do? His efforts to eradicate her had been half-hearted. Now he saw how wrong he had been, how right the soothsayers had been.

In one blow she had done more damage to him than anyone had since his reign began.

He would not allow it further. She would have to die. He knew her name. He knew the Empire had the audacity to parade their heroes in public. Soldiers such as these Furies ought to be kept secret, but the Empire liked its heroes, a vain people as they were. Moving forward, killing her would be the focus of his strategy. And with her gone, he would sweep aside both the last of these Mycenaeans and this upstart Empire of the North as well. And he knew just how to do it…

A word about the author…

Aside from being an author, Christopher J. Ferguson is a professor of psychology specializing in forensics. He has written several non-fiction books including Moral Combat: Why the War on Violent Video Games is Wrong, How Madness Shaped History and Catastrophe! How Psychology Explains Why Good People Make Bad Situations Worse. He has also published the mystery novel Suicide Kings with The Wild Rose Press. He lives in Orlando with his wife and son. http://www.christopherjferguson.com